I0577317

MAGGIE YORE

When She Breaks

First published by Maggie Yore 2025

Copyright © 2025 by Maggie Yore

All rights reserved. No part of this publication may be reproduced, stored, or transmitted in any form or by any means, electronic, mechanical, photocopying, recording, scanning, or otherwise without written permission from the publisher. It is illegal to copy this book, post it to a website, or distribute it by any other means without permission.

This novel is entirely a work of fiction. The names, characters, and incidents portrayed in it are the work of the author's imagination. Any resemblance to actual persons, living or dead, events, or localities is entirely coincidental.

Maggie Yore asserts the moral right to be identified as the author of this work.

Maggie Yore has no responsibility for the persistence or accuracy of URLs for external or third-party Internet Websites referred to in this publication and does not guarantee that any content on such Websites is, or will remain, accurate or appropriate.

First edition

ISBN: 979-8-9987987-1-9

Editing by Abbie Rutherford
Cover art by Pixie Thorpe

This book was professionally typeset on Reedsy.
Find out more at reedsy.com

For Adeline

Contents

Preface

Please be kind and gentle with yourself as you read this novel.

My intention in writing this novel is to display how disruptive, agonizing and debilitating it is to live with PTSD, C-PTSD, depression, anxiety, hormone dysregulation and gastrointestinal issues. I spent decades in and out of urgent care centers, hospitals, doctors' offices, specialists and holistic practitioners' offices with countless tests, imaging, procedures, supplements, over the counter remedies and prescription drugs trying to figure out why I have so many digestive issues, depression and anxiety.

It was only recently that I found doctors and specialists that all agreed on the same diagnosis and treatment. Diagnosis? Decades of trauma and abuse. Treatment? Self-respect, major changes to diet, intensive therapy and accepting that I was abused. That's when the real healing began. The validation and compassion that I was shown still brings tears to my eyes and warms my heart. I am so grateful for them. It changed the course of my future. This book was written during the most difficult part of my life, I didn't know that I was going to make it. By using Soshana as a fictional guide to navigate my healing, she gave me the courage to unleash a voice I knew I had but wasn't brave enough to release until now.

None of the contents of this book is meant as a therapeutic tool or meant for therapeutic use. This is a work of fiction and all opinions expressed are mine alone.

Information about this novel:

The main character's name was inspired by the Austrian abstract artist, Soshana.

The book cover is an original gouache painting by Pixie Thorpe Designs, used with permission by artist.

Font *Ascentis* by designer Emily Jing Sum Chan used with permission; commercial license acquired.

WARNING: Coarse language, descriptions of child abuse, descriptions of suicidal ideation and suicide attempt.

If you or anyone you know is considering taking their life, immediately dial 911 in an emergency or 988, the Suicide and Crisis Lifeline.

Life is worth living, you are worth loving.

1

Internalize

Restless but at the same time lethargic. It exhausts me, being frozen in place. I don't know what to do with myself most days. If I didn't have a job, I'm sure I'd be on the street. The world is falling apart, taxes are too high, I'll never be able to buy a house, my student loans are never ending and my left hip hurts. I eat too much cheese.

"Why do you feel 'frozen in place?' What is keeping you in that state?" Ms. Erling is a retired professor of Psychology at NYU and a former clinical therapist. She had given Soshana many assignments over the years, the most recent one was to write down exactly how she feels every day, without regard or hesitation, then read it aloud during their weekly 'off the books' sessions.

Soshana sighed, audibly. *Why does it matter?*

"My body feels tense all the time. But then I just sit there after my mind has run its course of agreeing and disagreeing with what it should and shouldn't do, I end up re-watching old movies and eating gummy worms."

"Is there anything that stands out while your mind is

running?"

"I don't feel like I'm where I'm supposed to be. I feel like I shouldn't be here."

"Here, where?"

"Here, physically in this spot, I guess. I don't know." She wanted to say, here on earth.

Ms. Erling pauses to digest the words.

"Let's work on that for next week. I want you to imagine where you would like to be. How you want your life to look. Focus more on positives than negatives, and don't leave any of it out."

Soshana placed a balled-up fist on her forehead, ready to pound it in.

"I have to leave for work soon. Thank you." Relieved to get off the phone, she hung up before Ms. Erling could respond. Irritation throbbed in her throat, anger caused her legs to bounce uncontrollably. What Ms. Erling didn't hear was the true inner thoughts, the ones that involved imagining turning the wheels of her car into oncoming traffic. Locating the vehicles that would cause the most damage, for a more immediate death. A glorious, blood-splattered ending to a pathetic existence.

Almost a year ago, Soshana had reluctantly accepted the supervisor position at a local convenience store in her hometown, northeast of Grand Rapids, Michigan. The pain in her abdomen was a constant reminder of that choice; she ignored it most days. "Actions have consequences," her mother, Marilyn, would often say, usually before delivering a gleeful punishment.

"In-actions also have consequences," her therapist retorted once, after Soshana had mentioned the excessiveness with which her mother used the opposite phrase. What a shock it must have been to Marilyn to be diagnosed with liver cancer after decades of heavy drinking.

Soshana took the first job she could get, one that was close enough to her childhood home, which later became her mothers' after their parents divorced. The convenience store, aptly named The Convenience Store, was six blocks away from where she lived now. Her studio apartment was around 450 square feet, just enough for her and Mr. Skittles, a middle-aged gray and white striped cat. She walked to work most days and bicycled others. Walking made her feel independent, capable of handling herself to a degree. She did anything she could to be outside to watch the trees move at the wind's command. Their waning brightly colored leaves had begun their annual pilgrimage to the soil.

Weather in late September in Michigan was always generally favored by most. There were days that were postcard perfect: a beautiful light breeze, deep blue skies, flower petals clinging on to dear life in the late summer months. The storms were something to behold. She liked to pretend the dark rainstorms held all her anxiety, anger and grief. When the clouds released their rain, she imagined they released her tears, all the ones she could no longer release herself. Soshana hadn't cried in years, not even when her mother died nine months ago.

She had moved back home from New York to take care of her ailing mother. She left her friends, her roommate, quit her stable decent paying job as a manager at a busy doctor's office and returned to the home and room she grew up in. Marilyn had a major stroke after completing cancer treatment. The nurses said she had stopped eating and was becoming violent towards the orderlies. Her doctor said she would most likely benefit from being in her own home, where she passed away within a few months. The oncologist and her primary doctor concluded her death was ultimately caused by alcoholism.

Derek, Soshana's brother, is eight years younger than her. He decided to follow in her footsteps by attending NYU, studying education. She didn't want him to be interrupted and miss that important time in his life by ditching school and moping around the stale frigid home just to watch their mother succumb.

Marilyn left her and Derek whatever was in her savings and the family home. Even though it was completely paid off, it was a wreck. It reminded them of the horrors of endless fighting, walking on eggshells, the smell of alcohol, and the way their father left them suddenly when she was twelve, leaving Soshana to care for her four-year-old brother. He was a handful, but nothing compared to dealing with Marilyn. She couldn't decide if she was angry with or jealous of her father escaping and abandoning them when they needed him most. He kept in touch and visited them once a month for a while, always meeting at a park or restaurant for a few hours. Marilyn, miraculously, was granted full custody. The visits became fewer and fewer and she hadn't seen or heard from her father in years.

You learn what kind of person your parents are when you become an adult. Choices are made, feelings are hurt and unexpressed. It was a miracle they survived, though Marilyn was an expert at hiding her alcoholism. She kept her job, kept up appearances in public and with friends and family, leaving the children to hide her secret as well. Marilyn worked in Lansing, where she purchased her alcohol. Small town rumors spread fast; secrets are best kept outside of it.

4

Derek and Soshana were at a loss when it came to deciding what to do with the house. It was not in sellable condition and neither of them wanted to live there. It was unkempt and outdated. The smell was enough to keep potential buyers away. He hadn't been home in over five years, even though they understood the state it was in when they left, those last few years showed the depth of Marilyn's alcoholism. Soshana thought Marilyn let the property fall into ruin just to piss off her ex-husband since he worked so hard to pay for it, then had to give it up to her. It was just another example of how her emotional instability led her to make selfish choices to satisfy her rage.

Soshana had hired a company to help make it ready for sale. They dealt with the deep cleaning, organizing and decluttering as well as carpet cleaning and painting. It took a crew of five almost four days to complete the job and cost them a small fortune. What kept her from selling the property now? It's in a decent area. She and Derek could split whatever they made off it. Her stubbornness or her will kept her from living there with no worry of rent or exorbitant mortgage payments. The small amount of money their mother left was going towards property taxes, insurance and upkeep. The mice had moved in instead of her. She knew she needed to make a final decision with her brother soon, otherwise the home would sit and rot. The investment would be wasted on ignorance and rebellion. These relentless and obsessive thoughts constantly bombarded her during every waking hour.

The holidays will be different this year.

Halloween was around the corner, then another quiet Thanksgiving, followed by her least favorite time of the year.

It wasn't just because the customers were always a bit on edge, or that her co-workers' kids were always sick. It wasn't the flashy lights, or uncomfortable gift exchange at the Christmas staff party. Without children around, the holidays seemed lifeless, useless. It was more that the memories produced great discomfort and reminded her that all of her family and friends were far away, silent, or dead.

She was only a few blocks away from work when her vision blurred, and her breathing became shallow and infrequent. Her stomach hardened, a sharp stabbing pain then nausea crept over her, saliva pooled in her mouth. She was sure vomit was coming so she stopped and leaned over the fence to her left, waiting for it. The feeling passed after a few seconds, she continued walking towards work and stalled, something felt off.

For a few blinks, the sun was in a different position in the sky, it felt like it was early afternoon. The street was quiet, the person that was walking ahead of her had gone. The barking dog had disappeared. The trees were full of green leaves. Her heart started racing wildly and her breathing was still shallow but more rapid and fervent. Panic. Taking a deep breath and with closed eyes, she spoke gently to herself, "It's nothing, nothing. Stop. Stop it." Her eyes flickered open, the sky bounced back, though the scene flipped back and forth rapidly between blinks before she saw what she had expected to see.

"Are you okay?" Joe, her co-worker, appeared at her side. He came up close and touched her gently on the shoulder. Soshana sprang up and yelped like a small dog that had its paw stepped on.

"Ope, sorry about that," he said, removing his hand.

"It's okay, I need to catch my breath." The leaves had returned to their yellow color, and she recognized that it was about ten in the morning, not three in the afternoon.

"What were you doing? I thought you might have seen an animal or something, but then you turned your head and I noticed that you were going to barf," he said hurriedly. Joe was an older man with big blue eyes and wisps of shiny white amongst the gray hair. He was large, at least six feet tall, with what looked like a basketball bloated in his belly. Over the past year, Joe had taken a liking to Soshana in a fatherly way. Patting her back when she stocked the shelves perfectly, giving high fives at the end of an especially difficult day, offering snacks and food, giving her a pep talk here and there. He seemed to have a sense of how to recognize the faults in others and turn them into opportunities of guidance, rather than belittlement. A trait Soshana admired and tried to emulate herself. She was never good at being kind to herself, but a champion when it came to lifting up others.

"I uh— I don't know. I'm not sure what happened there, I must have eaten something for breakfast that didn't agree with me, it's over with now." She looked to see if there was anyone else around. "Maybe I'll take a few minutes in the break room to compose myself."

Soshana has had her fair share of panic attacks. She was familiar with the sensation of when they were going to happen and what to do to stop them. Or at least make them bearable. Ms. Erling gave her 'tools' to use when she knew they were coming on.

"Find five objects and name the colors. Name three things that you smell and hear. Touch metal, plastic, glass and, if possible, go outside and touch plants, leaves, flowers, anything with texture and then describe how it feels. Take deep, slow, steady and meaningful breaths. You can handle whatever comes your way," she would say. She was an old coot, but for what it was worth, what she said was almost always helpful. That didn't always stop them from coming, though, and this time was something extraordinary, a waking nightmare. She couldn't believe it was real.

What the fuck was that?

Soshana sat at the plastic table in the cramped musty smelling break room for a few minutes, trying to figure out what just happened.

"One black refrigerator, two beige cups, three silver forks, four white chairs, five-" She closed her eyes and took another long deep breath in, then slowly let it out through her nose. She went to the bathroom, locked the door and checked to see if her pallor was still a pale green. She felt more tired than usual and noticed the wrinkles forming around her eyes, the darkness underneath them.

As she grew older, she looked more like her mother. The person that tormented and abused her the most. She was incapable of separating herself from her mother's appearance. A boiling hatred of herself grew every time she looked in the mirror. The pangs of disdain building inside her whenever a mutual acquaintance smiled at her and said "You look just like your mom! She was such a pretty lady." Staring intensely into her reflected eyes, she imagined her fingernails as sharp as knives, grasping the top of her forehead, pushing deep into the skin, deep enough to feel the skull. Pulling the skin over her eyebrows, then pushing the stained nails into her eyes, ripping the skin over her lips, scraping teeth, blood pooling in her mouth.

Blink. Focus. You're at work, you fucking idiot.

Taking another deep breath, she held it for a few seconds, then released it. Every so often she had to remind her out of control monkey mind to regulate her breathing. When she wasn't concentrating, her breaths were shallow and constrained. She tilted her head back and rolled her eyes back as far as they could handle.

Stop calling yourself an idiot.

She snapped into 'customer service mode', stepped out of the break room with a big toothy smile and greeted the workday with feigned enthusiasm. Just a few short years ago, when she was enjoying her life in New York, mutilating her face wasn't something she would think about. What happened to that carefree, senseless drone of a life? Everything, *everything* was too serious now.

Work ended around 7:45 pm. She went for a walk in the town center to grab dinner. It was a quaint little town, built in the early eighteenth century. Brownstone buildings, cobbled streets, lamp posts painted over many times in dark but cheerful green, cafés with stringed lights over the outdoor seating area. Typical midwestern 'nice.' Which meant passive-aggressive tones and fake smiles. People love to gossip and judge behind closed doors, in the comfort of their long-term friendships and close family members. Soshana didn't find enjoyment in speaking poorly about anyone, so she resisted as much as possible, which meant she was an outsider. 'Not any fun' according to those who found kinship when speaking ill of others. Everyone goes through something uncomfortable or difficult in their life, there is always an explanation as to why a person acts the way they do, so she never faulted them for it.

There was a familiarity and sense of reconciliation upon returning home after so many years—for a short while at least. The same people working at her favorite dirty spoon restaurants, albeit quite a few years older and not any wiser. There was still a sentimental feeling when recognizing some of the old haunts from memories past. But the town lacked a certain amount of diversity and progressiveness, especially coming back from New York.

"Soshi! Is that *really* you?" said a familiar female voice. It took Soshana a second to realize it was an old friend and she was near her favorite café growing up. Soshana had a tendency to drift into her thoughts and temporarily go 'blind,' even while walking when she knew she should be aware of her surroundings.

"Ah *shit*," she muttered under her breath. "Taryn! Hey, you! How are you?" she said with forced excitement.

Taryn exalted, "Girl, it's been so long, why didn't you tell me you were in town?"

They hugged; Taryn squeezed her so hard it made her see stars.

"I would love to get together and catch up, how long are you here?" Taryn said cheerfully with wide-open eyes that scanned over Soshana's body up and down like a judge from a beauty pageant.

"Oh, um." Soshana stalled and self-consciously rubbed her arm. "I'm here for a little while," she said sheepishly. How had she got away with avoiding her high school best friend for almost a year? The last time she saw her was at Marilyn's funeral. Soshana had not expected to remain in town, she hadn't been sure what to do so she stayed, then stayed away from everyone.

"Honey, I'm so busy but I will absolutely make time for you!" Taryn touched Soshana's shoulder while scanning and assessing yet again with a tinge of concern, perhaps pity this time. Taryn smiled at Soshana as she released her hand before she scrolled through the calendar on her hot-pink phone. Soshana tried to keep a composed countenance.

She's the one that asked to get together, why would she say she was so busy?

"How about Thursday at two o'clock? I have a few hours," Taryn said.

"Sure, want to meet at L'Addition, Merci?" Soshana loved that coffee shop, she imagined it was like being in a Parisian café.

"Sure! Oh, I'm so excited. See you then, gotta run!" Taryn gave her a quick side hug and cheek kiss before she walked off.

Shit.

They used to be close. Taryn had aged well; she looked almost exactly the same as the last day of high school. They kept up with each other on social media, texted on birthdays and holidays. She was tiny, standing about five feet from the ground when she wasn't wearing those stilts they call stilettos. She'd stopped dying her hair blonde, so the natural medium brown with some sun-lightened streaks shone through and looked nice. Everyone puts on at least ten pounds after high school, Soshana was no stranger to that, if not more, however, Taryn looked thinner. She dressed fashionably, always ready to make a sale. Being one of only a dozen realtors in the area, she had made herself into a small-town success. This is exactly the kind of person she would have been drawn to in the past.

Extroverted, confident, alluring and exciting. All of the things she is not.

A jolt of nerves bound at her core, Soshana was reminded of her former close friend, Mina, from when she was living in New York. The similarities were striking. She knew that she needed to be cautious, the damage from one relationship tends to bleed into others.

Taryn had a handsome husband, a young son and a stunning 3,000 square foot custom-built home. Soshana knew all this because of her Instagram: all the smiling selfies; the photos of her snuggling with her little one by the fireplace with a glass of rosé, her husband photo bombing in the background. No wonder Soshana wasn't interested in reconnecting. She saw herself as a loathsome failure. Single, broke and a college dropout. She never wanted Taryn's life, though she couldn't help the instantaneous comparison that happens when you see an old friend doing so much better than you. As hard as she tried to not compare, and find ways to feel grateful, she felt this as a blow to her healing process.

She grabbed a turkey sandwich from the deli next door to L'Addition, Merci and walked home to Mr. Skittles. Her studio was on the upper level of a red brick apartment complex. It was a small structure: six units; two larger apartments on the bottom; studios on the top floor. There were evergreens surrounding the building and a small, fenced courtyard at the back for the ground-floor units. She chose the upper level because they were a little smaller and the rent was cheaper. A square box, no balcony, no accoutrements. A place to survive.

The moment she unlocked the door, Mr. Skittles meowed

while rubbing his body against her legs as his tail vibrated to say, "I missed you."

"Hello, my little man. Mama's home, how was your day?" She loved the way he looked at her when she spoke sweet things to him. She would talk to her dog if she had one but couldn't imagine having another living thing in that small of a space, it would be cruel. Someday, she thought she could have a dog and a cat, maybe even a garden full of vegetables and flowers. Dreaming about a home she would most likely never be able to afford was the only luxury she could stretch to. As she sat on the lumpy old brown couch eating her sandwich, Mr. Skittles jumped up next to her and watched, his tiny breath on her forearm. He dove to snag the bits that fell on the floor.

After cuddling and watching some TV shows, she did some yoga, meditated for five minutes then headed to the bathroom. As she walked through the bathroom door, the uncomfortable dizzy feeling from earlier returned.

She let out a heavy breath, stood in the doorway for a minute and flipped the lights on. The lines of the tiles on the floor next to the toilet looked distorted, as if her eyes were watery. The distortion cleared once the lights fully illuminated the room. After blinking a few times, she decided she was just having some vision problems due to being tired. Mr. Skittles followed her into the bathroom as she sat on the toilet and brushed her teeth.

She looked down at her companion and said, "Why are we here? Can you help me with that? What are we doing here?" He sat in front of her, paws perfectly spaced apart between her feet. "Maaaww." He closed his eyes and opened his mouth to meow again but only a squeak came out. "Dammit, you're cute." He gave her every reason to genuinely smile each day.

The full-size mattress had old yellow sheets with a dark blue comforter. No decorative pillows or fluffy throws like her old friend Taryn has in her master bedroom. The clothes she wore three days ago were at the foot of the bed. She slept in her underwear and whatever T-shirt she was wearing that day, or whatever was left on her bed from the night before. It didn't matter; it wasn't like she was having sex with anyone. She hadn't been interested in having sex for a long time. She felt physically heavy, bloated, uncomfortable, uneasy with herself and if she was to be honest, she felt lost in every possible way. Emotionally, she was distant but always put on a smile and showed her best self at all times to disguise the frailty underneath. Putting herself out there was out of the question. These were the thoughts that regurgitated every night as she prepared to fall asleep.

Face, washed. Teeth, brushed. Hair, a hot going-gray mess. She hadn't bothered to look in the mirror and take in what was in front of her, not after fantasies of mutilating it into an unrecognizable human. How much was plastic surgery anyway? Wouldn't it just be easier to accept that she had no control over what she looked like? Maybe just a quick nose job would do the trick.

Sometimes she would remember to buzz off her mustache, shave her legs and armpits, cut her toenails and fingernails, brush her hair and scrub the bottoms of her feet. The bare minimum was as much energy as she could muster in order to be considered functioning. Makeup? Forget about it. Haircut and color? Not a chance. She didn't have the money for that kind of lifestyle, she often told herself, which was bullshit and she knew it. The cellulite that was forming on her butt and the underside of her thighs like dimples were a secret to her, someone who doesn't have the good sense to look at her own face in the mirror is not going to look at their own behind.

She despised the thought of presenting herself as a woebegone, depressed sad little thing who ached for attention. So, she faked her cheerful attitude so she wouldn't have to deal with people paying attention to her. She wanted to be seen as a kind, fun, outgoing and interesting person. She wasn't sure if that was how people did see her, even though she was excellent at knowing if people were telling the truth. A thirty-six-year-old average woman with nothing going for her and not much else to lose. She was one bad accident away from experiencing homelessness, since she wasn't considering her childhood home as an option.

Focusing on what I want out of life feels like a waste of time. There's not much I can do. I'm not sure what you want out of me. I am doing the best I can. I find it irritating that we are expected to just grin and be grateful, day in and day, out while the people in charge of the world are destroying it and we get to reap the seeds they sow. I don't know what I want my life to look like, I guess this is good enough. Maybe this isn't working.

Soshana can't imagine feeling any different than she does now. Writing her thoughts and emotions for Ms. Erling was becoming more difficult each time pen hit paper. How does talking about your past change your future? She knew it was all about staying present and focusing on the moment. All the experts, gurus, shamans, counselors, yoga instructors, teachers and therapists in the world combined couldn't convince her that someday she would find peace in her mind or body. The universe gave her the shit end of the stick and she wasn't going to be lucky. Some people's lives are just mediocre, and she was learning to be okay with that.

2

The First Episode

Thursday afternoon came too quickly. She had spent the morning reading a mystery novel with Mr. S on the sinking old couch. Her days off usually consisted of sleeping in as late as possible, lounging in whatever she had slept in until one in the afternoon, a quick shower, eating a very large lunch, then dinner around eight in the evening when she could no longer resist the hunger pains. If the anxiety crept up, she would go for a walk or long bike ride out into the countryside, weather pending. This day was going to throw her routine into the toilet.

It was hot and muggy out, so she allowed her hair to dry naturally into soft dark-brown waves. She wore a plain yellow T-shirt, to which she rolled the sleeves, yellow teardrop earrings, an old medium-length jean skirt with brown strappy flat sandals that resembled something a gladiator would wear. She looked in the bathroom mirror for a few moments longer than she normally would.

The tension began to well up inside her chest. What was she going to say to Taryn? How would she let her know she has been hiding away in her safe hole for nine months? Lying to Taryn was not going to work.

Taryn was late. This was not surprising. Soshana figured with Taryn's busy lifestyle and a kid to corral, she would give her some time. Soshana ordered a cappuccino and waited for what was surely going to be a draining event. After nearly thirty minutes, and when she was about to leave, in walked Taryn, full makeup, daisy duke shorts, crop top, sandal wedges and hair perfectly curled.

"Hey, you! Glad you could make it; I was about to text you," Soshana said brightly.

Taryn slapped her purse, one of her two cell phones and keys onto the table. "You won't even believe what just happened. Not only did Jeremiah have a full-blown tantrum right as I'm about to leave, Sean just had to take a dump right as it happened, and *then* I almost got into an accident! I just got that sedan! I'm sorry but this means our meeting has to be cut short, but I want to try and catch up as much as possible. Let me grab a cappuccino real quick."

Maybe she'll want to talk about herself the whole time. Soshana felt a surge of relief. *That's the plan, ask her about what she's doing and just give quick short and maybe slightly dismissive answers.*

Soshana's brain had been spinning since she sat down, it was good that Taryn was late and that she still needed to leave on time to get to her next thing. Soshana wasn't ready to hash it out.

"Great, he's texting me asking what to do about Jer." She huffed out a deep sigh. "Give me a second. So sorry." Taryn said this while not making eye contact and then tapped away on what could only be assumed was her personal cell phone, all while her probable business line was dinging, binging, buzzing and blinking notifications every few seconds. Soshana sat there, mesmerized at the alerts, her own silent cell phone tucked away in her satchel. She hadn't bothered to look at it until the moment before Taryn walked in the door. How awful it would feel to be addicted to two phones let alone one.

"Here's your cappuccino, ma'am." The barista placed it on the table.

Taryn haughtily exclaimed, "Ma'am? Seriously, no!" Then let out a short, sharp laugh that could have been mistaken for a sick Chihuahua choking on a cracker. Soshana's face must have been uncomfortable because Taryn, who finally made eye contact, realized why she was there. Her face dropped, looking perplexed to see her high school best friend sitting across from her. She smartened up and spread a fast smile and bright eyes at Soshana.

"So what have you been up to? Where are you living and what are you doing right now? I'm so glad we can do this, I feel like I have *so* much to tell you. Look at this picture of Jer! Isn't he the sweetest? He turns three next month. We're having a huge party with all of his little friends from day care."

Soshana tried to keep her face from showing shock at the speed at which Taryn spoke. Was she like this in meetings with clients? She looked down at Taryn's phone.

"Wow, he's getting so big, Taryn. He looks healthy and you all look so happy." Soshana was grateful that Taryn segued into talking about herself, so she kept that train running. "How's your business? Are you still selling real estate? And I'm so sorry, what does Sean do again?"

Taryn spoke faster, only stopping briefly to take a breath

and maybe two sips of the cappuccino. Before they knew it, her business cell phone alarm went off, telling her she needed to head out to an open house.

"Are you kidding me? That went by so fast, we have to do this again!" She got up and gave Soshana an awkward side hug and said, "You have no idea how much I miss you and I'm sorry I haven't said it enough." Taryn stared at her phone with wide-open eyes and smacked her hand to her mouth. "I have to go right now, they're starting early without me, it's unacceptable!" She blew a kiss to Soshana and left without her drink. It had gone cold and was mostly untouched. Soshana sat back down, she needed a moment.

"What the hell just happened?" she said aloud, unaware that the barista was listening the whole time.

"I'll tell you what happened," he said with an unmistakable southern twang as he walked towards the table. "She done held up the entire conversation without giving you a second to chime in. She's your friend?" He gazed towards the door. Soshana looked up at him, he was younger than her, tall, thin with long limbs, round metal glasses and tight curly hair that reached his neck. He was cleaning a mug with a white tea towel.

"She was a long time ago. I'm not sure what she is now."

He looked at her with a slight smile, a sense of concern and a slightly raised eyebrow suggesting *maybe you should find out for sure*, as he walked back to the counter. Soshana wasn't very good at socializing, but she felt that instinctual nudge that her abdomen gave her when she was not inside her own mind. She followed him.

"I'm Soshana, or Sosh. Thank you for the wonderful cappuccino."

He smiled and held out his hand for her to shake. He stared at her with wide eyes. He looked away, then back at her with eyes that were relaxed. "I'm Bernard, but please call me Barry."

She shook his hot damp hand; it was still wet from cleaning the mugs. "When did you arrive?" she asked.

He turned the mugs upside down and put them away on the shelf in front of him. "January. It was a sudden move, but I am glad I'm here. I'm sorry to cut you short, but we're closing. Maybe we can continue this another time? Assuming you live in town?"

Was he flirting? No. Too young.

Soshana left the café with a grin and a goodbye to Barry. The door jingled as it closed behind her, the conversation had sparked a tiny light of glee inside her. She decided to walk past her work to see if her subordinates, as she jokingly called them, were behaving. Peering into the window behind a sunscreen display that would hide her, she saw that everything looked shipshape. She kept walking and as she was about to pass the building, Joe popped out with a "hey!" She stopped but not before she did an eye roll and pursed her lips, hands on hips as she turned towards Joe. She relaxed her face into a smile. The banter they had at work was her favorite part of being there.

"Hey, you, how is everything going today?"

Joe clapped back with his hands on his hips. "Are you checking in on us, boss? I have this place running just fine. I wanted to check in on *you*. Are you okay? That was kind of scary the other day."

"You don't have to worry," she said with a chuckle and a small grin. "I can take care of myself, but it's nice to know someone cares about my wellbeing. I just came from a coffee date with an old friend and I'm about to go home and make myself a big bowl of cheesy pasta."

"Well, if that's all, then off you go. Don't get into any trouble, I'll see you tomorrow." He smiled at her, pinched her arm and went back into the store.

She shook her head and smiled. She was grateful to have someone who felt like a friend in her life. He must have been a caring father.

She hadn't heard from her own father since the funeral, which he didn't go to. They surmised he thought the ex-husband attending would make it awkward for his ex-in-laws. Whenever Soshana thought of her father, she felt an indescribable ache. You never stop needing your parents, even if they maliciously hurt you or abandoned you, it's a built-in mechanism. She wanted to cut it out with a dull knife so she could feel every piece of pain depart her body until it was completely gone.

Soshana had bought the items for pasta primavera at the deli next to the café; a woman on a mission. Pasta, cat cuddles and more mystery reading. That was the perfect evening. She waved to her elderly neighbor, Ruth, as she walked up the steps to her cozy apartment.

Mr. Skittles was waiting patiently by the window, he sprung off the ledge and came close to her feet for a pat on the head. She put down the bag full of groceries and headed to the bathroom. When she opened the door and flicked the light switch on, she noticed the lighting was not the usual bright natural tone, but a yellow, almost foggy, color. The dizzy spell came back, this time more sudden and dramatically intense. She closed her eyes and tried to take a deep breath, her lungs felt like they were collapsing. Her breathing was shallow and her chest felt as though it was caving in. Heart pounding and bile rising in her throat, it felt like a thousand hands were on her backside, pushing her down and forward at once.

Soshana had never felt this petrified in her life. She felt a deep sense of pain in her chest, the kind that is meant to break your spirit and force you to give into the torture. Again, she tried to take a deep breath, all that was coming in and out of her lungs were short and shallow breaths. She dared to open her eyes. The second she did, tunnel vision formed on the periphery of her sight and she felt as though she was falling forward endlessly, over and over into consuming darkness.

She landed on the floor, face down, her wrist folded underneath her abdomen, her right leg splayed out and the left tucked underneath, curled up in a half fetal position. Blood spilled from her nose after smashing into the toilet seat. She felt waves of sharp of pain on her face, but she was able to breathe a bit easier. When she finally felt brave enough to try to open her eyes again, she was not in her own bathroom. Her head was wedged between the bathroom counter and a filthy toilet.

She got up as quickly as her legs would allow, her brain was not putting together what was happening. Her body began to shake, first her head, then it shivered all the way down to her legs. The mirror changed shape; the lighting flickered and within seconds she was back in her own bathroom. Disoriented, she lost her footing and fell backwards into the bathtub.

3

Meeting

BAM BAM BAM BAM BAM. Soshana woke to the sound of loud banging. Mr. Skittles yowled and mewed. Disoriented, ears ringing, vision blurred and with a headache that could knock a horse unconscious, she shakily brought herself up to her hands and knees off the bathroom floor. *Her* bathroom. She recognized where she was, remembering she had, somehow impossibly, been somewhere else. Her heart started racing again.

The groceries from yesterday were still on the counter, untouched. She crawled out towards the apartment door and pulled herself up with the chair next to the door to look through the viewer. Two police officers and Joe were outside.

"Soshana, are you in there? If you can hear us, please open up, we're here to perform a wellness check," one of the offers said in a firm tone.

"Sosh, it's me, Joe! Please be okay, please." When she heard Joe's scared voice, she felt confident these people weren't here to hurt her. She opened the door and Joe pushed past the officers to get inside first. He hugged her and she let out a strained yelp of pain. Her arm, back and neck hurt. There was a line of crusted dried blood from her nose to her chin. Her eyes were dry, bloodshot and puffy.

One officer called for an ambulance while the other asked permission to enter to investigate what she assumed was a potential crime scene. Joe pulled Soshana away gently, the officer guiding him to place her on the sofa. "Ma'am, can you tell me your name and what day it is?"

Soshana mumbled, "M-my name is Sos-Soshana." Struggling to keep her eyes open, her shoulders came closer to her ears so she could gently turn her head towards the window to avoid increasing the pain from the headache. Looking towards a natural light source might give her a sense of what time it was. Her head shook slightly to tell the officer she did not know what day it was. The sun was bright in the blue clear sky, it appeared to be late morning. The air was crisp, cool and the perfect humidity. She kept staring out the window, searching for birds while intermittently bending over and vomiting.

The first officer, a large commanding woman, said to the room, "She needs to get to the hospital now, she probably has a concussion."

"I don't want to go, please don't make them take me, Joe," she said weakly, shaking. She didn't want to plead, she couldn't help feeling terrified. She couldn't afford an ambulance ride let alone an emergency room visit. Joe was doing his best to stay strong, this must have been excruciating for him, given that he lost his only child, his twenty-two-year-old daughter, to an overdose a decade ago.

"I think it's best that you go sweetheart. They're going to help you find out what is going on with you. Don't worry about Mr. Skittles, I'll make sure he is taken care of and work will be fine. It will be fine." He strained a weak smile, his eyes showed pain.

Joe helped the officers gather some of her personal items: a change of clothes, toothbrush, phone, purse and medications. He asked Soshana if he could have a key, she pointed at it on her key chain and he pulled it off. Joe patted her hand while she was wheeled out of the apartment. The female officer looked down at her with a smile that masked a grimace of pity.

The ambulance arrived, pulling up to a halt in front of the apartment complex. Soshana could hear the footsteps of the emergency crew coming up the stairs. Her mind begged for unconsciousness; the physical pain was all consuming. Three of them arrived and carefully looked her over and asked similar questions to the officers while shining a light into her pupils, assessing her neck and determining it wasn't fully broken, pleasantly smiling throughout. It was jarring.

"Where are you taking me?" Soshana said.

"To the closest hospital, they will assess you there. Can you tell me your next of kin? I'll let the nurses know once we get there." The paramedic's smile had faded.

Next of kin?! Soshana's body was beginning to violently shake at the words. *Am I dying?* The officer tilted their head down a little to indicate a response.

"My brother, Derek." She gave them his information then kept silent as they hoisted her onto the gurney. It was tricky getting down the stairs, and being picked up by the paramedics and jostled around caused her to fall unconscious from the pain and exhaustion.

She could hear the steady beep of the heart monitor as she laid with her eyes closed. Her breathing was back to normal, the sensation of her body barely hovering above the bed, while also feeling sunk deep into the mattress. The memory of the morning events felt far away, though she didn't realize it was the afternoon of the next day, in a different city. She had been airlifted to the University of Michigan in Ann Arbor. She was in the neuro intensive care unit and seated next to her was Derek. He was staring blankly at his phone, not looking at anything in particular. She opened her eyes and turned towards him. He gave her the warmest smile he could.

"Oh, Soshi. How are you feeling?"

She looked at him, crinkled her eyes and tried to form a smile back at him. "Derek?" she said with confusion, he registered this.

With a sigh, he said cautiously, "It's Saturday morning, you're at MSU Ann Arbor, in ICU. The doctors said you had a brain injury from slipping in your bathroom and hitting the tub." He was rubbing the palm of his hand on her forearm that did not bear any medical devices attached to it. He looked exhausted, older even. His hair was flat, unwashed and oily. He was wearing a beat-up purple NYU sweater that she had given him years ago. It had some cracker crumbs on the front. "You're going to be fine. I'll get a nurse and let them know that you're awake. They can explain more."

She gave him a small nod.

A nurse came in with a stern countenance, the look of someone who is obviously in charge. "Good afternoon, Soshana, I'm Carina and I'll be taking care of you this evening. You came in with a TBI, also known as a traumatic brain injury, from falling. The good news is you are here where we can care for you. The bad news is you have lost a lot of blood and are severely bruised. We have been monitoring you closely over the past twenty-four hours, and you will be transferred to the step-down unit in a few hours. Most likely you will be in the hospital for at least a few weeks. The doctor has been in to check on your vitals and will meet with you tomorrow. Do you have any questions?" This was said like she had memorized every word, a robotic staccato, cold and inattentive. Soshana had a hard time concentrating after the first few sentences. She looked over to Derek with concern and was hoping he understood what was said. Carina began to glare at the two of them. She demanded an immediate response and her full attention.

"She's probably hungry, when is dinner?" he asked with a scant declaration of attitude.

She couldn't help the laugh that came out of her mouth without warning. He always knew how to quickly defuse tense situations.

Carina was not amused. She walked closer to Soshana and put her hand on the rail next to her arm. "I will be back with some paperwork for you to review. It would be wise to appoint a DPOA. Do you know what that is? It's durable power of attorney in case you worsen. Now rest." She barked without giving either sibling the chance to answer, as if they were petulant, ignorant children.

She walked curtly out of the room, but not before giving Derek 'cut eye.' "What is up her ass? Jesus," he huffed, then continued, "You're okay, Soshi? I understand how serious this is but really?! A *DPOA*? You're fine." Derek shook his head. Was he trying to convince himself? "Anyway, I wasn't sure if you wanted me to call Dad, so I didn't."

"I guess he should probably know. I have to figure out who

is going to take care of-" Soshana stalled.

Derek interrupted, "Mr. Skittles? Your friend Joe said he's at your apartment twice a day, every day making sure he is happy, I was looking at your texts." Derek grinned cheekily, winking.

Soshana sighed in relief. "Don't wink at me like that, Joe's my friend at work. He's been so kind to me over the past few years. He's not my type, plus he's much older and has a girlfriend. And yeah, you can call Dad." She immediately regretted agreeing to it.

Derek made a very silly disapproving face that made her laugh again, and then abruptly stopped from the pain.

"Sorry, sis. I'm here for you until I know you are one hundred percent."

"No, you can't miss school, I'll be fine. I won't allow it. There are plenty of people here to make sure I stay alive."

He shook his head with another look of disapproval, sighed with annoyance and said, "You're always the one to take care of everyone else, but when it comes to you needing help, it's not allowed, it's bullshit. I'm staying until at least tomorrow night, whether you like it or not." Derek was always a quick-witted, strong-minded and confident kid. Now as an independent grown man of twenty-seven, tall, fit and classically handsome, she knew she wouldn't be able to tell him what to do. It was difficult for her to see him as a grown-up. He had proven over and over that he could take care of himself since he was a young teen. She was always so proud of him for standing up for himself and being exactly who he was. She took a breath in to dissuade the annoyance that crept up from his confidence, then nodded. The pain in her neck and the strain in her movements were building anxious momentum with each passing moment. Life becomes uncontrollable when you are incapacitated.

"Good. I was able to find a room at the closest motel. It ain't pretty, but it'll do. Do you want me to get you some of your favorite snacks or dirty magazines? I like the ones you would like so I can borrow them afterwards."

She started to argue that of course she didn't look at smut. *Not anymore at least.* The last thing she wanted to do was discuss images of hot sweaty naked men with her brother, she was entirely drained from the thought of arguing.

"Fine." She waved her fingers toward the door. "Please grab some toothpaste, lip balm and no dirty magazines, you turd!" she barked after him.

Derek waggled his thick eyebrows and grinned from ear to ear as he giggled and skipped out of the room. Soshana fell asleep almost immediately.

The next time she woke up she was in a normal-looking hospital room. For the first time in what was apparently two days, she felt starved, stomach aching, her mouth was parched dry, as if she had been chewing on sand. Grateful for the water bottle next to her bed, she guzzled down half of it in one go. She smacked her lips, wishing she had lip balm. She felt dry inside and out.

"Where is that little asshole with my snacks?" she said out loud. Behind a curtain, she heard an unfamiliar response.

"He ate most of them," a mans voice drifted from behind the curtain to her right. "He told me to tell you to... 'deal with it'?" He spoke carefully with an inflection on the last words, making sure it sounded like a question. His voice had a deep resonance and a kind tone.

Soshana's eyes and mouth popped open in horror, her face burning.

"Oh my god, I'm so sorry, I thought I was in a room by myself!"

The man next to her chuckled. "It's totally fine, I was kidding around. Most people don't get separate rooms in this hospital. He did bring you snacks and gave me some as well. I think he may have been flirting with me. Who knows ha ha! Check in the drawer next to you."

Soshana leaned over to her right to reach into the drawer and found a few books, toothpaste, lip balm, deep mauve lipstick, a brush, some potato chips, licorice and chocolate chip cookies.

"That dirty bastard," she whispered to herself. He left an erotic male magazine flipped upside down with a note on the back that said *Don't you DARE throw this away, I want it back!* She huffed to herself as she opened the chips and stuffed her face.

"I heard that too, you know," the voice retorted.

Soshana responded sternly, laced with irritation and chips spitting out of her mouth, "Can you hear me eating too? Should I chew quietly?"

The only thing she could hear was a ringing in her ears, a sign to cool her temper.

"Sorry. It's been a rough week and I'm doing my best to keep myself entertained. I'll mind my business." His voice was stoic and flat.

Embarrassment set in. She rarely showed her angry side to people, let alone strangers, especially if she couldn't see their face. In fact, most emotions that weren't considered pleasant were not expressed.

She paused and said calmly, "No, I'm sorry. I'm just exhausted and hurting. My name is Soshana." She did her best to say this with a smile, her face felt funny, numb and tingling in different areas, while her head and nose throbbed, pulsing with pain at each breath.

"Hello, I'm Kieran, and I'm exhausted and hurting as well."

Soshana's face fell. "I'm sorry we're both here. If you don't mind my asking, what happened to you?"

He let out a sigh. "I had a tumor removed from my brain."

The silence could have been cut with a knife. Her heart sank. She said she was sorry, he said it's fine. Shaking her head, she took a few bites before an orderly came in to take their dinner orders.

She ordered a cheeseburger and salad. "I'll have the same, hold the onions," Kieran told the orderly.

They sat in silence for about fifteen minutes. Curiosity must have got the better of him. "I'm so sorry but what are you doing over there? Are you sleeping? Please tell me to shut up if you need rest."

"No, I am just checking my texts. I haven't looked at my phone in several days." One was from Derek, saying he was on his way and would be there as soon as possible, the other was from Joe, he said *we're becoming fast friends, please don't worry all is well. Speedy recovery and please keep me updated!* and included a photo of Mr. Skittles lying on the couch. Mr. Skittles was her world and she would do anything to have him there, being comforted by his velvet fur and purring. Soshana responded to Kieran, a bit distracted and, if she was being honest with herself, a little annoyed. *Who is this guy?*

"What are *you* up to over there?" she asked genially.

An obviously eager response came back. "*I'm* reading a

vintage issue of *Reader's Digest*. Did you know that you can use mayonnaise as a mask on your scalp for added moisture?" They both chuckled. "If you could read anything else besides *Reader's Digest*, what would it be?" he asked.

Personal questions, or any questions about herself were taken with a front of skepticism. She figured it couldn't hurt to be distracted from the mess she was in. *He could be safe.* Someone who'd had intensive surgery and she would probably never see again wouldn't have the chance to hurt her. Knowing this was an opportunity to work on her rapidly declining social skills, she responded reluctantly. "Anything mystery, some science fiction or fantasy. I don't mind a bit of classical romance either. What about you?"

"I love mystery! Classical romance, huh? Like Jane Austen or Charlotte Brontë? I read one or two. The prose and dialogue are fascinating compared to today's use of language, don't you think? Although I enjoy TV shows too, any kind of medium that allows for great storytelling. What do you do for a living?" Bursting at the seams, hasty and giddy with his responses, he sounded genuinely interested, like he couldn't wait to ask questions, and was grateful to have someone to talk to.

Needing a moment to recover from the rapid-fire responses and questions, she took a moment to think. *He's read period piece novels?*

"Let me ask you this first, why do people ask what you do to make a living rather than asking what you love doing with your life? I think it's much more meaningful."

"I'm not happy with my career either."

Soshana was unsure how to respond and felt a twinge of offense. *Don't assume,* she thought.

"I mean, I'm assuming that's why you didn't want to tell

me." he said, words spitting out quickly as if to clean up a mess he didn't intend to make. "I haven't spoken to anyone besides the hospital staff in days, my mouth doesn't have a filter right now and my brain isn't working the same these days either. I'm really sorry if I offended you." He stayed silent for a few moments, Soshana was calculating her response. He continued, "You don't have to say anything if you don't want to." He sounded ashamed. She could tell by his tone he was also desperate for human connection.

Soshana was overwhelmed with exhaustion, pain and confusion. She wasn't sure what to say for a little while. "It's okay. I wasn't sure how to respond, I don't think my brain is working quite well either. I won't hold it against you."

He breathed a sigh of relief. "Thank you. I'll try to be more mindful."

Her nose itched, she brought her fingers up to her face and without thinking, rubbed underneath her nostrils then let out a yelp of pain.

"NURSE!" Kieran yelled. The nurse came running in, around the same time Derek walked in through the doors to the unit. Soshana had forgotten that she landed on her face the day before.

"Your nose is broken, please don't touch it." Carina grabbed some gauze and gently held it up against Soshana's nose.

"You hadn't mentioned that during your briefing. Is there anything else I should know?" Soshana replied curtly while holding the broad side of her index finger to the underside of her nose, suppressing the blood as a few drops curled it.

Carina grabbed a mirror from the tall white cabinet and handed it to Soshana. She looked at the nurse with deliberate bitchiness before she peered into it. One of her eyes was blood red and a dark purple bruising had begun to form underneath her bottom eyelids. Her hair was messy and her skin was pale, she looked like she had been brought back from death. She stared with her mouth open, her eyes wide from looking at someone she didn't recognize. She clamped her mouth closed tightly and swallowed. The only respite that came from her staring at a face she didn't recognize was that the mutilated, morphed features looked nothing like her wicked mother.

"Sis, it's okay. The bruising and swelling will go away and your nose will heal. Does it hurt?"

She nodded.

Carina, in all her abundant wisdom and compassionate nature, without saying a word injected some pain medication into her IV bag and brought her an ice pack for her face. "This will make you drowsy for a few hours. I'll come back with your dinner and wake you up." She turned and left the three of them in the room without saying another word.

"She's a ray of fucking sunshine," Derek said. He sat next to Soshana and held her hand while she adjusted herself, preparing to fall asleep in the most comfortable position.

Soshana had always been more of a mother to Derek than Marilyn. He loved his mother, but she wasn't the type to be affectionate and open. Derek and Soshana could talk for hours on end about any subject they enjoyed. He loved that he could be a comfort to her during this time. She was always the one comforting him through life's challenges. Keeping her struggles to a minimum during conversations because she didn't want to burden anyone or stop them expressing their needs. She fell asleep nauseous, head splitting, feeling lost but not alone.

When Soshana woke up a few hours later, she called for a nurse to help her walk to the bathroom she shared with Kieran. She walked past his bed; the sheet was drawn all the way around it towards the window so she couldn't get a look at him. He must have been sleeping or drugged up, because he wasn't talking. She wondered how old he was, his voice sounded young, but his choice of words was old enough to have some life experience. Having a brain tumor will provide a humble personality, one would think. She relieved herself easily enough and returned to her bed.

The kinder, gentler nurse that helped her back into bed asked if she was feeling okay and if she needed anything. Soshana tried to smile but it came off as a grimace, as she said. "No thank you, I'm fine for now, I think." The nurse left and closed the door quietly behind them. Soshana sat upright in her bed. She examined the off-white sheets with her right hand, then she noticed that the back of her hand had some bruising, and her nails were brittle, broken in some places at the tips. Her breathing became shallow, fast and erratic. Her mind went silent, not out of her own accord, but out of necessity.

"Soshana?" Kieran said groggily.

Unaware of any sounds, the ringing in her ears and unsettled breathing closed her mind off from interruptions.

"Are you okay, Soshana?" Kieran said with more effort and concern.

Startled, she responded, "Fine." She made an attempt to revive her stagnant mind. "How about you?"

"Ah. I'll be fine. I'm sorry I'm so talkative. I usually don't talk *this* much." He took a quick breath and let it out faster. "I think I'm nervous. Might be the drugs. I guess I lost about five days and I hadn't talked to many people, even before the surgery. Is it okay with you if we continue the conversation? I think it will help me with tr-trying to forget about all this." He stammered the last part of the sentence, sounding insecure.

She felt worse for him than she did for herself. She wondered what kind of tumor and what he meant by 'losing five days.'

"Of course. I think it might help me too."

He blew out a "phew" and chuckled lightheartedly.

She continued scrambling and searching for something to ask him from her addled mind. "I have to say, I'm a bit jealous of your window, I get to watch the nurses run around and I would much rather look out into the world."

He stated plainly, "It's a brick wall, so ya know you're not missing out on much. Sometimes a bird will fly by. Other than that, it's boring."

"Ah. That would be boring," she said. "To bore you even further, I will answer your question from earlier."

He interrupted her again, "I'm sorry to cut you off, I don't need to know your occupation, I would much rather hear what you love to do with your life. You're right. It's so much more important than how you make money to survive. Sorry again."

"It's okay. Thank you for understanding," she continued, a little annoyed about being interrupted again. Though being courageous enough to open up about herself to a stranger gave her a bit of renewed energy she hadn't felt in a long time, or possibly ever. She thought perhaps it would be a good day to start practicing what her therapist asked her to do, several years ago, which was *share your life, be open and vulnerable. Listen and act on your quiet, reserved instincts. Learn to discern between the anxious signals and the real instincts.* Or something to that extent.

She recognized in that moment that she needed permission to be vulnerable from an adult, an older, wiser adult. It irritated her that she was a grown woman, taking care of herself and yet still sought out permission and guidance to just be herself.

He was immobile, she didn't know him, she couldn't even see him. *What harm could he really do if I don't allow a conversation to harm or affect me?* She reminded herself, as she often needed to when it came to meeting new people. *What better time than now?*

She began slowly, thinking about her words carefully. As the thoughts and ideas came out, it led to her remembering more things. She continued to elaborate, he listened silently, which encouraged her more. Talking about her upbringing in Northeast Grand Rapids, how she loved being outdoors in the natural world: gardening, biking, learning about animals, playing with her cousins on the beach at Lake Michigan in the summer, reading, her amazing cat, how she wished she had a home where she could have a yard and a dog. She missed her friends and her life in New York, she loved trying new food at eloquent and upscale restaurants with them. She stopped herself before she went too far and mentioned why she had moved back to Grand Rapids and what happened before and after the move. She wasn't ready to dive into that tender wound.

Kieran stayed silent for a while after she finished speaking. She wondered if he had fallen asleep. "Kieran, have *you* passed away?"

"Not at all, I'm enjoying hearing the passion in your voice.

Thank you for telling me all that. Can I ask you a very serious question, Soshana?" She could hear the smile on his face, growing as his sentence ended.

"Sure," she replied.

"Will you have dinner with me tonight? My treat."

She laughed cautiously. "Yes, especially since you're paying," she responded playfully while smirking carefully, still feeling the strangeness around her face.

Is he flirting? Am I?

She had no idea anymore and didn't know what to think of him. What was his aim? What did he get from keeping himself entertained by a strange woman? What did he gain by having these small, insignificant interactions? She hated that her mind went to those places when she met new people. She never knew what they wanted from her unless they were direct, which rarely happened as people don't say what's on their mind. It was also beginning to dawn on her that she was flustered that she couldn't see his face while she was talking with him. How could she know if he was sincere if she couldn't read the tiny but important expressions? Why hadn't he interrupted and said things about his life? *"The world is not straightforward, one has to learn how to navigate through the charisma, silence and accusations of everyday people."* Ms. Erling came into her mind again, without warning or warrant.

They continued their small talk, which almost made her more uncomfortable than talking about personal experiences. He mentioned how he felt cold after the surgery, and before he was always borderline roasting in a T-shirt and shorts most of the time. He figured it must be the drugs and lying around.

Dinner came within a few minutes after pausing their chat. It was no foodie's dream, but it was edible and gone within minutes.

"And how was your meal?" Kieran asked playfully.

"Perfectly okay. 3.5 stars on Yelp, at best. How about you?" she responded.

"Meh," he muttered.

She imagined his mouth contorting, his upper lip curled in mild disgust. She needed to see him; she couldn't stand not being able to watch his facial reactions. But she didn't want anyone to look at her, the attention and fuss would send her reeling. It's bad enough Derek had to be there.

Derek came back to say goodbye as visiting hours were ending. "Where were you? And take that smut mag out of my drawer, I don't even want to touch it!" she demanded. She could hear Kieran chuckling behind the curtain.

Derek laughed. "You kill me, Soshi!" He looked at his sister with deep concern. "I hate to leave you. Are you sure you're going to be all right?" Derek said while patting her arm lovingly.

"For the last time, yes. I promise I'll let you know if anything changes. I am so grateful that you were here for me. I love you."

Derek gave her a quick peck on her forehead and said his goodbyes. "Go to sleep, I'll text you when I get to my apartment," he said as he left.

Kieran said, "He's a good guy, your brother. We spoke for a little bit before you woke up. He wanted to see the scar on my skull. I'm a right mess, but he didn't care. 'Bless him,'" Kieran said in an English accent. "I'm going to request some debilitating drugs right about now and promptly pass out, it was a pleasure, Miss or Mrs.?"

She replied, "That's Miss, to you, sir. Sleep well." She

imagined the scar on his head. What did that mean? Did he have a scheduled surgery, or was he in a terrible accident and they happened to find the tumor? The thought of it gave her dull, aching shivers and pressure in her chest, similar to when she heard or saw someone getting hurt. Her thoughts became disorganized. Eating a full meal, conversations with a stranger and the medications made her body feel ten times heavier than normal, and her head buzzed with the anticipation of falling asleep.

4

Seeing

She dreamed of running outside as a teenager, stopping to look up at the trees, watching the light catch each leaf in the wind as they twisted and turned, the chattering and whispering of the leaves as the wind passed through them. The wind would pick up intensity and cause the evergreen branches to sway, and the leaves on the silver maples would dance and twist more fiercely. In her dreams, there were times when she could almost smell the warmth of the earth as she laid on the grass looking up at the magic that nature created. When she was alone with the trees, she would think, *someone-something could have made this for me, just so I can marvel at your beauty.*

Soshana became aware that she was dreaming and hoped to stay there for a while longer in peace and comfort. There was no pain, no anxiety and no worries about anything. She wished she could feel this way in her waking hours, the thought of having that kind of contentment warmed her chest. She eventually let go and drifted into a dreamless sleep.

Soshana woke up feeling worse than she had the day before. She assumed it was the drugs wearing off. She reached over to take a drink of water and pressed the nurses' button. It must have been around six in the morning. She could tell by the light from the window and the dampness in the room that it had rained, or it was about to. There were small, steady intakes of breath from Kieran, his heart monitor beeping steadily along with hers.

A nurse walked in gracefully, she was tall, trim and broad-shouldered. "I'm Josette, darling. I'm here, what do you need?" Her voice was soothing with a deep resonating tone. She was considerate in her manner to not awaken those in the room.

Soshana smiled at her and in a voice slightly louder than a whisper and said, "Good morning, I need to use the restroom and I'm uncomfortable and in a bit of pain. Can I have something for it, please?"

Josette responded in the same whispered volume, "Of course, let me help you up." As they walked past Kieran's bed toward the restroom, the curtain around his section had been pulled in so she was able to get a few seconds glimpse of Kieran sleeping. The immediate and obvious feature that caught her attention was the large bald patch with a curved line of scabbing, a stitched incision along the right side of his head. He was thin, had a patchy dark brown beard, broad shoulders, wavy and curly dark hair, a large but not overwhelming nose. He wasn't unattractive, or attractive, she supposed she couldn't quite tell. She thought she imagined some gray hair on his temples, and on his left hand, a ring on the fourth finger. He must have been in his thirties, or maybe forties. She knew all too well how being thin from cancer treatments made you look older. In the few years that she hadn't seen her mother, and to the point when she went home to take care of her, it looked like she had aged twenty years.

As she left the bathroom, she hoped she could get a better look at him, but the sheet was closed when she walked past.

Josette was gentle, sweet and had a calming energy. Soshana wished she could be her full-time nurse instead of 'Crabby Pants Carina' as Derek had named her. Soshana remembered that she still hadn't seen a doctor yet. It was a bit concerning to her as she had been in hospital for three days now. "Josette? I haven't met the doctors yet, can I please meet them?"

Josette nodded and with a genuine smile, pumped her full of drugs and told her she would grab one of her doctors in the next few hours. She also asked if Soshana wanted to go back to sleep or be propped up. The kindness she was being shown was enough to cure her. She wasn't sure, so she asked to be propped up with the option of sleeping that way. She drank more water, put some lip balm on and grabbed the first book in the drawer. She must have fallen asleep for a short while after a few pages.

She woke up thinking about the ring on Kieran's left hand. She had not heard a spouse, nor anyone visiting him. That seemed strange. She tried to figure out a way to ask him how he ended up here, where he was from and if he was married. She heard the rustling of sheets and groaning coming from Kieran.

Brrrrrrriiiip.

Soshana became alert, eyes moving back and forth. *Did he just fart or was that me?!* Her face was beet red and hot with fear. She sniffed the air.

Nope. Not me. Phew. But then she started to giggle, as painful as it was, the feeling of wanting to laugh coming from her chest was irresistible. She wouldn't want to embarrass him by announcing it, though maybe he would find it humorous. If it were her that released the noxious gas from her anus she wouldn't want to admit it right now. Too fresh of a relationship.

He started to cough and she heard him press the nurses' button. Josette came in within thirty seconds and helped him up to use the bathroom and administered more drugs for pain. He sounded awful, she felt for him, she hadn't heard him complain once.

Breakfast was arriving, she smelled coffee and eggs. She closed her eyes for a moment and pretended she was at home, cuddling on the couch with Mr. Skittles.

"Here you are. Would you like cream and sugar?"

"No thank you," she responded.

"The crew is coming in today!" the orderly said with a smile.

"What does that mean?"

"The therapy pets. I wanted to ask if you would like a visit. We have Oscar, he's an English pointer, and Sugar Baby, a Bombay long-haired cat. They are the sweetest!"

"Yes, please!" Soshana said loudly, almost leaping out of her bed with excitement, forgetting every pain, bruise and cut, before the inevitable sharp reminder. Kieran was back in his bed. "Do you want to have a visit from the therapy pets too?" Soshana asked him, even though it was the orderly's job, she couldn't help it.

"Yes, I would love that!"

So he's an animal lover too, Soshana thought to herself.

"Good morning, Soshana," Kieran said after breakfast had settled. "Soshana, means lily, correct?"

"Yes, it does."

45

"Do you like lilies?" he asked sweetly.

"I enjoy all flowers, but they aren't my favorite. Did you google my name last night?" she asked him in a flirtatious tone without recognizing her action.

"Yeah, I did. How are you feeling this morning?" he asked.

"Kind of you to ask, I feel like a pile of shit that someone stepped on. A swollen pus-filled carcass of a human. And I'm sure I look like it too. How about you?" This was the truth. She was astonished by herself. She was continuing to be open with him, maybe just to see what would happen, maybe because she ached for it.

"Jesus. Well, I'm thinking I look and feel just about the same. I'm trying to picture how that would look, and *I'm frightened!*" he said in a goofy voice, then laughed at himself for being outwardly silly.

She laughed with him. "Well, that's how I feel. I haven't taken a good look since yesterday. It could be worse, that's what they say at least."

He replied with a breath that was sucked in between clenched teeth. "Jeez, yeah. I'm really sorry, it sounds painful. I hope it gets better for you real fast."

Josette returned with a fresh set of towels, a generic robe, clean slippers and some off-brand toiletries. "Ready for a shower?" Soshana almost fell out of bed with excitement. "Me first! Yes please!"

Josette laughed with a smile made of starlight and said, "It's the little things in life, huh?" She helped Soshana over to the bathroom and asked if she needed any assistance.

Soshana felt comfortable with Josette, even though they had just met, it was her warmth and genuine sense of care that helped Soshana feel safe. "Can you wait outside the door just in case? I feel more confident today."

"Of course, darling." Josette said while softly patting Soshana's forearm.

Soshana grabbed a fresh set of clothes and undergarments. She hadn't worn a bra in several days so that was going to feel interesting.

Water sprayed out from the industrial hospital shower, releasing the smell of bleach and artificial fragranced cleaner from the plastic shower walls, a smell she detested since it was harsh and unpleasant. Right now, nothing could matter less. She stepped gingerly into the stall and let the water fall over her head, avoiding the cut on her nose and jerking her body when it touched the back of her head and base of her neck. It was soothing after a while. She allowed herself to take a long deep breath and close her eyes. She reminded herself that she was safe, that Josette was watching out for her, and that she didn't need to worry. Scrubbing her scalp, washing her body and face carefully, brushing her hair out and braiding it to one side was a luxurious kind of satisfaction. She was so grateful that she had a packed bag filled with her essential toiletries, especially her face moisturizer and body balm. Joe was aware of what she needed and that was something she wished she recognized and appreciated more in people.

She clipped her jagged fingernails, then her toenails. She was ready to come out, almost feeling like a new person. How incredible it was to take a full shower after several days in an unfamiliar place, it helped her feel at ease and gave her a boost of confidence.

"The Crew" came to visit in the late morning, going by too fast as they had a lot of other patients to visit, but those few minutes really elevated their spirits. Soshana could hear the smile on Kieran's face as he talked to them. She didn't want the therapy pets to leave, hoping they could come back around before they left. Soshana wanted to keep that smile on Kieran's face but wasn't sure how. Making people happy was a drug to her.

Kieran was onto her, he also wanted to keep the uplifting atmosphere going so he asked, "How about this? Let's play a game. You describe to me, in as much honesty as you can, how you look. I will do the same. And someday, hopefully not too long from now, we will get to properly meet each other and we can see who told the truth." Soshana was hesitant to respond. "If you're comfortable with that, if not, no worries. Just trying to pass the time."

She hadn't thought how odd his question was. Then she started to think about her appearance. She hadn't concerned herself with her image in a long time, it didn't matter to her.

"Um, sure. I am about five feet four. I have long dark wavy hair. I'm fairly average-looking, I guess?" Her eyebrows furrowed, eyes darting from left to right. She pulled in her lips involuntarily, not wanting to say more. She was becoming uncomfortable but sat with that feeling and continued reluctantly. "Um. My eyes are grayish green. My face is oval-shaped." She was unsure of what else to say.

"Nice," he said as kindly as possible. "Thank you for humoring me. Um, let's see. I'm around five feet eleven, I have brown eyes, brown hair and my body is in the shape of a skeleton who wishes for death! Oh and I'm half bald."

She laughed; it eased the static in the air.

"You sound quite lovely, Soshana, Lily of the Valley," he said.

She replied, "Thanks, I guess. I'm sorry about your baldness. Is that a temporary thing, or are you experiencing a rare form of male-pattern baldness?"

He chortled. "Thankfully no, and hopefully temporary. The chemo and radiation ended three months ago and I worked hard to grow it back to where it is now, until the surgery just last week, of course."

Soshana's heart dropped, her face and ears flushed with heat. She paused from speaking for a few moments, unsure how to respond, unsure why she had such a reaction hearing about it.

She finally replied, "I'm so sorry, Kieran, I didn't know."

He coughed and said in a small voice that turned brighter as he spoke, "You don't have to be sorry. I'm going to be fine; it was in the early stages of cancer. They weren't confident with the labs after the treatment, so they decided to operate to clear the margins. It's just scary. I wasn't sure if I should tell you, but for some reason talking to you makes it easier. I don't feel judged or overly criticized by you. No stranger danger vibes."

Silence. Her eyes darted back and forth. Her face was still hot and her blood pressure was only just beginning to go back down.

Cancer.

Of course, this set off the feelings she had when she found out about her mother's cancer. The helplessness, concern, anxiety and fear of losing her crept up but was quickly quieted.

"I would never judge you in that way, you are going through a very difficult..." she trailed off. *What do you say to someone who just recently went through cancer treatment, someone who just got out of major surgery?* "...transition. In life. I am happy to be your crutch." She felt fifteen per cent okay with that answer. A lifeless and dull response, but adequate for the time being.

Josette was back in the room with a wheelchair. "C'mon,

darling, let's get you up. The doctor is ready to see you now." Josette helped her out of the bed and into the wheelchair. Soshana took notice of all the aches from sitting still for so long, and all the pain that was inflicted from the accident. She didn't want to leave Kieran hanging, she said whatever she could come up with in that moment. "I'll be back and we can continue." It was another awkward response. She rolled her eyes at herself.

"Okay. Good luck," he said.

She was wheeled into an elevator and down to the floor below. They entered a small office with a large floor-to-ceiling window that had a great view of buildings, trees, the courtyard and gardens. It was a relief to finally see the outdoors. She desperately wanted to go outside and get some fresh air. They waited several minutes for the doctor. Josette hummed a familiar old pop song Soshana couldn't pick out, but she enjoyed hearing it anyway and could easily tell that she must be a talented singer.

The doctor walked in after knocking on the door twice and looked at his laptop. Without making eye contact he said, "Hello, I'm Dr. Weathering, neurologist, I hope you're feeling better, Ms. Jones. I wanted to quickly go over why you are here." He looked up at her for a split second, let out a short sigh that told her he was tired and maybe annoyed, then looked back down at the laptop. "You had what is called a TBI, traumatic brain injury, from collapsing. There are no signs of stroke, seizure, heart attack or amnesia. Your upper back is bruised, no fractures, same with your shoulder and arm. It looks like you have a small fracture on your nose that should heal fine in a few weeks without any consequence. Are you able to recall what happened?"

Soshana felt a little underwhelmed with his lack of concern, and also worried about telling the truth, so she told a half truth. Dr. Weathering clacked on the keyboard and checked his watch.

"I believe I slipped on some water in the bathroom once, and then again after I got up. I must have been very disoriented the first time."

He replied, "And that's it? No illegal drug use, alcohol abuse, or maybe you'd been at a bar and someone slipped something in your drink?" He dipped his chin lower, lifted one of his eyebrows and parted his mouth slightly, as if no matter what she said, he was not going to believe her. This is not the first time Soshana has been treated like this by a doctor: accusatory, belittled, degraded.

She looked at him with a straight face and declared with a pointed tone, "No. And wouldn't you be able to tell with the toxicology reports? I'm not sure why you're asking me these questions. I don't know what happened."

He looked down at his laptop, typed a few sentences, checked his watch again, snapped the laptop shut and stood up.

"We will be monitoring you over the course of the next week or so. Let us know if you need anything." He left without looking at her or saying another word.

She decided she wasn't going to let it bother her, most doctors think most people are inept and lack a certain level of intelligence. Whatever she was going through, these knuckleheads in the hospital were not going to figure it out. She would have to seek out a specialist. Josette tapped her on the shoulder to signal she was about to move her out of the office. Soshana was upset but not surprised. She did her best to leave her emotions in the room.

"Everything okay?" Kieran asked when she returned.

She really didn't want to talk about it. To assuage his question, she answered, "I don't know, I suppose. I might be here for about a week; it all depends on how quickly I recover." She tried to sound more positive. "Let's talk about something else. What's your favorite movie genre?"

Kieran and Soshana hit a spark of conversation that was easily motivated by each film they brought up. It was an enjoyable, lively chat as they laughed and criticized each other about their most cherished films and the memories that came from the experiences they associated with them.

"What's your absolute favorite movie? You have to choose one. Quick! No time to think," Soshana playfully asked.

"*Alien.* Oh God. It was the first one that popped into my head. What *must* you think of me?!"

She laughed then said, "Well mine is *The Princess Bride*. What does that say about me?"

Without hesitation, he mimicked the priest. "Mawwiage is what bwings us togevah."

Soshana burst out laughing and as much as it hurt, it felt even better. He laughed along with her.

Carina popped her head into the room and said each word as sternly as a pissed off schoolteacher, punctuated and deadly. "I need you both to keep it down. You *should* be resting." She left without another word.

"Oops," Soshana said with a grimace. They kept their conversation going regardless, lowering their voices a few notches.

"What about TV shows?" Kieran asked.

"I don't really like any. Well... Hmm, I take that back, I do like food shows," Soshana replied. Which then led them into talking about their passions for baking and cooking. "When you get out of here, what's the first thing you're going to eat?"

"I'd love to make myself a hearty meal, something like boeuf bourguignon with a glass of red wine. I'd love to go to France and experience that. What about you?" he asked cheerily.

"I want to eat a big bowl of pasta with salty, briny capers, spinach, butter and shrimp," she said with a weak smile. She was anxious to see him, to look at him while she spoke. It helped her to watch facial expressions and body language to match the tone of their voice so she knew if people were being truthful. She wasn't sure how to ask, since she was feeling extremely self-conscious about her own appearance. At least she was able to shower that morning, brush her hair and put on her comfy oversized pink sweater. That gave her some courage. She felt a wave of bravery, something she hadn't felt in many years.

"Kieran, I have a request."

"Anything," he replied happily.

"Can I see you, please?"

This time, he was silent. "I'm not sure. I guess if you don't mind showing yourself in your state, I can show off my Frankenstein scar. The last thing I want to do is scare you. I don't normally look like this. I haven't shaved my beard in a while and…" He was rambling now; she interrupted him by getting out of her bed and pulling back the sheet separating them.

He was sitting upright with his head facing forward. He looked fine, she was facing the left side of his head, the side left untouched. First his eyes moved towards her with a tense look, his face softened at the sight of her gentle features. He turned his head fully towards her with a small smile.

"Hi."

"Hi," she replied with a warm smile, keeping her eyes on his eyes.

He looked back up at her, pausing to observe her face. "You lied," he said with a hint of snarkiness, eyes narrowing.

Her face must have shown some remorse and confusion because he changed his expression to show he was joking. She could tell he was adjusting to comfort her change in attitude. Most people told Soshana they couldn't tell how she was feeling or what she was thinking. It was her job to keep her face composed in order to prevent any kind of reaction from others. It was better that way.

"About what?" she said.

He let out a cautious laugh. "You said you looked like, and I quote; 'a pile of shit that someone stepped on. A swollen pus-filled carcass of a human.' Or something like that."

Her mouth popped open, she rolled her eyes and then guffawed. "The audacity!" she said with a big grin. She looked at his face, his eyes were calm and sweet. She may have stared at him for a moment too long as he started laughing and made a silly face to snap her out of it.

His smile was a bit crooked, possibly from a crossbite, but not altogether awful. She always noticed people's teeth and gums; it was a marker of how they took care of themselves and could tell you a lot about a person by their hygiene standards. His were a healthy color. She continued to observe him, hoping he didn't notice. It was a great relief to be able to watch his face, his lips moved in a pleasing way when he spoke.

He stated in a grateful tone, "Thank you for being the first one to rip the Band-Aid off, I was afraid I'd repulse you and then you would run away screaming and I'd have to talk to Carina for the remainder of my hospital visit."

"Oh, that will not happen on my watch. You're not grotesque by the way." She smiled at him. She was beginning to feel grateful for him, to have someone to commiserate with. She walked over to his bed and pulled the hospital chair next to it. "Do you have any pets?" Soshana asked.

He looked at her in a way that showed her he was watching her carefully, curiously, cautiously. She was in full view of the Frankenstein incision on his right side. She took no immediate notice; she observed it without fully staring. It was alarming but she kept her face in a reserved state for him. She took note of a small pink object on his nightstand. It looked like a plastic heart. *Odd.*

"No, I wish I did though, I love dogs so much. Cats too. I would love to have a little farm someday, get out of the big city and settle down with a pack of 'em. How about your cat, how is he/she doing?"

She thought of how much she would love to have that too. A nice quiet place to rest, and someone to share it with. "He's great, want to see Mr. Skittles?" She didn't wait for him to respond; she got up and grabbed her phone from her nightstand and pulled up the photo that Joe had sent her earlier.

"He's handsome," he said. Kieran talked about a cat he had as a child and how it would curl up next to his feet on his bed at night and 'make biscuits' on them.

Lunch and dinner came and went very quickly that day. They had talked and laughed their way through the misery and discontentment of being in a hospital, recovering.

Soshana felt uneasy and fatigued. "Oh, I think I need to lay back down," she said.

"Absolutely of course," he replied.

"Do you want me to close the curtain?" she asked.

"Nope. Do you need to rest?" he said with a look of deep sincerity and concern, his eyes locked onto hers. Soshana didn't respond yet, she laid down on her bed first, carefully on her side, facing Kieran. Her hands were underneath her face, like a child sleeping sweetly, she wasn't sure what else to do with them. She watched his face for a few seconds, studied it without making a move on her own. She swallowed and steadied her breathing.

He isn't bad looking, actually.

When she responded, she said it quietly with intention and did not make any facial reactions except a gentle smile. "What would you like to talk about?" She had a way of relaxing anyone in her presence, no matter the situation.

He visibly relaxed. "Tell me your favorite childhood memories."

Her stomach dropped and blood pressure rose. She wasn't ready to divulge her tumultuous childhood with this man she just met. Even though she was good at calming others, she had a terrible time trying to calm herself.

She decided to go into safe territory, detailing her adventures in the woods, watching animals in their habitat, and the pets she had growing up. Kieran relaxed further, his eyes were soft but wandering back and forth over Soshana's face. She watched him to see if he showed signs of boredom, disinterest or apathy. There was none. She continued to talk for a while longer, then asked him the same question in return.

He gladly reciprocated, talking about learning how to swim and fish in Lake Ontario in the summers, rollerblading with his pals after school, taking the train to New York City with his parents, building snow forts and playing hockey with his older brother, Abrams, in the winter. He has a six-year-old niece, Sadie. 'A little spitfire.' They continued to share pleasant and mostly positive stories until they both fell asleep, facing each other.

5

The Courtyard

"Josette, can I please ask the biggest favor of you?" Soshana put on her best smile, the one that seemed to win over her old crotchety customers at the store. She only pulled it out when she really needed something. "Is it possible for Kieran and I to have some time outside? I believe I'm developing cabin fever and anxiety from being stuck indoors."

Josette didn't respond immediately but gave a nod of acknowledgment. She directed the assistant to clean up their breakfast dishes and put the clean sheets and towels down on the waiting room chair by the bathroom. She turned to look at Soshana, darted her eyes at Kieran's direction and grinned but also sighed, this wasn't a good sign. Soshana was desperate. Her throat and chest felt tight, as if an invisible wrap was around them and every time she took a breath in, like a boa constrictor, it would tighten further. In addition to that, she started having restless legs, shaky breathing; chattering teeth; a buzzing, rolling feeling in her veins; and a general unwellness in her body. Going outside and feeling the wind and sun on her skin and looking at nature instead of the pale-yellow walls of the room would give them both a well-deserved respite from their current scenario.

"Please." This time her award-winning smile faded and was replaced with genuine pleading.

Josette looked out the window, pondering what to do. Soshana saw a plan forming in her eyes. She came up close to Soshana, looked out into the hallway and said in a hushed voice, "I'll tell you what. Let me take my lunch first then I'll cover Carina's. She takes about an hour. I'll come and get you both, but you have to be in your wheelchairs ready to go by 12:15 pm sharp, got it?" Josette looked at Kieran's curtain, concerned.

Soshana quickly nodded her head. "Kieran, did you hear that? Can I open your curtain?" She didn't wait until he responded, she was too excited. She froze at the sight of him, the smile fell from her face when she saw he had been crying. His eyelids were puffy, his face blotchy and red. He took deep breaths.

"Sorry, Soshana. Sometimes it's just too much. I appreciate you making an attempt to escape outside, but I just don't feel up to it today."

Soshana's heart started beating faster, coldness washed over her body, and she felt strangely disappointed. She didn't know how to respond. He turned to look at her, his face was complacent and neutral, wet and flushed.

She sat next to him on the empty space on his bed, heart still beating faster than usual. After a few moments, she carefully and slowly placed her hand on his arm. She couldn't lift her eyes to look at his, so she closed them and just sat. She squeezed his arm gently, imagining that her touch could steal his misery. Her eyes opened when she felt his hand on top of hers. She couldn't help twitching when she was touched, especially when she wasn't expecting it.

Looking at each other, he smiled warmly at her, fresh tears forming. "I've never known anyone like you. You're so genuinely kind and caring, aren't you?"

Accepting compliments was a challenge given that she rarely believed them. People always wanted something when they complimented you. How could he possibly know who she is, when they only met a few days ago? She felt defensive and skeptical of him. He definitely wanted something from her, but what?

Looking down at his hand on top of hers, he continued, "I know we haven't known each other long, but I've been on this earth long enough to know the difference."

This did make her chest feel unexpectedly warm, given the fact she had just decided against his good intentions. She wanted to believe him, just like she wanted to believe it when others said it about her. She knew it was true, but her mind always took her to a place where it ran with disbelief.

Curiosity overruled the anxiety. "What can I do to help you right now?" Trying to convince him that taking a few moments outside would be incredibly beneficial, she thought of what else she could do.

"I can't ask you for anything, you've already wasted enough of your recovery time on me. You should be resting." He removed his hand from hers and turned his head, taking a breath that sounded defiant and hopeless.

The sting of his rejection, after just being so kind, jolted something inside her. A reminder of how she felt rejected when her mother would say something nice, then rip it away with a smarmy remark.

She sat up straight, face calm and complacent. She knew that speaking her feelings was important, she also knew it needed to come from a place of compassion and honesty. This was another thing she was told she needed to practice preventing her emotions from ruling her life. Here was her chance, with someone she was getting to know, someone she found she cared about and also a person she may never see again. She leaned in slightly and spoke firmly. "You don't get to decide how I feel about spending time with you. If I didn't like you, I would have asked for a different room by now."

He clenched his teeth; she saw his jaw muscles moving. His eyes drew towards the ceiling, it looked like he was trying not to cry again. His eyes closed. She could feel he was uncomfortable, defeated. She sat up and turned to walk back to her bed.

He grasped her wrist gently. "Please, I just don't know what to say right now. My head hurts. It isn't my intention to upset you."

She was facing her bed as he was speaking to her, her wrist clasped by his warm hand. Chills spread down her body from her head to the tips of her fingers, her chest tightened while guilt stored itself in her abdomen. She turned towards him, he dropped his hand from her wrist, more tears rolling down his cheeks. He closed his eyes again, she reached for some tissues and blotted away some of the escaped tears. She knew what she needed to do, it's what she always did in these scenarios, she became the caregiver.

Soshana grabbed her novel and moved to the chair close to the window on Kieran's side of the room. While she read and sipped coffee, Kieran got up, brushed his teeth and changed into some sweats. His hair and beard were a scraggly mess.

She watched him get in and out of bed, taking care to notice if he had experienced any imbalance, just as a nurse would. They did not talk much; she could tell he was having a terrible day. She felt a growing sense of empathy for him, to the point of feeling responsible for his wellbeing. Still, no one had come to visit him. There was one short phone call a few days ago that sounded like he was arguing with someone he could be close with, maybe a partner or a co-worker, she couldn't tell.

With that thought, a text came in from Taryn.

Hey, girl! I'm so glad we got to meet up the other day. I realized that I spent the entire time talking and you were so patient listening to me! I'm really sorry about that, I hardly get time with my girlfriends anymore. Please believe me when I say I do actually want to know how you're doing! Let's set up a time when I know I won't have a meeting afterwards and the boys aren't going to bother me, what do you say?

Soshana was thrown off by this text. She had forgotten she had met up with Taryn. Part of her wanted to ignore the message. Avoiding people wasn't the answer but it sure was easy.

Hi, Taryn! I have some stuff going on right now, let me get back to you next week, hopefully. She pressed send then added *thank you for reaching out. Looking forward to catching up more.* This wasn't the time to drop a pity party on Taryn with her current issues.

She wasn't great with open communication, especially with women. She told herself she would get better at it, later.

When Josette came into the room at exactly 12:15 pm on the nose, she put her hands to her hips and shook her head. She was wearing a bright blue sweater over her light blue scrubs and large gold hoop earrings that sparkled as her head tossed from side to side.

"Don't you remember our little agreement, my darlings?" she whispered.

Soshana looked at her apologetically. "Kieran isn't feeling up for a field trip today."

Josette made an incredulous face, walked over to the opposite side of Kieran's bed, her hands firmly on her hips, and stared at Kieran. She pursed her lips, her head down in disappointment, batting her eyelashes. He turned his head towards her cautiously and stared back. She looked him up and down.

As dangerously and sickly sweet as possible she demanded his attention. "Looks like you were able to get yourself up and tidied. It would certainly be no problem getting you into a wheelchair and out for some fresh air. What do you say?"

He stared at her blankly, took a half-assed breath and let it out dramatically. "I suppose, especially since you asked so *kindly*," he said with an air of sarcasm. Soshana shook her head in disbelief, she couldn't convince him to budge, but one hard look from Josette and he was good to go. Josette had more self-confidence than Soshana could bear to withstand in herself. She thoroughly enjoyed and admired Josette.

Josette grabbed the wheelchair from the hallway and winked at the orderly that was on staff, signaling their agreement. The orderly was of medium height, portly and had a neatly trimmed beard. He had a friendly demeanor, Soshana could tell Josette and him could get into all sorts of trouble, but in a way that wouldn't interfere with the importance of their jobs.

He grabbed the other wheelchair, turned it towards the door, pointed to Soshana then down at the seat. She placed herself into the seat and looked backwards at Josette and Kieran.

Kieran's face was solemn, and he moved slowly. Her smile faded a little, he was really struggling. She could always tell when a person was being deliberately dramatic for attention and there was no hint of it on his face or body language. She looked at her hands. The plum nail polish had worn off. She paused her mind at the sight of them, lost in a moment of remembering the days of painting her nails black and glittery. That younger version of herself was tucked away and she now looked forward to a future where she wasn't in a hellscape of twisted thoughts. That young girl was brave, but not smart.

Kieran was wheeled behind her and the orderly began to push, but not before he checked the hallways for anyone that might disrupt their plans. They all fit into the large elevator at the end of their hallway. It smelled like cheap fried food.

Kieran didn't look at Soshana. She wanted to see his face and read his emotions but instead, she remained staring at the buttons as they descended. Josette popped her head out when they landed on the ground floor, quickly looked right and left, then pushed Kieran forward with a steady confidence. They went through the lobby and out to the courtyard where Soshana had seen the beautiful trees from the doctor's office.

The instant the sun hit Soshana's face, she could feel her body's tension ease, the bright light moving through her head down to her toes. She closed her eyes and breathed in deeply through her nose. The noise of relief that escaped her mouth was louder than she anticipated, it made the orderly chuckle a little. The wind blew through their hair and clothes, it had a slight chill that struck the skin in warning of winter's approach. Soshana grabbed her pink sweater and wrapped it tighter around her waist. They planted Soshana and Kieran near the tree, on a sidewalk that led to a gazebo.

Soshana looked up at the orderly. "Thank you so much, I really mean it."

He smiled down at her, then said, "I'll be back in thirty. Enjoy."

Josette patted Kieran's shoulder and took her leave.

There was no one else in sight. It was a small courtyard surrounded by shrubs, a few large oaks and some well-appointed orange and yellow flowers that were in the last stages of summer bloom. They were quiet for a long enough time to feel uncomfortable.

"Are you feeling okay?" Soshana asked sweetly but also with a hint of encouragement.

He shrugged and didn't respond but kept looking at the gazebo. The passive responses were starting to bother her. What was he playing at? Yesterday he was all too eager to ask questions, making her believe he was interested, and now she was getting the silent treatment, something she knew she had a hard time handling.

"Soshana, why are you trying?"

Startled by the question breaking their awkward silence, she replied as carefully and without emotion as she could, though it was difficult. "What do you mean?"

He asked again, with a damning tone, "What is the point of trying, why do you care? You'll leave soon, go back to your life and your home. You'll forget all about me. I just don't see the reasons for your efforts today."

The words stung, but she showed no reaction on her face. She'd played this game before, with her friend Mina, with her mother and with her ex-boyfriend. They wanted attention and sympathy. She couldn't believe this was his intention. She didn't see it or feel it coming from him. It was coming from a place of suffering.

She took a very intentional breath in and then exhaled, repeating the process until her heart rate slowed. He turned his head towards her during the last few breaths she took.

She got up from her wheelchair and walked toward the gazebo, up the steps and to the opposite side where she could view the old oak tree more closely. She stood for several minutes before she felt the warmth of his body close to hers.

He spoke slowly and quietly. "I'm sorry. You told me not to assume your feelings or thoughts, and I went ahead and did it again. I guess I just want to know why you're choosing to put your time into a stranger. It's surprising to me."

She felt a ball of energy in her core that welled up close to her throat then sat there. He was too close for comfort; she took a half step back and looked into his eyes. He was taller than she imagined, though she didn't imagine him very tall at all. He was thin and weak-looking, and it made him seem small in his bed.

This wasn't about her. This was about him, his insecurities. She felt a kinship in this, since she tended to push people away when they started to get close.

"It's surprising to me as well, but I like you, Kieran." He looked bewildered.

She continued, "I will have you know, I like very few people, but when I find them... I do the best I can, within my ability..." She trailed off, looked past Kieran at the empty wheelchairs, then at his chest. She could see his heartbeat through his white T-shirt. It wasn't steady and calm, her eyes traced up to the artery in his neck, the vein was visible and copied what she saw on his chest. This was confusing, why was he reacting like this? Was he not feeling well or was he upset?

The wind passed between them, she could smell his body and feel his warmth, it made her dizzy. Her mind wandered to summer evenings, the humid air, the stars popping into existence in the darkening sky, a kind of peace she hadn't felt in a long time.

Kieran spoke up first. "Your ability to trail off and float into space?"

She refocused and shook her head. "Sorry I was just… thinking or… something." She smiled to neutralize her distraction. "What I mean to say is that I am your friend, if you will have me."

He cleared his throat and eased down to a kneeling position in front of her. She caught his eyes and forcefully put on a charged grin.

"What are you doing?" Panicking, her eyes moved left and right over his face, looking for some kind of sign. He grabbed her left hand. Her eyes widened, the tension between them was palpable.

"M'lady. Will you please forgive my attitude and henceforth be willing to accept my friendship, as well?" He bowed his head while still holding her hand.

"What? Oh hell. Get your ass up." She laughed at him; he smiled for the first time since yesterday. A great relief that washed over her. He got up too quickly and wobbled. Soshana instinctively grabbed his arm and pulled him closer to her.

"Steady, steady. Let's go sit back down," she said, easing into caregiver mode. His body steadied with hers but remained in place. She looked up at him to make sure he wasn't about to pass out.

His gaze was alarming, intense but curious. "You didn't answer my question." He spoke softly, his eyes darted back and forth across her face, observing for any sudden imperceptible changes in her expression.

"What question?" She thought for a moment and then laughed, uncomfortably. "Oh yes, yes of course. I accept." He leaned in closer; she wasn't sure what was happening. Was he trying to kiss her? What was he going to do? Her brain was screaming.

"Good, now that we're friends, I have a request, but only if you're comfortable and I mean it. I'm choosing to trust you to tell me the truth."

Soshana was frozen in place, this happened to her much too often, she declared in her frazzled mind. She couldn't breathe properly; something was being triggered in her memory and her mind was too scrambled to register. She reminded herself that no matter what it was, she was safe, they weren't alone and that Josette and the orderly would be back shortly.

He must have noticed the stiffness in her body and backed up while releasing her hand. He waited until she took a breath then asked as genuinely and sweetly as he could, "I would love to give you a hug. To say thank you."

At the words, she began to melt. *A hug.* Wanting hugs and then always pushing the thought away.

Which thought was more powerful? Which action did she need the most? It was dangerous and altogether too important to miss an opportunity for touching. We don't understand how important it is to touch, to know that we are present, to let the other person know they are visible, and worth touching. Nothing sexual about it, just a promise that you are with them, and they are with you.

"Oh, sure," she responded slowly. She gave a quick smile and went in for a quick hug. She wrapped her arms around his back, he placed his arms around hers, relaxing his cheek on her head. She tried to let go after a second, but he held on to her.

As he held her more tightly, he sighed. "Thank you," he said as he pulled away and held her by the shoulders at a friendly distance.

She dared to meet his eyes, to read what he was displaying. It was cheerful, friendly and calm. She mimicked his expression to show complacency, her body telling her the opposite. Buzzing, shaking, she worked on returning to her normal state of frail anxiety and doubt. The mind pushed to be bold.

Say something funny to break the ice...

"You farted in your sleep the other night." It spat out of her mouth like she had a bee in it, she grimaced as she hoped his humor matched hers.

His mouth dropped open; his eyebrows scrunched. In panic? Agony? He chuckled, then cackled loudly, bracing his stomach, throwing back his head.

"Aww, man! I'm so sorry!" He laughed again and she laughed with him.

They walked back to their wheelchairs, her arm holding his for balance, one of his hands on his head from the throbbing of laughing. They pulled the chairs forward to hit just the right amount of sunlight. Soshana spoke up first, feeling more courage now than ever.

"Now that we are officially friends, can I ask *you* for a favor as well?" She wanted to ask him why no one had come to visit, or called, or at least sent some sort of token of love. He gave her a smile. She hesitated; she couldn't ask him that after the day he'd had. Instead, she came up with a lighthearted question, something they hadn't talked about yet.

"Do you like playing board or card games?"

He laughed. "That's not what you were going to ask!"

Her mouth dropped open. *He's incorrigible, a mind reader.* She gently smacked his arm with the back of her hand.

"Yes, it was!" She winked. "I was wondering if you wanted to play a game of cards when we get back, after lunch?"

"Yeah, sure. Okay." He spoke softly. "As you wish."

Josette and the orderly returned to take them back upstairs and serve lunch. Josette had grabbed Soshana this time and wheeled her a distance ahead of Kieran. "So... how did it go? Did Grumpy Gus lighten up?" Soshana felt a static energy in her body that caused her to shiver. "That bad, eh?"

"Oh it was fine, he came around."

"You know, we're all rooting for you two."

Soshana looked up at her. "Thank you, we both want to survive this and get better."

"Yes of course we want that, but we mean you two maybe, you know, getting together."

Soshana froze, bewildered and confused. She was tired of these strange people causing her to have such alarming reactions.

"What? No!"

Josette cackled, then leaned down and whispered, "You know he's sweet on you, right? Can't you tell? A pretty young thing like yourself."

"Pretty? *Young?* That is just not true." Soshana brushed off complements like dust off a table.

"I know it isn't appropriate, but I couldn't help myself. He's such a gentleman, so thoughtful and caring. He deserves a person that matches his heart." Josette squeezed her shoulder.

"He might be married or with someone. What if I'm with

someone?" Soshana tried her best not to balk out the words.

"Are you though? I'm almost a hundred per cent positive he's single. And even if you were, what's the harm of making a friend at least?"

"We are friends. Funny you should say that, we just agreed to it. I think he would make a great friend."

"Mmm. Okay, darlin'."

Josette hummed and danced while she wheeled Soshana back to the room. With Josette's words running in her mind, Soshana's heart was now pounding out of her chest and she feared she may have a stroke. She practiced her four-count breathing pattern to slow it down before Kieran came back. He waved at her as he passed her bed.

Lunch was brought immediately. Meat loaf, mashed potatoes, canned green beans, and a brownie for dessert. She was getting tired of hospital food. Thoughts of cooking Kieran dinner crossed her mind.

Don't be silly.

"Not bad, I thought it would taste like mushy cardboard. Not bad," Kieran said.

Soshana replied with "Yeah." They were silent again. She couldn't focus on anything because of what Josette had told her. Confusion clouded her thoughts.

He piped up, "I asked Josette if they had a deck of cards, what do you say to blackjack?"

She knew she couldn't avoid him with enough time to organize her thoughts, so she pushed them aside for now. "Sounds great, thanks for taking the initiative."

Josette returned shortly after lunch with the cards and handed them to Soshana, but not before she mouthed, "Go for it." With a wink and a spin, she left the room humming another pop song, this time with a dance routine. It made Soshana laugh.

They played for about an hour and talked about familiar subjects. He talked about animal rights and how it's mind-blowing how North America treats farmed animals. How he wished he had the funds to be able to return to college and become an attorney for environmentalists and scientists facing persecution from corporations. He was a kinder, more compassionate person than she had even imagined.

She dared to look at his face again and took in more of his features. His eyes were large, lids shadowed above his cheekbones. She assumed the slight acrid acidity to his breath came from the medications. His hands were masculine, somewhat worn but with neatly trimmed nails, a scar on his right index finger gleamed differently to the rest of his skin.

He noticed she was looking and offered her a kind smile. "What are you thinking about?" he asked gently.

"I'm not sure. I don't know what to think. It's beginning to make me feel crazy."

He nodded in agreement. "I felt like I went crazy about six months ago, and now I'm in a full sprint towards insanity."

She couldn't agree more. "Do you ever think, 'what am I doing with my life?'"

He stopped shuffling his cards. "All the damn time. I think 'what is the point of anything?' I don't know where I'm going with my career, I have nothing to look forward to. Am I just going to keep working at the same job, stay in the same relationships, get up, shower, work, eat, sleep, repeat until 'lights out?' Getting older is awful."

"So how old *are* you then?" She was playing along with him now.

He gave her a crooked smile. "If I tell you, would you mind telling me? I hate guessing but I know it's taboo to ask a woman her age."

"On the count of three we both say it, promise?"

He nodded with a tiny smile. An intuition grew inside her chest. She took note of it and felt the warmth of her trust. While acknowledging her accomplishment, she silently made a promise to herself that she would only be honest and vulnerable with him from now on.

"One... two... three... thirty-six."

"Thirty-four," he said. "Wow! Thirty-six? You look so much younger than that. I thought you were in your mid to late twenties, good job."

"Thanks, I think?" She wouldn't dare say anything negative to him at this time, he looked older than thirty-four unfortunately. If he had a few more pounds on and wasn't recovering from cancer treatments, then his age might match his appearance.

"Well, no wonder we have so much in common, being basically the same age, right?" He grinned at her, the glint in his eyes playful and encouraging.

As each exchange of dialogue brought new stimulus, she wanted to try a different conversation with him, with some reservation. She kept her eyes low, focused on the cards.

"I had a pretty rough childhood, I guess. We were talking earlier about childhood memories, and I skipped over most of it. I think I've been brushing it off most of my life, telling people 'Oh it probably wasn't that bad. They did the best they could.' I forgave my mom, so everything is cool. She said she was sorry and stuff, you know. That sort of thing. I think I forgot how bad it was until recently. And I mean, within the past few weeks recently. It might be hitting me in a way I don't recognize." She stalled, her eyes fixed on the space between them.

He was engaging when he spoke but said in such a way that it caught a sob in her throat. "I'm so sorry, Soshana."

She nodded her head quickly to prevent crying. She continued, distancing herself from her experiences so she didn't have to feel the pain it caused. The pain that was currently culminating deep in her abdomen.

"It's funny how parents say things like 'kids are resilient, they bounce back.' How do you bounce back from being called a fucking bitch when you're a child? Or being beaten because you misbehaved as children do, or didn't have the right look on your face?"

"Those kinds of people will tell you that's how *they* were raised, and look how they turned out, 'just fine!' And then call you weak and ignorant for not beating your own children." He shook his head. "If you were to go up to another grown person, as an adult, and just beat them because you didn't like their attitude, wouldn't you get charged with assault? When was it ever okay to beat a child? Please, do tell." He gestured in the air to an invisible crowd.

"Right?" she responded. "I'm sorry, all that just kind of fell out of my mouth." She regretted apologizing immediately.

He shook his head. "No, no apologies from you."

It was time to look up, to look at him. Soft, warm eyes greeted hers. His face was alarmingly calm, eager to listen. Maybe she was dreaming, because she had never experienced anyone giving her this kind of intentional attention before. The tightness in her stomach loosened, so she continued, instinctively knowing it was safe to do so.

"When my mom apologized, she said 'I don't remember doing or saying those things. I'm sorry you felt that way. I love you.' And somehow, after never hearing her say the words '*I'm* sorry' or '*I* love you,' I easily forgave her. It was always 'love you' to my back, never to my face. When you add 'I' in front of it and look people in the eyes, it holds you accountable for your actions. But at the time I thought it was sincere."

"She didn't apologize. That was *not* an apology." His eyes were menacing. Not directed at Soshana, she knew, but at a faraway place, possibly imagining saying that to a person.

"No, it wasn't a true apology, I would find out years later in therapy. She was awful most of the time. It was difficult because she provided for us, she took us on trips, she bought us stuff, but it always came with an emotional tag. 'I did this for you, you owe me. You're both so spoiled. You should be grateful.' And I should feel grateful, I grew up with food on the table, a roof over my head, I was provided for... so why do I feel like I was robbed of my childhood?"

"Does she still treat you that way now?" he asked.

"Nope. She died. Almost a year ago," Soshana said with no remorse or emotion.

"I'm sorry."

"Don't be. I'm not. She can't hurt me anymore."

"Maybe not."

"What does that mean?" Her eyes darted to his with sharpened interest.

He hesitated. "I don't mean it in a bad way, but when people deliberately hurt us, it tends to take a long time to heal, to recover from. Especially if it was family. That's all."

She nodded her head, sneering at the thought that her mother could still get at her from the grave. But she recognized his words, deciphered and decoded their meaning.

Did he have this kind of experience too?

"I feel honored that you felt safe enough to tell me that personal history. I'm sorry to say that my mom and my dad were pretty boring. Though, I can't say that about my adult life so far." He made a face that screamed 'it's been rough' but did not elaborate.

They had a lot in common, and the sense of his growing attachment to her was becoming stronger as they chatted and played cards until dinner arrived that evening.

Before they went to sleep, Kieran apologized again for his attitude and behavior earlier in the day. She thanked him and told him, "Rest assured, I will never be perfect," and hoped that was okay enough for him. He requested some pain medication from the nurse, closed the curtain and went to sleep, but not before saying goodnight to Soshana.

She sat up in bed for a few hours, unable to silence her racing mind. She thought about what she had said about her mother, how it made her feel guilty and deeply ashamed. She had always protected her. Told people she was eccentric and passionate while constantly making excuses for her behavior towards her. Now, she didn't have to. It felt strange being this honest.

Then she thought about what Josette had told her. Did Kieran tell her that he liked Soshana directly, or did Josette assume?

She picked up her phone and noticed a missed call from her father but no voicemail or text. "Typical," she whispered to herself. She texted Derek and Joe, then turned her phone off and placed it back on her nightstand.

She stared at Kieran's closed curtain for a while. She knew

how important it was to organize her thoughts.

Why was I upset to hear that Kieran liked me?

The negative thoughts were always the same but they didn't make sense. There was nothing Kieran could get out of Soshana that mattered. If he did like her in that way, there was nothing they could do about it. They lived too far away from each other, or did they? He still hadn't told her where he was from, who he worked for, or if he was in a relationship. What about the ring she thought she saw? It hadn't appeared over the past few days. There wasn't anyone that visited or called.

He could be texting people of course.

Wait, why do I care?

She followed her thoughts again. She remembered his scent when she was hugging him earlier. This sent a jolt of pleasure through her core. Some indescribable feeling, words she couldn't pull to the front of her mind, it was all so disorienting. She thought about his sweet, sparkling eyes and smile. She hadn't received this kind of attention before. He was so different from everyone she knew. He was different, that was fine, and it was enough for her to find a calm space in her head to tuck the thoughts away for another time. She felt the pull of sleep sitting heaving on her eyelids and limbs, but as she drifted off she could tell something was off.

6

The Second Episode

She was dizzy, lightheaded and nauseous. The room started to spin.

Please, please not again.

She was standing in a different hospital. Her breathing rapid and fast, her heart pounding. She closed her eyes. "No no no no no no! Why is this happening!?" she screamed into the abandoned hallway.

Opening her eyes, she practiced the routine to prevent a full-blown panic attack. "Five windows. Blue tile, gray ceiling, yellow countertops..."

This was not a typical panic attack. This was delirium, a hallucination. Another episode, though it felt entirely different from the first one in her bathroom. Terrified, body violently shaking, the routine wasn't helping. She stopped and looked around. She knew where she was: the hospital in Grand Rapids where her mother received chemotherapy treatments.

Breathing deeply and tapping her left hand on her right arm and vice versa, her courage recovered as she walked down the hallway. She knew exactly which room her mother was in: 112. Before she could stop herself, she was in front of the door. Distant monitors were beeping, it sounded distorted, crackling in the cold air. She swallowed the bile in her mouth. Closing her eyes and breathing as best she could, she pushed open the door.

Nothing could have prepared her for what she saw.

Her mother, laying in the hospital bed, sleeping. The chair next to it contained a shadowed outline of a person with no face. Soshana's body felt hot and tingly, weak and shaky. She opened her mouth to scream as she felt the pull of gravity coming from behind.

She remembered the event more clearly this time. She hadn't fallen or hit her head, it happened without any warning as she was already laying down. When Soshana woke, she yelped out of fear, not knowing where she was and reeling from the episode. Carina came running into the room and repeatedly asked her to calm down. Soshana was so afraid to open her eyes, she yelled with them closed. "Derek! Derek!"

"Ma'am, you need to calm down otherwise we'll have to sedate you again. Soshana, please look at me, this is Carina, your nurse."

Soshana slowly opened her eyes. Blinking a few times and controlling her breath, she remembered where she was.

"I'm sorry, I'm sorry, I don't know what's going on. I... I was in a different hospital and I saw... I saw..." she sputtered before vomiting into the trash can next to her.

"These things can happen with TBI. We're going to change your pain medication in a few hours just in case it's causing issues, and I'll get you something for the nausea, all right?"

Carina stared at Soshana with what appeared to be concern.

"Yes. Can I have some water, please?"

Some surprising tears came next, it was involuntary, kind of like breathing. It scared her and was physically painful.

"Soshana?" Kieran called softly. His curtain was drawn.

"Yes?" Soshana weakly replied.

"I'm sorry you're going through whatever this is. If you feel comfortable and want to talk about it, please know that I will listen without judgment."

She thought without responding. This was possibly a hallucination, an out-of-body experience that she couldn't predict or control. How could she tell him or anyone without sounding insane? She didn't have the energy, nor did she want to discuss it.

She mustered up the emotional energy to give the bare minimum response. "Thank you, maybe later." She felt guilty. This person had shown her a level of kindness and potential friendship she was not used to and it upset her in a way she couldn't understand.

Derek phoned. "The nurses called me and told me you had an episode. What does that mean? Are you okay? Jesus, I leave for a few days and see what happens?" He tried to tease her without upsetting her as best he could.

"I'm okay, I think. I don't know, the doctors are doing their best, right?" she said between shallow breaths.

"How could I leave you while you're in this state? They said this kind of episode could have happened at your house, they suspected a seizure, but there was no indication of one." There was a note of panic in his voice. He did not do well when the status quo was shaken.

"Please, please don't come back. Of course I'd love for you

to, but I promise if anything bad happens they'll call you."

"I won't argue with a maniac. You win this time. I'm texting you every hour on the hour and I expect a response within five minutes."

"I'll do my best," she said, sounding like she had little energy left.

"I love you, Soshana," he said and hung up.

Soshana was given more medication and told it was vital for her to rest, there would be more tests done in the afternoon to rule out further complications or medical issues. Soshana rarely cried and never when in pain, but she had to fight back tears. Though she was feeling better in her shoulder and neck, her face throbbed. Being away from her own space and her cat was causing unease and restlessness that would only be cured by returning home.

Soshana slept for a few hours and before being wheeled away for more tests. She laid in the MRI and PET scanners listening to the whooshing, beeping and creaking sounds. She couldn't care less when the technician attached the stickies around her breasts and down her body for the EKG. She had been poked and prodded so often over the past few days.

All she could think about was how it would come back normal and the "cha-ching cha-ching" once the hospital and lab bills arrived in three to six months' time. Healthcare in America is a hungry beast and must be fed, feeding on the people, their panic to avoid it at all costs, because it will cost them their life.

When she returned to the room, she felt hunger pangs from missing breakfast. Lunch was eaten in silence. Soshana secretly wished Kieran would say something, ask her a question, make a noise, anything. All she could hear was the fork scraping against the plate, faint chewing and the wiping of a napkin against his lips. Yesterday was so different, they were talking and joking like old friends who had years of catching up to do. She believed she scared him last night. *This is not good for his recovery; they will most likely move him to a different room.* The thought of losing her entertaining roommate made her heart heavy.

She had to figure out how to keep these events from happening. She thought of calling Ms. Erling. She seemed to have answers when Soshana couldn't piece them together herself. She could tell her anything, even if it sounded bonkers. They had only reconnected recently after several years of not being in touch with each other. Soshana had felt their work was finished: her panic attacks had stopped; her anxiety was at a manageable level; and her depression, although clouded by a thin veil of uncertainty, was manageable. She had ceased writing her thoughts since the recent accident, knowing it would have to resume after their next conversation.

Soshana waited until she had finished her meal and was certain Kieran had finished his. Gathering her courage, she decided to tell him at least some of the reasons why she was in there.

"Kieran?"

"I'm here," he said with assurance, but quietly.

"Hi," she said meekly.

He replied with a gentle response. "Hi there. How's it going?"

She replied, "We'll, I'm here, aren't I?" She exhaled and closed her eyes as she replied. He retorted with, "Same."

She continued. "Since we may be here for a while, I'll tell you why I ended up here. And also because you asked so kindly earlier in the week. I don't remember much, but apparently I slipped on some water in my bathroom, landed on my face, woke up disoriented, slipped again and fell backwards into the bathtub." She paused for a second. "Ta-dah," she said while spreading her arms out, pretending to bow.

Kieran stayed quiet for a few seconds. "As much as I wish you weren't hurt, that must have been quite a show you put on. What I would give to see that spectacle. Bravo!" he said loudly while slowly clapping.

Soshana smiled, then grinned, then started cackling, hard. She pictured herself flailing in the bathroom. She laughed harder and harder, she couldn't help it, even though it damn well hurt like hell. Kieran started laughing too. She hoped it was in empathy rather than sympathy. Imagine if laughter could be the medicine they needed in order to heal. It just felt so good.

I could get addicted to this feeling. She thought about how she hadn't heartily laughed like that in a long time. Long enough to not remember when.

"I enjoy your laugh, Soshana, it's so full of life. I appreciate you being so open and kind with me over the past four days. You really are something special and I hope you know that."

She didn't know what to say except, "That's a really nice thing to say. I want to believe you, Kieran, but I don't know how."

"I don't want this to sound presumptuous or righteous but I could tell you have a hard time with compliments. It's a fact, Soshana. You are kind and sweet and lovely."

There it was, a welling of pain in the back of her eyes, in the depth of her throat. It could be the end of her years of numbness; a force that could break the spell she was

83

under. Feeling emotions was exhausting, she remembered how painful it was as a child. It hurt too much.

He continued pointedly, "Please believe it, if not for me, but for yourself, you deserve it." His words were fraught with anguish, as if he was saying it for himself as well. "You need to rest, Soshana. I want you to get better. I'll leave you alone." His final words came out like an epilogue. Soshana found herself wanting more from him, while also knowing he was right.

They both remained quiet for the rest of the day. She fell in and out of consciousness, and every time she woke, she wondered what he was thinking, and if he was thinking about her.

Dinner arrived early, without warning, at 5:30 pm. Lasagna, salad and corn. Carina came shortly after Soshana had finished eating to administer the new pain medication along with extras for deep sleep. It was only six in the evening. "Expect to be sleeping for at least eight to ten hours. We'll be checking on your blood pressure and monitoring your vitals every hour. The doctor and I feel it will be beneficial for your brain and body to rest, this may help to prevent further episodes." She capped off the IV bag and left.

"Brr, was there a cold breeze that just blew in?" Kieran broke the silence with a joke.

"Haha… yes. Hope it's warmer now the ice queen has left," she said.

Kieran replied in a whisper, as she dozed off to sleep, "Goodnight, Soshana."

She woke up nine hours later at around three am, in a different room, by herself. She felt weird but not worse. She figured the doctors thought it would be best if she was away from Kieran so she didn't disturb him. She laid there for a long while, fighting off a terrible urge to see him. It didn't last.

Carefully and quietly, while holding her IV bag as a cane, she went to the bathroom to make sure she didn't look like a nightmare, brushed her teeth and combed her hair. She became dizzy, not the kind that made her leap into another dimension, just the kind that came from many, many drugs. She splashed some water on her face and drank some from the tap, swooshing some in her mouth and spitting into the sink.

She crept towards the door and looked into the hallway for the nurse or night staff. He was facing a computer, the light shone past his head, he was sitting still, distracted. *Perfect.* Her mind oscillated between *what the fuck am I thinking?* and *I can do this.* She felt a surge of bravery after she popped on her slippers and with the light on her phone, she sneaked out into the night like a child to find their presents on Christmas Eve.

The IV bag hit the side of the wall with a soft thud. Soshana froze, hardly daring to breathe, she waited with her eyes closed, prepared for the trouble she was about to get in. Nothing, no noise, not even a shuffle of feet or chairs. *Phew.* She slowly let out a quiet sigh. She found the room easily. Kieran's curtain was drawn on the side where her bed was. *Damn,* she thought. She carefully walked over to the other side of the bed.

She felt a sharp pang of horror as she gently pulled back the curtain.

Oh God, it's the wrong room.

Instead of fleeing, she paused and observed the strange man.

Except it wasn't a stranger, it was Kieran. He'd had a shave and combed his wild hair. She stared at him for a long time, not believing how much of a difference it made. He looked younger and quite handsome. She could see that he had a strong jawline and full lips. She hardly believed he was real. He was kind, compassionate, funny, understanding and now irritatingly attractive. Her heart pounded at the sight of him.

She sat on the chair next to him as quietly as possible. She kept looking at his face and lips. She panicked and thought about leaving before he woke up. For a brief and fleeting moment, she thought about kissing him and then instantly switched to thinking how absurd that was. She had known him for less than a week. Can strong feelings form that fast?

The urge to hold his hand overwhelmed her, however. That was platonic and caring, right? Her heart started to beat a little faster. Her skin began to tingle and her whole body felt like she had walked into a furnace, palms becoming sweaty, face completely flushed. She wondered what she was doing, it was unlike her to sneak around at night, looking for a man. But she felt like they were true friends considering the conversations they'd had and this would be okay. This reassurance convinced her to reach out towards him. She could have been pushing a hundred-pound rock across gravel with the tips of her fingers as she inched closer, taking tiny breaths while staring at his hand, sweat and heat forming in unusual places around her body.

The moment her hand touched his, Kieran's eyes opened. She jerked her hand away. He turned towards her and smiled. Her heart was now pounding in her ears, her eyes darting to his, she gulped and spoke to him in a hushed whisper. "I didn't mean to wake you, I just wanted you to know that I'm here and I didn't want to leave you. I'm sorry I got kicked out."

He looked at her with reverence for a few moments. She could tell he was exhausted but clearly pleased to see her. "Come here," he croaked softly. She didn't understand until he sleepily scooted his body towards the edge of the bed and lifted his right arm.

He wants me to lay next to him.

Panic seared through her. This request from him was the last thing she had imagined. Her mind whispered, *Something has to change. No,* she fought it back. This was strange. She must reason with her panic. She hadn't been that close to a man on a bed in many years and wasn't sure she wanted to right now. "Please," he said sweetly.

Her body moved without her consent, her brain reeling, heart racing. She climbed over the rail slowly and carefully and laid on her side close to him, with her right arm tucked beside her body. They had to be mindful of their IVs and the many cords that were attached in various places. She put her head on his shoulder, he leaned his head towards her and pressed his cheek against the top of her head, then wrapped his arm along her back and the curve of her waist. A gentle touch through a single layer of fabric was too intimate.

I always run away or disassociate from uncomfortable situations. He hasn't hurt me; he won't hurt me. He won't.

She repeated it over and over until her breathing steadied.

She lifted her arm; it hovered above his waist as she hesitated. Making the decision for her, he lifted her elbow for encouragement, then placed her arm around his waist. He took a weighted breath then exhaled while humming a deep comforting tone.

"Are you okay? Is this okay?" he whispered, causing shivers

and goosebumps along the back of her neck, back and arms.

She nodded her head into his shoulder and chest to give him affirmation. It must have been good enough for him because that was all he asked.

Soshana felt the warmth of his body next to hers, it was exciting, nerve-racking and soothing all at the same time. She indulged in the sweetness of his scent, masked under the smell of hospital and cheap detergent. He seemed to fall asleep fairly quickly. She laid awake listening to his heartbeat, fast at first, then steady. Her heart was still pounding away. The thoughts of *what am I doing?* faded after ten minutes or so. This gentle moment created a spark of curiosity that she now desperately wanted to explore further. Sleep came swiftly, blackening and heavy.

Thankfully, Josette was first on the scene around seven in the morning. She tapped Soshana's free shoulder and asked her to get up and back to her room, wheelchair ready. When she had laid next to Kieran just a few short hours earlier, Soshana had blissfully forgotten that her back, neck, shoulder and arm were bruised from her accident. It was a harrowing task not to moan in pain from the position she was in for those few hours. She did it without waking Kieran and put the blanket back over him. She looked at him before she left and felt her chest warm at the sight of him. Insecurity with small bursts of energetic hope at the same time.

"Now, darlin', you know full well that *that* can't happen again. I will let it slide this time," Josette said with a smirk. "I have to tell you, between us girls, I think you're helping him somehow. I'm not a doctor, but since you came into the room he has been eating well, smiling more and sleeping better. I'll ask the head nurse to either let you visit him or be brought back into the room, okay, my dear?"

"Thank you, Josette," Soshana said, hope established.

7

The Escape

*lept with a strange man... just kidding. We literally slept.
I actually felt safe enough to tell him about my childhood.
His eyes sparkle when we talk, he truly listens. I feel like I
might be going insane. Maybe I am. I question everything: motives,
smiles, words and gestures. I am tired of questioning everything
and everyone. I want my mind to be silent.*

She felt a thrill of excitement writing in her journal for her to
share at the next therapy session. Soshana had forgotten that
she had left Ms. Erling a voice message the day before. She
had returned her call in the morning but of course Soshana
had missed it due to her circumstances. Ms. Erling's voicemail
message was the same as it always was. "You've reached
Professor Erling, leave a message." It made Soshana shake
her head.

She had been retired from NYU for over fifteen years
and did not want to be called doctor, she said it was too
pompous. Ms. Erling led a simple life, had never married,
had no children and preferred to stay in solitude. Odd
as that was, since she was a professor of psychology and

philosophy for over thirty years, and you would think she'd want to be surrounded by many strange and wildly weird people. Soshana had taken several of her classes while she was studying and ended up staying behind to ask her questions about existence.

Ms. Erling was not intrigued by her at first. Soshana was sure she was annoyed because it was her last year and she wanted nothing to do with obnoxious, immature students. She had eventually been convinced that Soshana was different. Mature beyond her years, seemingly more grown up than most of the professors she worked with. She gave Soshana a chance and guided her through her severe, and at times debilitating, panic attacks that came from being emotionally abused and assaulted by her now ex-boyfriend.

Much of Soshana's anxiety also came from growing up in a volatile household, which was somehow overlooked during her first few sessions with Ms. Erling. Dodging household items, insults being thrown at her, screaming at all hours, her mother's uncontrolled rage from mental illness and alcoholism were all part of her upbringing. Soshana had to be a responsible 'grown-up' at all times and be a parent to her younger brother since her dad worked ridiculously long hours before they divorced, which she assumed was to avoid being at home.

The last time Soshana met in person for a session with Ms. Erling, it had been about her best friend and roommate, Mina. Soshana had always been there for her friend, through all of her new boyfriends and break-ups, moving several times into bigger and bigger flats. Picking up her groceries, cooking for her because 'Oh, Sosh, you're such a good cook!' and various other tasks that Mina just couldn't handle because she was 'so stressed out' and tired from her demanding job as a corporate lawyer.

Loving Mina was easy. She was outgoing and entertaining, tall and pretty in an other-worldly way with a million-dollar smile that could knock the boots off a snake. Mina had grown up in a home that demanded success, and she let everyone know it. Soshana moved in with Mina after the break-up. Mina's friends and family became Soshana's. Their favorite haunts became hers. Mina showed her a world that was so far removed from her own. She owed Mina a lifetime of gratitude because of it, so it seemed.

But over the next seven years, living with Mina had changed and emotions curdled into a sour resentment. It takes an immense amount of work to come to the conclusion that who you are is directly correlated to your upbringing then actually take that on board to improve yourself, so naturally Soshana was proud of herself. But when she would discuss her past or current accomplishments, as minuscule to most as they were, Mina would cut her off and go on about how much more stress she had and how much harder she had to work to get to where she was in her career. That continued for years, eventually falling into the rhetoric of 'Soshana didn't have it as bad, her job was easy and fun,' that Mina was 'floating her, paying most of the rent' because Soshana couldn't afford it. More accolades were pinned to Mina as reminders to Soshana, such as the diverse and charismatic group of people who were only friends with Soshana because of *her*. Once again, introspection at a loss, Soshana was controlled by her fear of disappointing others.

The last straw was when Soshana's mother was moved into hospice care. Soshana explained she had made the decision to temporarily return home so she could help her mother transition.

Outraged and spitting mad, Mina threw her anger as daggers while Soshana was packing her things.

"Are you fucking kidding me? This is so like you, Soshana, you're selfish and only think of yourself. Go. Help that bitch that did nothing but fuck you up. Look at you, look at yourself. You're a fucking mess. You won't even talk about it."

I can't because you won't let me.

Mina huffed, coughed out a few disgusted laughs. "You know what? Fine. Just fucking fine. Go, be a doormat. Don't expect me to help you ever again, you need to grow the *FUCK* up!"

Violently shaking and brimming with rage, Soshana held her tears in until the belt buckle clasped on the plane to Grand Rapids from Newark. Devastated, her entire body ached for days after their one-sided fight. This was more than just the typical sense of heartbreak. The only way to describe it was an unbearable, painful emptiness. Her bones felt fractured, muscles overused, organs and limbs missing or not operating. Her mind and body felt disconnected, and she was unsure how to put everything back into place. How does one function without the whole body? Today, the sting of being rejected in that way still lingered.

There were times when she wouldn't think of Mina or her mother, those days were peaceful. If only she could just forget them. Other days it was like a freshly salted wound, imaginary fingers covered in jagged salt, rubbing into the cuts, maliciously, slowly, intentionally. Mina had been her close friend for fifteen years. The family gatherings on holidays, some with Derek, were unforgettable. She didn't understand how she could have missed the signs that led to this 'break-up.' Her mother and ex-boyfriend treated her the same way: gaslighting, demoralizing, blaming when she presented opposing thoughts, facts, opinions or ideas. Loving and complimentary when Soshana was useful and compliant.

Ms. Erling was the one that presented the idea of Mina's true colors. "She's a dirty, dry, diseased cunt," Ms. Erling said quite matter-of-factly. Soshana had called her right after deplaning while waiting for a taxi to take her to her mother's house. She could still remember how she felt in that exact moment. The words that came out of Ms. Erling's mouth, someone who was supposed to be a professional also happened to be human. Laughter broke her out of the painful reality.

Her therapist was on her side. Soshana had complained about Mina over the years, and was an expert at coming up with excuse after excuse for her behavior. Ms. Erling reminded Soshana why she was allowing Mina to treat her that way: trying to stay safe, protecting herself from physical and emotional harm by making excuses for her behavior, it was because of what she went through in her childhood.

"People who suffer from this kind of childhood trauma often try to replicate their abusers in other relationships. Don't blame yourself, you only did what you thought would help the relationship. The hard part isn't over, though. You're going to question every relationship, the ones you are currently in, and the ones in the future. Not only are you damaged from your mother and Mina's relationship, but also the experience you had with your ex. It is up to you to take this as a lesson instead of falling back into the same patterns in relationships. If you want things to change, *you* have to change, Soshana. The world isn't going to do it for you and you have the power to do so."

This was hard to hear. She thought she had healed from her childhood trauma and changed into a more informed adult. She had spent years working on this.

"A wise person once told me the moment you stop learning, you stop living. Never stop learning and evolving, Soshana."

Ms. Erling returned her call shortly after 9:30 am. It had given Soshana enough time between leaving the message to properly shower, blow dry her hair, braid it, shave her legs and scrub her face. She felt so much better that she forgot about her episode and accident for a few moments.

"Hi, Soshana. You called? Sorry we missed each other." Ms. Erling spoke with a lightness in her voice.

"Hi, Ms. Erling, thank you for calling me back. How are you doing?" Soshana replied.

"I'm fine, thank you. How are you? Everything okay?"

Soshana winced and squeezed her eyes shut, lips pursed in self-irritation. *I am not a burden.*

"Well, no actually, I don't think it is. I was wondering if we could schedule a session as soon as possible." She exhaled, not thinking about the fact Ms. Erling could hear it over the phone, she knew Soshana well.

"It sounds like you need one right now, I can talk for a little bit. What's on your agenda?"

Soshana did her best to explain exactly what she remembered: the bathroom scenario, the most recent episode in the hospital. She did not hold back and didn't leave any detail out this time, letting slip in the smallest most insignificant way possible that she'd had suicidal thoughts.

"Hmm," was the first thing Ms. Erling said, pausing.

Soshana stalled, unable to grasp the weight of revealing her most wounded thoughts. "I'm sorry to hear you have considered taking your life. This is something new, I'm assuming."

"No." She didn't know how to talk about suicide. In all fairness, most people thought of slamming their head into a spiked fence as hard as they could every once in a while, right?

"I want you to know that I care about you like a dear friend. I need you to know that I am here for you at any time, however, I feel this may be out of my wheelhouse. I'm going to reach out to a couple of my colleagues and get back to you. Can you request your medical records to be faxed to me?"

"Yes, of course. But Ms. Erling, what's your initial reaction?"

Ms. Erling took a moment to reply. She sighed into the phone. "I'm not actually sure, Soshana, but I have a hunch. Give me a few days."

Soshana's anxiety spiked sharply. Ms. Erling always had an answer, and most of the time it was quick and confident.

"I'm beginning to get worried. This last episode was worse, terrifying. I did end up remembering it better than the first, not sure if that makes any difference." Soshana recalled the incident when she was walking to work. "Oh, I forgot, actually I'm not sure if this counts or if it has anything to do with these episodes, but I had a similar feeling with light distortions on my way to work last week."

Ms. Erling replied, "Anything helps at this point. Tell me more."

Soshana finished her story with as much detail as possible. Ms. Erling told her not to hesitate to call her home line at any time with updates, she would review the findings and get back to her as soon as possible, without trying to sound like this was a severe situation. Soshana could tell it was, though, and feelings of panic and wanting to escape invaded her thoughts.

They said their goodbyes and hung up.

I need to get out of here.

It had been almost a week since she arrived at the hospital. With the smell of the room, cleaning agents, and the stench of the pain medication leaking out of her skin, her head started vibrating and shaking, a panic attack emerging to be sure. She sprung up quickly from her chair in the office where she took the phone call and started walking fervently towards her room. She became unsteady and vertigo set in. Taking a deep breath and steadying herself against a wall, she was determined to make her body do what she instructed it to. She grabbed her sunglasses, pen and notebook, then put on her red knock-off Converse shoes and searched for Josette. Carina was the only option.

"She's on her break, what do you need?"

Soshana knew Carina wouldn't let her go outside without a chaperone, or possibly at all. Soshana calmed her face, stood with confidence and spoke clearly while looking directly into her eyes. "I am requesting to take some time to walk around outside, with your permission of course."

Carina stared at Soshana for a few seconds before looking away and saying, "Fine. You can have one hour, you have a final appointment with Dr. Weathering at 2:00 pm sharp, I expect you back up here for lunch at 11:30 am."

Soshana couldn't believe it. She thanked Carina and set off for Kieran's room first. Like magnets drawn to each other, she felt an incredible pull to him for comfort.

Walking towards their once shared room, she recalled

their conversation from the other day in the courtyard, the warmth of his hug, the way he smelled last night as they were embracing each other. *We technically slept together.* Her body was momentarily set on fire. Not wanting to believe what it meant.

She peeked her head into the room, his curtain was closed, but she heard videos playing on his phone. "Knock knock," she said.

"Soshana?" Kieran's voice came from behind the curtain.

"Can I come in?" she asked tenderly.

"Of course, yes, please." He pulled the curtain back and gave her a smile that nearly sent her flying. Her body caught her off guard, she was frozen at the sight of his freshly shaven face. Though he was gaunt, pale, unwell and in recovery, his smile felt like warm sunshine in her chest.

"You're looking well! I almost didn't recognize you." She motioned with her thumb and index finger around her upper lip and down towards her chin while focusing on his lips. She moved forward and grabbed the chair next to him.

"Yeah, I was tired of my scratchy beard." He stopped the video and put his phone down on the nightstand. He looked up at her, in a whisper low enough to decipher he said, "I was so drugged up last night, but I wonder if I had dreamed of a lovely woman lying next to me."

Soshana felt the heat moving from her chest to her cheeks, a smile crept across her face. "You weren't dreaming." She watched his lips move while he spoke, becoming entranced by his features, Derek was right. Kieran was attractive.

Kieran's smile faded. "I'm so sorry for what you're going through. Do they have any answers?"

Timidly, she replied, "I'm meeting up with the doctor later

this afternoon. Supposedly the tests they ran yesterday should give them some clues as to why these episodes are happening. At least I was in bed for the last one, they make me feel like I'm going to fall into a black hole, my whole body being sucked down into intense gravity." She paused, accepting the weight of her life right now: it was a mess.

"Wow, that sounds horrifying, I'm so sorry." He placed his hand on her forearm.

"Carina said yes to me going outside. I was wondering if you might want to join me again? If you're up to it. Maybe she'll let you go too, I asked real nicely."

"I can't, but I really wish I could. I have a meeting with the doctor in a few minutes, and I have some boring phone calls to make. You go ahead and enjoy some sunshine for me. Can you tell me all about it during lunch?"

"Sure, sounds good. Good luck with the doctor." Soshana got up to leave but hesitated. Her body's initial reaction was to hug him. Instead, she awkwardly patted his shoulder and smiled.

"See you later," he said as she left his room.

Soshana didn't want to register the despair in his eyes as she exited. She shook it off and went straight to the gazebo and sat down with her notebook. The trees had lost more of their leaves, though most were still attached, some still green with browned tips, some yellow gold, burnt orange and blazing in the sunlight. She watched them moving in the wind, glanced at a passing bird and observed the dark blue of the sky between pillowy clouds. Her energy was focused on trying to identify the first indicators of her episodes. Thoughts of Kieran kept interjecting her stream of ideas. She knew she needed to focus. Implementing the four-square breathing technique while concentrating on the smell of the fresh air and sounds of birds happily chirping helped her thoughts flow more easily.

The outline started with the first episode outside of work, then writing down every detail she could remember from the subsequent episodes. When she finished, a memory from being in the hospital with her mom surfaced. Marilyn had abruptly stopped drinking. This is what caused the stroke. Soshana watched Marilyn decline quickly. At the hospital she was still lucid and had some of her memories. Marilyn had asked Soshana why she stopped calling and visiting.

"I'm… busy. Sorry." Internally, she wanted to scream in her face.

"What did I ever do to you, besides provide you with a home, food and paid for you to go to college, don't forget that I co-signed that loan so you could leave me and fuck off to New York. Now your brother has done the same."

Soshana was always apologizing and making excuses instead of speaking the truth. No matter how many times she kept the peace and lied to keep her mother off her back, she couldn't fathom the pain and damage she was accumulating. For a stark, brief moment, she thought these episodes could have something to do with not expressing her feelings to her mother before she died, rather than the fact that she had died. The thought passed. She continued writing what she remembered from being in that hospital, in that room, the conversations that passed between the nurses, doctors, her mother and herself.

She remembered the car ride home, silent, stagnant. She helped Marilyn out of the car, while she batted her daughter's hand away. "I'm not an invalid, I can walk." Marilyn wouldn't know it then, but that was the last time she would be able to walk on her own. Soshana braced herself before she walked into her childhood home. It was dark, windows shut and all blinds drawn. It smelled of musty cigarettes, old dust and layered filth. The kind that told you there were dishes left in the sink for days, a possible recent discovery of mice shit underneath the sink, maybe even a deceased rodent in the walls. There was trash in the corners, some in plastic bags and small bins. Soshana made no mention of any of it as they walked in, she knew better. Marilyn had gone straight upstairs. Soshana heard the bed creak. "Honey, can you please bring me a glass of water?" Marilyn had the energy to snip at her daughter, but not enough to stop in the kitchen before she headed upstairs. Soshana complied immediately.

The dark stairway had pictures of her and Derek as kids on the wall, one was of them playing outside in the summer, Derek had the hose pointed towards Soshana, she was sitting in the small plastic pool, huge smiles on their faces. Other photos of them were more sterile, including school portraits, pictures in front of the Christmas tree, the forced grins on their faces. She remembered how drunk Marilyn was when she was taking one of the photos, it had been 8:00 am and she was fuming, practically flammable. Her drink of choice that morning was Irish coffee. The dust and spiderwebs that collected on the frames of the faded photographs were signs that these memories had long been dead. Buried and forgotten. Soshana felt nothing when she looked at them. She saw the light coming from the window to her old room. She ascended the stairs and headed straight to her mom's room and handed the water to her. "Is there anything else you need? Are you hungry?"

"No," she said sharply and dramatically with a small huff. "I'm fine. Close the door on your way out. I need to sleep." Marilyn's face was upturned and pleading pity.

"Okay, Mom, rest well. I'll be here if you need me." She left, closed the door and whispered, "You're welcome."

Soshana peeked into her old room. It looked nothing like it did when she left for college at eighteen. The world map poster with star stickers on wish list locations was gone, along with the photos of her and long-lost friends, stringed lights, and the patchwork vintage quilt her aunt made for her. Any sign of Soshana was apparently forbidden, as if she'd died or never existed. Upon Soshana's departure, Marilyn had immediately ripped off the old wallpaper and repainted it an ugly taupe. She'd pushed the bed to one corner and replaced sheets and duvet. She had put her book collection in the room along with a reading chair and some bins that didn't fit in the storage unit. It became Marilyn's room, no longer a place where her daughter could comfortably come back to visit during her breaks at college. It had felt like she was invading her mother's space. She had to ask permission to come home and sometimes it was an inconvenience if Marilyn had a man over, one of the many strange men that stayed there.

Soshana didn't feel like cleaning. If she went overboard and cleaned a little too much, Marilyn would have a conniption. Nothing could be out of place, even though everything was in disorganized chaos.

She needed her own money. Her mother had reluctantly given her money for food and expenses. Marilyn often told Soshana how grateful she should feel that she was supporting her while she was so ill. That's when she decided to get a job and to take the first one that was offered just to get out of that hellhole. Not having to feel the constant shame and guilt was worth being poor.

Marilyn had fallen down the stairs and suffered the final stroke that would end her life only after two short months of being home. Soshana had moved into her apartment just the week prior to the incident. She ran over and greeted the day nurse after they had called the ambulance. She followed them to the ER and in the stuffy waiting room, numbness crept over her distorted mind. She reverted back into caregiver mode, cold and unfeeling, professional as a nurse, only to stow away her feelings for later so she could get by during this time.

Marilyn stayed in the intensive care unit for several weeks, then was transferred to a hospice care. In that before Marilyn had the final episode, Soshana was alone in her childhood home. Her body began to show signs of distress and disease. Food wasn't digesting properly. Sleep was irregular and inconsistent. Each day after work she stared into the empty liquor cabinet, wishing to have a drink. She didn't think much of it. Instead of putting two and two together and calling a doctor, she went out for walks or runs when the restless legs began their vibration. She felt better afterward, yet no long-term improvement.

She couldn't bring herself to care for the home, she was angry at its very foundation. The worn stainless steel kitchen sink reminded her of the time she vomited cheap red wine into it after a party in twelfth grade. The poorly patched up hole in the hallway from her bedroom to Derek's was a reminder of their father's fury over Marilyn's drinking and her eventual admission to cheating, though she had always blamed him for cheating when he was only working late to avoid her.

The home reminded Soshana and Derek of how their father emotionally abandoned them, while also relying on them to take care of their mother as children. They didn't understand how a relationship could go from being in love, to getting married, agreeing on having children, then complete misery. Love was eternal, love was kind, sweet and loyal.

No, it truly wasn't. Love was a fucking lie. Love is fear, pain, suffering, worrying, needy and unreliable. Why do humans desperately seek it in order to be crushed by it eventually?

Soshana looked at her phone, it was 1:52 pm. "Shit." She'd completely skipped lunch and needed to be at the doctor's office in eight minutes. She wouldn't have time to stop by Kieran's room. Her stomach was in knots, her heart rate jumped. She gathered her things and walked briskly to the elevator in the lobby. She made it to the doctor's office with a few minutes to spare.

"Soshana, please sit down," Dr. Weathering said directly but with a calmness she hadn't heard from him before. "I'm pleased to tell you that we couldn't find anything abnormal from your tests or imaging."

Soshana felt numb. Shock took over, then anger. "What?! How is that possible? What are you saying then?"

He replied calmly and repeated, "There's nothing coming up from the results. I suggest you schedule an appointment with your primary care doctor when you get home so you can get any additional help that you need. Do you have any further questions?"

Soshana was stunned. How could they possibly think nothing was wrong? "Well, what do you think it is? Do you think I'm making this up?"

This time his face showed subtle signs of frustration. "No, I do not think you are making this up, Ms. Jones. I am simply explaining our findings. I don't have a straightforward answer for you. These events could be connected to a number of things. We are an emergency hospital. According to the bloodwork and imaging, you are fine. We're going to release you tomorrow. We have written instructions to follow up with your primary care doctor next week."

Knowing full well that she would not be getting any solid answers from him, she stood up and left without saying a word. She was afraid if she spoke, she would call him a fucking asshole. She also knew that he was right. There wasn't much else they could do. She was so irritated at the fact this was not the first time she was told by a doctor she was fine. In fact, it had happened multiple times in her life. She had to figure out most of her ailments herself.

Soshana walked quickly back to her room to drop off her things. She sat on the edge of her bed, shaking. After a few minutes she started to feel weak and lightheaded, she was very hungry. Lunch must have been taken away since she wasn't there. She silently thanked Derek for bringing her snacks on the first day. She ate some cookies and chewed a piece of wintergreen gum then set out to find Kieran to apologize.

Soshana became concerned as she turned the corner towards their old room. As she walked up to it, she noticed the door was closed and the blinds were drawn. She tried to open the door but it was locked. She knocked, waited, then knocked again. He could have been sleeping. The door was never closed though.

"Kieran?" Soshana said in a medium-toned voice, hoping to reach through the locked door. She waited for a response.

Nothing. Soshana looked around to try and find an orderly or a nurse. There was no one around. It was eerily quiet. Panic set through her body. Was she in an episode? She usually found herself alone in them, but this felt too real.

She walked further down the hallway, then crashed into Josette coming out of the room two doors down from theirs.

Exasperated, Josette spoke quietly and seriously. "Oh goodness, I didn't mean to run into you. Where have you been? Did you see the doctor?"

"Yes, yes, it's fine. I'm approved to go home tomorrow. Is Kieran in the room? I need to speak to him."

Josette took in a sharp breath and looked empathetic. "Oh dear. I..." She trailed off and looked around the hallway. "I can't tell you much, but he's not here, he was transferred to the surgery center just an hour or so ago."

Soshana couldn't breathe. A hellscape of chilling energy sent shockwaves through her body. "What... what happened?"

"He became very ill and was sent back to the surgery center. I really can't tell you any more than that. I could get into trouble." Josette's face said something other than the professional manner in which she spoke.

"What do you mean? I just saw him not too long ago!" Soshana did her best not to scream. She was at breaking point.

Josette said sincerely, while placing a hand on Soshana's shoulder, "There's nothing else I can tell you since you're not a direct relative, I'm sorry."

The lump that had formed in Soshana's throat welled up until the pain from it burst like a busted dam. Trembling, she pulled her palms to her face and sobbed painfully, holding back as best she could. She slid to the floor and put her knees to her chest.

Josette looked around, found a box of tissues and sat on the floor next to Soshana. "I'm so sorry, my darlin'. I wish I knew more and could tell you more. Can I give you a hug?" Soshana nodded. Josette gave her a tight side hug and gently shushed her, like a loving mother would if a child fell and scuffed their knee. Josette gently brushed away loose strands of Soshana's hair and tucked it behind her ear. "Let's get you back into your room and get you ready. Think about how you will see your kitty soon and be at home in your own bed."

That did help a small amount. They returned to the room quietly. So much had happened over the past few hours, Soshana didn't have the will to process it.

"Can I get you anything, sweetheart?"

Soshana stared blankly, tears still forming in her eyes. "No." Josette tapped the frame of the door and turned to leave. "Josette?" Soshana pleaded.

"Yes, dear?" she said sweetly.

"Thank you."

Josette smiled, nodded and left.

Soshana sat alone in her room for what could have been hours, she couldn't tell. The sadness she felt was too much. She began to panic, thinking her upset could cause an episode, a vicious cycle. A wild thought emerged, could her emotions and stress be the cause of them? She hadn't felt severe stress or anger for a while, she'd kept it well under control. These episodes were happening *to* her, not because *of* her, right?

Remembering to take deep breaths when she found herself breathing shallowly, she thought about Kieran. Desperation crept over her body, she needed to move, her leg started shaking. Though she was better than last week, she was still dizzy and fatigued. Bolting up from her bed, she quickly packed all her belongings, checked her appearance and sprinted down the hallway towards the elevator in the lobby.

She ran to the gazebo, sat and pulled out a few blank pages from her notebook. She began to write a letter to Kieran but wasn't sure what to say. Something in her chest felt uncomfortable, almost unbearable. It wasn't familiar and it had frightened her over the past few days, yet she was pulled towards him. She kept thinking to herself that it was just a fluke due to the episodes. She decided to talk to Ms. Erling about it when she got home.

Her hand flew to the back of her neck to scratch it, mindlessly forgetting about the scab that had grown there. It broke free and a small amount of blood was released from the wound. She pulled her hand back and saw the bright red splotch on her fingertips. Her mind told her, without warning, *this is proof you are alive.* It was a jarring thought. She didn't feel much alive and hadn't for a long time. She wasn't even sure what it was like to feel 'alive.' "What does that mean?" she said aloud to herself.

She continued the letter on a second page, deciding to keep it short, be honest and leave it up to him if he wanted to continue speaking. She still didn't know him very well. She wasn't exactly sure where he grew up, though she knew the general area. He never mentioned a spouse or partner, and didn't talk much about his current employment or what he was doing with his life before cancer took over it. Her heart sank. This made her think he was purposefully hiding something, but for what reason? She didn't feel he was lying in any way, she could typically sense that. Although some people were talented liars and exceptional at getting away with it.

A wind blew through the gazebo; the warm sun was glaring through the cracks of the banister. She knew what she had to do, what she had been practicing with him since being there.

Kieran,

My therapist is demanding that I be violently vulnerable. I need to rip my heart out, put it on the table for all to see, so here goes.

I have never enjoyed spending time with someone as much as you. My face hurts from smiling and laughing. Thank you for bringing some joy into my life during this difficult time. My hope is that we can remain friends, after all this is over. I don't want to leave you, especially now since...

Tears fell onto the paper and blurred a few of the words. Instinctively, ashamedly, she went to crumple the page and start over, but she stopped. The tears were part of her vulnerability, she shouldn't leave them out. She waited until the feeling passed and continued.

...you are back in surgery. I have to leave tomorrow because I was cleared by the doctor. Here is my number 616-555-4859. Please call/text anytime, and I mean it. I want to be there for you, just like you were for me. Please, please, please take care, rest well and recover fast.

Your friend,

Soshana

That would have to be good enough, wet dimpled tear stains and all. Feeling some small resemblance of relief, she got up from the gazebo floor. She closed her eyes and imagined the previous day when he stood so close to her. She could almost smell him, feel his ephemeral warmth. He must have made such an effort to get out of his wheelchair and walk over to her, that warmed her heart more than she had felt before. *Stay here in this moment for a while longer. This feels different.*

Still, her thoughts wandered to the darker, more pessimistic places quite quickly. She shook those foreboding thoughts off her mind and went back to her room. As she waited for her last meal during her tenure at the hospital, she devised a plan. She knew the surgery center was across the street in another building. She knew she'd need a reason to be there and an excuse to wander the halls, searching. She racked her brain to come up with one. She could be his wife. The image of a gold ring on his finger flashed in her mind. She knew his last name, but she didn't have a ring. She could keep her hand in her pocket. She would escape after dinner. The plan was set, she would give Kieran her letter in person, so she knew he had received it.

Evening crawled closer and closer. Dinner finally arrived at about six, a little later than usual. Visiting hours ended at seven. She ate fast, which she regretted later. She put on her pink sweater and running shoes, waited and watched for the orderlies and nurses to thin out after dinner had been completed, and set off for the elevator.

"And where do you think you are going?" Carina called out from behind her.

Soshana's neck hairs stood on end. She relaxed her body and said, "I just need some fresh air, please."

"Twenty minutes," Carina called back.

Soshana, shocked at how easy-going Carina had been all day, waved her hand and said, "Thank you."

She couldn't believe she'd got away with it. She needed to look confident as she walked out the front doors, past the lobby and in the opposite direction of the courtyard.

The front desk staff couldn't have cared less, they were looking at their phones, sharing photos of Halloween costume ideas and laughing.

Soshana knew exactly where the surgery center was as it was the adjacent building across the street from the main hospital. The day was fading fast, only the last few glimmers of sunlight held close to the earth as pink, purple and blue melted into one. Her courage returned and she jogged up the steps. Confidence and bravery were the only two thoughts she had in her mind.

"Hi, I'm here to see Kieran Summerland. I'm his wife, Rebecca Summerland."

"Sure, he is recovering in room 193. You have twenty-five minutes before visiting hours are over."

The desk attendant didn't even look up from her computer. *What is the world coming to?* That was too easy. Anyone could have come in and say they were a relative or spouse. This wasn't right. But she didn't care at this point. She got in and she would get to see him, hopefully not for the last time.

Soshana braced herself as she approached his room. The door was open, and the curtains were open. She heard the steady beeping of the monitors, then her heart started pounding when she saw he was hooked up to a breathing machine. He was unconscious. Her body was vibrating and trembling again, this time more intensely.

"No." slipped from her mouth. She walked carefully over to him and observed what she could. They had only shaved a small portion of the area that had previously been worked on and there was a tiny amount of blood. She looked over his hands, neck and face. He didn't look much different than he had earlier in the day.

Knock, knock, knock. Soshana quickly turned around to see a kind-faced short man in a white coat. "Hello, ma'am, we were hoping you would come in today. I'm the nurse on staff tonight, I can give you a quick update before visiting hours are over in a few minutes."

Soshana thought with a panic, *they were waiting for 'me,' meaning his wife?*

"Nothing to worry about, he's stable, though we did put him in an induced coma for today just to be safe. He had some excess fluid, which was causing headaches and pain. Normal for this kind of surgery and recovery. We'll continue to monitor him for the next week." He gave a reassuring smile and asked, "Do you have any questions?"

Soshana couldn't think of anything to say, so she shook her head.

As he walked out the door she said, "Thank you!"

He turned around and said, "He was trying to say something, but," he chuckled, "it almost sounded like he was shushing us. 'Shuh… Show…' Who knows? Keep a positive attitude for him, will ya?"

He left Soshana alone with Kieran. Had he been trying to say her name? Maybe he did have a wife? *That doesn't matter, I guess.* Her thoughts turned dark. She shook her head and, with a heavy heart, touched his hand, then squeezed it gently. "Kieran, I'm here." She didn't say her name out loud just in case. He didn't move. The tube forced down his throat was unbearable to witness. She imagined kissing him on the head then surprised herself by moving forward towards his head. She leaned in slowly watching his face for any signs of movement, nothing. She gently kissed his forehead.

He wasn't very warm, like the day before. His smell was still there, though it wasn't as powerful. She needed to leave before someone else walked in to warn her visiting hours were over. She found his coat in the closet and tucked the letter into the pocket. She turned to look at him again. This was goodbye and she knew it.

She made her way to the main hospital and got into bed. She laid there for hours, not daring to move. Her heart felt like it was breaking in places she hadn't realized it could. She felt heavy, terribly uncomfortable, and melancholic. She dozed on and off all night before she decided to get up and shower around 5:30 am. Josette was not working that day, and another nurse she didn't recognize was covering the shift. Soshana was ready to leave around seven and planned out her bus route back home. Joe would be picking her up at the station.

Sitting upright on the bed, backpack on her shoulder, body feeling so heavy she didn't want to lift it for fear of falling to the ground, she thought, *I have about fifteen minutes, I could run over there and see if...* Her thoughts raced in then trailed off. This time her unconscious mind said something so extraordinary, so unlike her, that it felt like it had begun to feel *for* her. *What I would give to see his eyes, his smile one more time.*

STOP IT. Just stop.

She headed downstairs and waited in the lobby for the taxi to take her to the bus station. This was her final chance to see him. She stared at the building. She told herself he would still be in a coma and there would be no point. The taxi arrived early and she willed herself into the cab. No goodbyes, not from anyone. No finality, just alone in her silence.

8

No Answers

I am really upset with myself that I forgot to meet Kieran for our lunch date. I didn't realize I was going to be released the next day, then he had emergency surgery while I was with the doctor and at the gazebo. I snuck into the surgery building to see him and left him a note. I almost don't recognize myself and my actions, I pretended to be his wife and they trusted me! I don't know what I was thinking. I wasn't thinking, I was acting. And I don't know what the consequences are and I'm afraid.

The bus ride was quiet except for the scribbling of pen to paper. The sun shone brightly in the late-morning sky. She watched the trees as they passed in a blur, then blurred further as more tears came unannounced. As they drew nearer to home, she straightened up and wiped the dampness from her face, surprised at how much she had cried in the past twenty-four hours. She felt she was on the edge of tears at almost any minute, and she hated it. She wanted to bury it, push it away. There was no time for crying, not now. She thought of all the work she would need to catch up on, how she would need to clean her apartment, return all the texts and calls she had got from various people, not many of them were important but she did not want to disappear from anyone. Not to mention calling her doctors and setting up follow-up appointments to hopefully figure out what caused the episodes and what she needed to do to stop them. A small bud of energy filled her body, knowing she could keep herself busy for a while and put away any thoughts or feelings from the past week so she could deal with them later. It was too raw and uncomfortable right now.

Joe was standing outside the bus station, leaning against his dark blue 1999 Ford Taurus. He caught a glimpse of her and waved frantically. She couldn't help but smile wide as she saw his enthusiasm. He ran up to her as she got off the bus and without asking, hugged her so tightly she almost couldn't breathe.

"I can't tell you how happy I am to see you upright and looking better, you can hardly tell anything happened! Look at you! Only some minor bruising. How are you feeling?" Joe said with a grin that could light up a football field on a Friday night.

"Oh haha, I'm okay, I think. I don't know, I have some follow-up appointments, they couldn't find anything." She gave him a weak smile. "I don't know how to thank you for taking care of my little munchkin and for picking me up."

He patted her on the shoulder. "No need to worry about that, let's get you home." He drove her to the apartment complex and parked outside the main entrance. "Do you need me to help you upstairs or are you good?" He handed over her key.

"No, I am okay, I promise." He gave her a look that could

only come from a father. "I will text you if I feel even the slightest bit off." She gave him a reassuring smile.

She got out of the car and took notice of how she felt at that moment. She felt different, something had changed, her apartment building was exactly the same, albeit a few more leaves had fallen from the maple trees and the grass had grown a little more, but all was relatively the same. She walked up the stairs to her apartment and felt a growing sensation of strangeness as she put the key in the lock. Was this the beginning of another episode? No, this felt different, almost the opposite. It still gave her terrible anxiety, not knowing when and if an episode would happen. It was energy, positive or negative she was unsure, but it was an energy she would have to decipher later.

Mr. Skittles ran up to her chattering like an old maid who hadn't spoken to anyone in years. "My baby!" She dropped her bag on the floor and scooped him up. He was purring and chirping so loudly she couldn't hear anything else. He licked her face as she nuzzled her cheek into his. She swayed with him in her arms and started to hum as he rubbed his head into her face over and over. She sighed and went to put him down, but his claws grasped on to her shoulder. "All right, dang," she said aloud. She bent over carefully with him in her arms to close the door and pick up her backpack.

Her apartment was immaculate. Joe must have cleaned her entire place while she was gone. She glanced around her living/dining area, kitchen, then went to her bedroom. The bed was made, clothes that were in the hamper were washed, folded and placed carefully on the bed.

She dared to enter the bathroom, the scene of the crime as she told herself, it was also perfectly clean. No evidence of any accident.

This made her uncomfortable, as no one had ever done something like this for her before. She was always the one to take care of others. She really didn't know how to thank Joe.

Mr. Skittles finally let go of Soshana's shoulder and she placed him on the floor. He looked up at her, lovingly, slowly blinking his eyes and still giving her little meows and chirping between purring and rubbing his body on her legs.

Feeling useless, she was unsure what to do with herself. She sat on the couch and looked outside. Mr. Skittles followed her and leapt onto her lap. Before she knew it, she had fallen asleep, her face pointed towards the sky.

It was early in the afternoon. Her stomach grumbled. She got up after skillfully moving Mr. Skittles off her lap onto the couch. Forgetting how much her neck and back still ached, she groaned and wobbled to the kitchen. In the fridge, there was a meal in a glass container with a note on top. *Carol insisted she cook for you, bon Appetit!* She opened it to find leftover coq a vin. Soshana couldn't put it in the microwave fast enough. While she waited for her delectable meal, she smelled its aroma and felt the love and care from someone she has only met a few brief times.

What would she do if she actually allowed herself to be loved and feel it? This was unheard of, she was the one that gave all of her love but never allowed it to set in her heart from others. "Maybe because it would hurt too much, or maybe because deep down you feel like you don't deserve it, that comes from the deep childhood wound of being mistreated." Ms. Erling's words.

Her mind felt like it had been unlocked and this cruel

but accurate monster was walking around in it, just saying whatever the fuck it wanted. Was this truly her subconscious mind, or was she becoming seriously mentally ill? Was she already? How far of a reach would it be since her own flesh and blood was severely mentally ill?

Her phone rang, it was Derek.

"Hi, sis, how are you feeling? Are you home yet?"

"Yes, I'm so sorry, I got home and the little man needed all of my attention, then I fell asleep on the couch for a few hours."

The microwave pinged three times.

"Hey look, I need to eat. Can I call you back in a little bit?"

"Yes of course."

Soshana ate so fast it gave her heartburn. She knew she needed to slow down and chew but this was just ridiculously delicious. She texted Joe to tell Carol *thank you SO much, I am very full and happy. You guys are wonderful. And I can't believe you cleaned my entire apartment!! That was too much. Thank you times a million.*

She texted Derek to see if he was available to chat for a few minutes. He called immediately.

"So tell me what's up, what did the doctors find out?"

She told him they couldn't find anything abnormal or out of the ordinary beyond the traumatic accident.

"What in the actual fuck? Are you kidding me? What about that whole thing that happened in the hospital, the second episode?"

"Yeah, I guess it was nothing. But it felt like I was thrashing about and then falling. It felt like my body was shaking. The nurse said I was frozen in place and my eyes and mouth were wide open, like a silent scream. After about ten seconds I passed out and stayed like that for hours. The nurses said these kinds of things could happen with a TBI, which sounded like bullshit to me."

"That sounds terrifying, and it doesn't sound like nothing. Soshana, this is serious. What happens next?"

"More testing. I have to make a few appointments. Speaking of which, I need to get on that."

"Wait, wait, wait, hold up, sis, don't think you're going to get away with not telling me about Kieran."

At the sound of his name, she felt a pang of sadness.

"Yes. Him. There's not much to say, really. We did talk quite a bit and spent some time together outside. I needed to breathe and demanded he join me. Right before I was released, he ended up needing another procedure to remove excess fluid. I didn't know he was in so much pain. I didn't get to say goodbye to him." Soshana sighs at the thought.

"I'm sorry to hear that, please tell me more. What did you guys talk about?"

She recalled some of their more exciting conversations, the way he listened so intently, how he laughed with her. She described him in a way that made him sound platonic, safe, and left out any discernment.

"Huh. Sounds like you like him."

"Derek!" she half shouted.

"Well sorry, I mean by the second day I was there, he seemed like he couldn't wait to talk to you, but of course he didn't want to move too quickly. I just dove right in, you know me."

"Yes, I know. God, Derek, I do like him but I don't know if in any other way than someone I want to be friends with." Lies oozed through her gritted teeth.

"C'mon, there's more. I can sense it."

"Bloodhound! He asked me to hug him at the gazebo. Then

119

that's the night the episode happened. The next day they put me in a different room after they administered the drugs, I didn't know they were going to do that. I got up, snuck into the room to see him, I didn't want him to think I'd requested to be moved. He asked me to… I mean, I guess to sleep with him? Next to him, in his bed. No sexy stuff. It was wildly uncomfortable, yet kind of exciting. I don't understand."

"Holy shit, Sosh, he likes you. It's so obvious! Ha ha! I was right! He is, for sure, recovering, but I can tell if he just cleaned up, gained some weight, he would be a knockout. Not to say he isn't now, but I mean, he looked so unwell, you get it."

"Yeah, he kind of is. He shaved his face, I stood there staring at him, gawking."

"*Hell* yes, I knew it. Sosh, you gave him your number, right? You guys need to keep this good thing going. How long has it been?"

"Derek, you're treading dangerous waters right now, that is none of your business."

"For fuck's sake who cares, you need to tell me all the details. What did he look like? I bet those lips are gorgeous," Derek said. She could tell when he was smiling over the phone.

She talked about Kieran for a little while longer, all the while feeling the warmth growing in her chest. This was such a new and raw feeling she wanted to run away from it and careen towards it.

"All right that's enough, butthead. I have to go, I need to call my doctor to set up an appointment."

Derek reluctantly said goodbye and she hung up. Her thoughts racing back to Kieran, she checked her phone for messages, either a text or voicemail from a strange number. Nothing. She called her primary care doctor, the one she'd had when she lived out here many years ago. They said they had no new patient examinations open for three months and she would be put on a waitlist to be called back as soon as there was an opening. She hung up, frustrated and unsurprised. But this was serious. She called back and asked to speak to the office manager, a person she knew from high school who had been the position for a long time. She was able to get Soshana in the following week on an emergency basis. That would have to do.

Soshana changed into fresh clothes, they felt a little baggier on her than usual. She walked to the local grocery store a few blocks past her work. Fresh vegetables, fruit and some protein sounded good. Nothing in particular was appealing in regards to nourishment. When she had collected her items in her reusable bags, she stopped in the convenience store to get some things she'd ran out of and check in on her co-workers.

Joe was there; he waved excitedly at her. It made her laugh. "Hey, lady! What are you doing? You should be resting!"

"I know, but I just missed you all so much! I also needed to make sure I still have a job, you know..."

"Hmm, I don't know, state laws and such... Let's see if Wendy's around, she's in today."

They found Wendy at her desk in her office. She was a middle-aged woman with dark frizzy hair that was always up in a bun. She wore the same polo work shirt and blue slacks to work every day, no one knew who she was outside of work. She was pleasant enough, but always serious and work oriented.

"Hi, Soshana, it's great to see you upright and breathing. How are you feeling?"

"I'm fine, I think. Fatigued and still bruised. I should be

good to come back to work in a few days, I can bring the doctor's note in."

"Glad to hear you're recovering, yes bring in the doctor's note and just let me know what day and I'll get you scheduled in. Joe kept us all updated with your progress. You gave us a good scare," Wendy said with a dullish tone. She wasn't one for sentiments or emotion, Soshana was okay with that, but sometimes she couldn't read Wendy.

Joe followed her around the store, chatting about some of the events that happened while she was away. A local teen with a gun had threatened one of the clerks, it wasn't loaded but they still called the police on him and he was arrested. "I'm so glad you weren't here for that, it was terrifying. I just don't understand why."

I know why. There's no hope left.

"Wow, yeah. It's such a quiet small town where not much goes on. So sad." She felt terrible for the clerk or anyone that had to deal with that kind of distress.

He led her to the front cashier, she put in her employee ID for the discount.

"Now, I want you to go home, get in your jammie jams, put on a good movie and rest." He gave her the dad look again.

"Yes, sir, I promise."

"Good. I'll see you in a few days when you're back. Take it easy."

"Thank you again for the delicious leftovers. Carol can cook for me anytime!"

"And she would love that."

Soshana said, "See ya," and left for home.

Over the next few days, Soshana checked her phone at least a hundred and fifty times. The growing sense of dread, anxiety and disappointment would have led anyone to insanity. A physical gaping hole in her body would have been less painful than the poisonous phantom that had crept its way into her.

In an act of desperation, she called the hospital in Ann Arbor.

"May I please speak to Josette, she's a nurse working on the second floor."

"What's the reason for your call?"

"I… I just need to speak to her, it's personal."

"I can't let you just speak to a nurse without a reason."

"I think I left something in my room and I need her to check it."

Silence.

"What's your name? We can have one of the orderlies check for it, what was it?"

Soshana scrambled to come up with something original. "Um, Soshana Jones. A book, it had a picture of a mountain on it, I can't remember the title."

"What room were you in?"

"Number 213B"

"Hold, please."

It sounded like she was being transferred, the line beeped three times, then paused, then beeped three times again.

"Soshana?" A familiar voice sounded through the line. It was the orderly that took Kieran and her to the courtyard.

"Hi! Yes, it's me."

"How are you doing? You left so fast, none of us got to say goodbye to you!"

"I'm okay, thanks for asking. I was wondering if Josette was around? Can I please speak to her?"

"Yes, she's with a patient but should be done in a few minutes, can you hold?"

Soshana waited, listening to her own heart pounding. She needed to know how Kieran was, maybe her life depended on it at the moment.

"Darling! It's so great to hear from you, so glad you called. How are you?" Josette said in a hushed tone, happy nonetheless.

Soshana was getting kind of tired of telling people she was fine when she damn well knew something was very wrong with her.

"I'm… fine, I'm alive. I'm so sorry I didn't get to say goodbye to you, everything happened so quickly."

Josette spoke more hurriedly and quietly. "Did you get to say goodbye to him? Did you find him?"

"Yes, I did. Carina actually let me go outside, I told her I was going to the courtyard. I snuck over there and… and I pretended to be his wife."

Josette wheezed out a laugh. "Oh! Shocked to hear that, actually. You don't seem like a rule breaker to me, but what the hell do I know? Tell me, what else happened?"

This was middle-school gossip, silly girls spilling silly secrets.

Soshana laughed a little with her. "He had to have another procedure. He was put in a coma. I did get to leave a note in his jacket pocket, though. Is he there? Is he okay?"

"No, he's not here, must be back home, I guess. He ain't dead, otherwise we would have heard about it." Josette must have heard the sharp intake of breath from the other end of the phone. "That was blunt, I'm sorry, darlin'. He hasn't called or texted you yet?"

Soshana spent a moment in her thoughts. So he was awake,

out of the hospital, he could have seen the note by now and could have called her. What was he waiting for? Maybe all that conspired between them was just a passing fancy, not good enough for a real connection.

No. I felt something, I read what his face and body language was telling me. It couldn't be nothing.

"Soshana, are you still there?"

"Oh yes, sorry. No I haven't heard from him," she spat out.

"Give him time, love. I know you might not believe me, but there was something between you. You're a smart woman. Such a beauty too, he'd be a damn fool. Whatever it was, you two are connected and bonded now. Don't give up!" She paused.

Whispering quickly, Josette continued, "Shoot! It's Carina. Hey, I have to go. It was so great hearing from you! I wish we had more time."

Stifled out of a closing dialogue with Josette, she felt another small loss. He hadn't called or text. What did it mean? Was he purposefully ignoring her, or was it possible that he didn't get the letter? Maybe it fell out of his pocket when he put it on. And damn that Josette for renewing hope in their fleeting relationship, *she* even saw there was something there. It greatly disappointed her he had left and Josette wasn't able to give her any information, or that she couldn't leave any.

She went back to work the next day, glad to have a distraction, not wanting to think about the silence coming from her phone.

Overwhelmed, and definitely not happy about the amount of work that was left for her, the day went by extraordinarily fast. She had an appointment with her PCP the next morning then she had a call in the evening with Ms. Erling to go over the lab work, test results and imaging from Ann Arbor.

The doctor was no help the following day. She was bewildered when Soshana openly and confidently explained everything that had happened, just as she had explained it all to Ms. Erling.

"Let's get a full panel and see if we can start solving the puzzle. Other than that, you look fine. Keep drinking lots of water, rest as much as you can and when possible, light exercise and a well-balanced diet."

"My fucking landlord could have told me that, for free," she shouted in her car, in the parking lot of the doctor's office. "*You look fine*, give me a break."

She popped home before returning to work and surveyed what apparently "looked fine" in the mirror. There was some yellowish green bruising lingering around her nose and eyes. At the back of her bathroom drawer, she rooted around for some long-forgotten concealer.

Might as well blot on some blush and mascara while I'm at it. Hag.

Stop it. Stop calling yourself names, you aren't twelve anymore.

Shelf stocking day. This was her favorite job as she could focus on the placement of the items, lining them up neatly. Each item placed was a chess piece, a game of her own making, one that was won only by perfection. It was an escape, one that she was being paid for, free of any hangovers from narcotics or alcohol. Free from most interruptions, it took her mind off everything that day until a familiar tune pulsed into her subconscious. Finding herself looking at a bottle of shampoo, staring into nothing, her upper lip curled in disgust and her eyebrows creased together. Memories brushed across her mind like a paintbrush dipped in the inkiest crimson red over blinding white paper. The lyrics to 'Orinoco Flow' floated in the air.

And there was her mother, flailing her arms, dancing with yet another abusive man, twirling in forbidden bliss, wine glass in hand while the merlot splattered on the walls of the dining room. Soshana watched her, thinking all the while, *I get to clean that up. Thanks, Mom.* Twirling and splattering. Laughing and cursing. No doubt dreaming of sailing away with that man, away from her responsibilities, her emotions, herself.

I'm at work, it's not 1999. Another great opportunity to take a deep breath. For the ten thousandth time, it's not happening right now, it's over with. Soshana resumed her monotonous work chores, focusing on nothing more than the fact that no new memories involving her mother could be made.

When she got home, she plopped on the couch and scratched Mr. Skittles' head. The phone rang, the number came up as unknown, sending her into a tailspin. Her heart pounding out of her chest, she braced herself for a split second then answered.

"Hello?"

"Hi, Soshana, it's Ms. Erling."

Damn it.

"Oh hi, this isn't your usual number."

"No, I'm calling from a colleague's office, Dr. Linds. We've been working on your case together."

"Wow, thank you. What have you found?"

"Everything looks hunky-dory. How have you been feeling? Has anything happened since the last episode?"

Hunky-dory?! Now she really couldn't believe it. She had at least five doctors from various fields looking at her lab work, images and documents, yet they still couldn't find anything. These so-called professionals.

"No. I mean, other than the usual, I suppose. No new episodes."

"Did you see your doctor today, what did they say?"

"She said exactly the same, that I'm fine. Or that I looked fine, but she did order more lab work. I feel like a guinea pig; a lab rat being experimented on."

"Yes, yes. Okay," Dr. Erling responded, sounding distracted.

"What should I do in the meantime? I don't know if there's going to be another episode, and I never know when they're going to happen if there is. Am I going insane or am I already there?"

Ms. Erling laughed.

"THIS ISN'T FUNNY! I feel like I'm going to die! My heart is constantly racing, I can't keep my thoughts under control and I'm just... I'm just fucking angry all the time and you're laughing?!" Was this to become her life? All questions unanswered, no hindsight, no foresight, all allusions. Smoke and mirrors.

"I'm so sorry. I wasn't laughing at you, just the situation and how you said it. No, Soshana, you are not insane. This is an anomaly. I believe you, I truly do." Ms. Erling had an edge of sympathy to her tone, something she rarely showed.

"Fine. Is there anything else I can do in the meantime?"

Ms. Erling sighed. "There's not much. I'll report this to my colleague, Dr. Linds. He's very curious about you. Is it all right if I give him your number? He may want to chat with you further. He works in a clinical setting where they are performing research on victims of PTSD. He's the leading doctor of the study and found your case to be comprehensive and daunting. I hope it's okay that I spoke to him on your behalf."

"Yes, of course."

"Good, thank you. I suggest you follow what your PCP says and call me immediately, I mean anytime, day or night, if you have another episode. You most likely will. You need to be prepared by quickly finding a safe place on the ground then just let it happen. You'll need a note from your doctor explaining that you're prone to passing out and that work needs to accommodate you. I also suggest that when you are lucid, write down every single minuscule detail. I'm right here. I promise I'll do whatever it takes to help you. Do you understand?"

She often talked to Soshana as if she were a child, but over the years, and understanding Ms. Erling better, the resentment had faded. She was direct and wanted to know if you truly did understand and comprehend what she was saying.

"I do. Thank you."

They ended their conversation and Soshana was, again, left alone with her thoughts, her fears and now even more confused than she was a week and a half ago.

9

Each Memory, a Moment

Vivid dreams of Kieran tap, tap, tapped into her restless sleep. They were walking in a park, not unlike the courtyard in the hospital. It was early summer, in the late morning, warm, and bright sunlight blinded her gaze. The flowers were waiting to burst open; some were in full blooms of red and yellow, the tulips on their last days, their petals spread wide and wilting. Flowers of any kind caused a temporary distraction from reality, a drug of sorts.

Kieran looked young, healthy and vibrant. His smile was not the same as she remembered, his teeth were more separated, but his face was full, showing health and radiance. She was talking to him softly, with coyness, but he wouldn't respond, he would turn to her, smile, blink, nod his head and then continue looking ahead.

She woke up sweating. She rolled over to the nightstand to check the time. It was 4:23 am. No possibility of falling back asleep. She'd taken the early shift so she could grab more groceries and do some baking after work. Her mind drifted back to the sensations of the dream, how healthy and handsome Kieran looked in the sunlight, how light and free she felt walking beside him, not caring that he wasn't responding to her, just knowing that he was listening. Wouldn't it be something if people had the sense of smell in their dreams?

She switched to thinking about what she would get at the grocery store after work and bake for her co-workers. This was safer. It wouldn't upset her and it made her happy that she would finally be able to give to someone else, rather than everyone else fussing about her. The attention she was getting lately was enough to make her want to peel her skin off.

Pumpkin spice bread. Cranberry, orange, and butterscotch cookies. Blueberry ginger scones with a sugar drizzle. Snicker-doodle, vegan gluten-free cookies for the people at work that had particular diets and intolerances. She loved a challenge and loved how much they appreciated her making something special they could actually eat. It gave her purpose.

After work she walked home and went to the garage where her green sedan was parked in her designated tenant parking spot. She rarely needed to drive since she hardly went anywhere besides work and the small grocery store next to the cafe. She realized how much of a hermit she had become. The past year had been a blur of working and sleeping. A dull and lifeless routine that acted as a safety net.

It looked neglected. Much like her life. She neglected and ignored as much as possible. She paused in front of the driver's side door and stared blankly at it. She had continued numbing herself on purpose and been unwilling to give time or energy to work through it.

Were these episodes a wake-up call?

The engine sounded gruff when the key turned over, the battery could be going out. "Another thing to add to the never-ending list of things I need to take care of with the money I don't have," she said aloud, knowing how obnoxious and whiny that sounded.

She drove to a proper grocery store to pick up the ingredients needed for the cookies and treats. They had freshly made meals, so she picked up four to last her a few days. When you live by yourself, it's difficult to cook full meals without having to eat leftovers for a week, which would make anyone gag by day five.

During the drive home, she listened to some pop songs from the mid-2000s and was surprised to find herself singing along, delightfully and freely. She stopped. She used to love singing and had been in the high school choir with her friends, going to competitions across the state. Singing distracted her from reality as she focused on the small muscles in her throat, contracting and changing to adjust the tune.

One part of her wanted to do things that were enjoyable, creative and expressionistic, and another part of her wouldn't allow it.

When she got back to her apartment, she wrote down the strange occurrences: staring blankly at the car, singing without realizing then suddenly stopping. They could be something; they could be nothing. Her instincts told her they were important.

She turned on the radio and started to prepare the ingredients when the lights started dimming. A buzzing sound came from inside her mind and the room started to spin. She didn't have much time to react, but she now knew what was going to happen. She quickly put the utensils down on the counter and bolted to the couch to lay down. One second longer would have been too long.

While in this state, she recognized she had a little bit more control over her body. She decided to ride it out, even though it was utterly terrifying. It made her mad: she didn't get to just do whatever she wanted, she was a victim of these random episodes. Her life was not her own.

Taking in her surroundings, she immediately knew she was in her mother's kitchen. Soshana looked around for the dark omniscient figure that seemed to loom during these episodes, the one that also brought her back out of them, back to reality.

Taking gentle steps around the kitchen, she jumped when her mother appeared from the dining-room, looking many years younger. She was pointing to a tray of burnt croissants; she slammed her hand on the counter and screamed, "What the *HELL* is wrong with you? I told you twelve minutes for the timer! GET IN HERE, *NOW!*"

Soshana was shaking. She didn't remember this happening. Was it her she was yelling at? It had to have been. Her father never baked; Derek was too young. In the corner of her left eye, she caught a movement, and a shadow appeared. It was the same dark figure as in the other episodes but shorter, smaller.

She felt the pull towards it, but it wasn't as strong as it usually was. It moved slowly, the faceless head tilted down, it shuffled its feet towards Marilyn. Once it stopped in front of her, Marilyn turned and grabbed the still hot tray of croissants, and screamed, *"TURN AROUND."* She swung the tray then beat the shadow across the back and bottom with it as the croissants flew across the floor. The dark figure fell to the floor and the pull to Soshana became undeniable, slow at first then slamming into her. As she fell into the gravity of the figure, Marilyn's scathing words and vile tone echoed into Soshana's memories. "Get *UP!* Move your hands away from your ass or I will move them for you!"

Soshana felt like she was the one that had hit the floor, not the dark figure. She was out of breath, sweating, nauseous and dizzy. Back in her physical apartment, the sun had completely set, she panicked again. She tapped her hands to her chest, legs, and back to her chest, needing to physically feel her body to know she was in the present moment and not locked into the episode.

Loud sobs choked out of her mouth. That *did* happen to her. She had forgotten the time when she had been beaten with the hot oven tray. She remembered that her mother had severely burned her own hands, hoping the beating would have hurt her insolent child as well. Soshana felt more pity for her mother's injuries than she did for herself. It sickened Soshana to think about how little she cared for herself. It was what she was taught, though. What good could come out of regurgitating this horrific memory? Now, more than before, Soshana was petrified of what episode would come next, would it be an even more devastating memory?

Carefully moving herself to an upright position, she looked at the clock in the kitchen. 8:47 pm. She had lost a few hours. It had only felt like several minutes.

I hate this, I fucking hate this! I don't want to live like this!

She got up slowly, acid burning in her stomach, her face and neck soaked with tears, still dizzy and shaking. She gulped several glasses of water then went to her journal to write down every detail, as much as she could remember. She thought about what Ms. Erling had said, "Call me, anytime, no matter what." Soshana hesitated. She wholly loathed putting anyone out, but this might benefit Ms. Erling and her colleague, so it was for them, not just for her.

Soshana couldn't remember where she had left her phone. Thinking it was on the counter, she accidentally tripped over Mr. Skittles, who had laid on the floor next to her feet. "I'm so sorry, sweetie!" Guilt dropped to her core; she hated herself for not noticing him.

She found her phone on her nightstand along with her purse. She had several missed calls: one from Taryn, and another from an unknown caller. There was no voicemail from either. Her heart raced when she saw the unknown number. She wished there was something she could do about this terrible feeling of... she didn't know what it was. *It's all chaos now.* She used to be so good at identifying what she was feeling and why. Ms. Erling had taught her that, but it had been many years ago.

She called Ms. Erling on her home number, the one she was familiar with, and she picked up within two rings.

"Hi, Soshana, what's happening?"

There was no time for niceties or small talk. "I just came out of another episode."

"Tell me everything, start with the beginning of the day. Well, tell me how you slept the night before and if you had felt funny yesterday. And tell me what you ate."

Exhausted, her mind and body spent, Soshana told her everything with as much detail as possible, including the things she may not consider part of the episode.

"Do you remember what actually happened to you in the kitchen? With the tray of croissants?"

Soshana tried her best, she couldn't believe how much of her childhood she had forgotten. Or tucked away. She had told herself and Ms. Erling over the years that she was busy and it was time to forgive and move on.

"Yes, I think so."

Ms. Erling replied with a harumph.

"How did you feel this time, coming out of the episode?"

"Well I didn't throw up. I guess that's an improvement? I also wasn't out for as long."

"Okay." Ms. Erling sounded as if her questioning had concluded.

"Hey, Ms. Erling, how long will this go on for? I can't lose time like this. I can't continue to lose work. I can't even imagine how much the hospital bills are going to be. I need answers, I need help."

"I hear you, I really do. I don't have answers for you, not yet. Let me have Dr. Linds call you. He's the one that may have different solutions. Tomorrow afternoon all right?"

"Yes, I'm off tomorrow. Thank you. Ms. Erling."

"You're welcome, my dear. Please call me Ellen. You don't have to call me that anymore."

"Okay, goodnight, *Ellen*." Soshana chuckled, so did Ms. Erling.

Soshana reluctantly put away the ingredients for the baked goods, brushed her teeth and passed out cold in bed.

She woke up early the next morning to Mr. Skittles gently tapping his paw on her face. She had forgotten to feed him last night. "Shit, I'm sorry! I'm failing at everything right now." She got up and fed him, guilt and shame once again rolling over in her intestines like food poisoning. It delighted her a minuscule amount that he purred as he crunched on the dry nuggets of food.

Parched, as if she had crossed the Mojave Desert without supplies, she drank several glasses of water, filled a third and sat on the arm of the couch. She took a deep breath, feeling remorse and upset from being so out of sorts in her own body.

Had she really been ignoring her feelings, emotions and reactions for the past few years? She thought she had her trauma and issues all sorted out, she had done 'the work' as her therapist, life coach and friends had told her over the years.

"More so than I ever have, or anyone I know for that matter! You should be so proud of yourself, Soshana," one of her friends from New York told her one night in a bar.

Soshana had it 'all figured out' back then. A young, naive twenty-something. Thinking she had more life experience than her counterparts. She didn't know how much she would despise her life in a few short years. The train wreck that she was now, was never what she imagined.

If you have it all figured out, you should be happy, content, full of joy and optimism, even in the face of tragedy, loss and hardships.

She felt well enough for a walk and needed the fresh air the next morning. Some days she felt the nagging ache in her neck, her nose never quite healed properly, the smell of some things, like celery or laundry detergent, seemed off. After each episode her body felt dysregulated, detached in some regards. For example, she would look at a shirt and not know how it should be worn. The muscles knew what to do with the shirt. One arm in this hole, the other in that hole. The big hole is for your body, the small hole for your head. It went on just fine, but her mind questioned it. *Something is wrong.*

Stuck in the routine of work, sleep, eat, repeat, that kept her going. The drone of life. The capitalist machine must be in working order otherwise what are we? Do we even have a purpose without a career, money or relationship? Must get back to work. Must buy things. Must get married and have babies. We all must accept that this is life. No answers, just gaslighting us into believing this is how it has to be. No questioning, just silence and acceptance. Just like she was told to forgive her mother, forgive and accept. There wasn't enough time in the world to learn how to forgive her.

The itch to run away, or at least run outside, bubbled up in her chest. Much like the feeling of being stuck in the hospital for almost a week, she needed to act now before it turned into a full-blown panic attack.

She ate some toast and peanut butter, put on sweats, a baseball cap and her running shoes, gave Mr. Skittles a pet and promised she would be back soon. Her bike was stored by her sweet elderly neighbor downstairs. There was a storage closet that she had access to since she was the building's owner and administrator for many years. Soshana called her Nana, by the woman's request, but her name was Ruth. She looked to be about seventy, all her children were grown and moved out of state.

Everyone adored her, they were always asking her if she wanted to play bunco, making her dinner and helping her with the gardening in the courtyard. The tenants had agreed to the front area maintenance being done by a hired professional, but the courtyard was theirs. They had a community vegetable garden they planted together every year. Soshana hadn't participated, she kept mainly to herself and was disinterested in it, even though she wanted a garden for herself and enjoyed the spoils of the harvest this year.

Soshana went downstairs to Nana's apartment and knocked on her door. It was around eight and she knew she was up already with her cup of joe and English muffins dripping in butter and strawberry jam.

"Look at you! Looking better and better every day, how are you, Soshana?"

Nana wanted to chat, but Soshana's insides were buzzing with energy and anxiety, she needed to leave before she scraped her skin off from the crawling waves of anxiety.

"I'm feeling much better, how are you doing?"

"Oh, you know, I'm all right. What brings you down so early?"

"I need my bike, please. I want to ride to the park."

"Yes, yes, yes, okay, okay, let me get the key."

Soshana's leg started shaking and she tapped her foot to release the energy.

"I'm coming, I'm coming, give me a minute."

"No that's not, I don't mean…" Soshana scrambled her words, pressing her hand to her forehead, exhausted by the shame she constantly felt in almost every scenario. She didn't want to seem in a hurry, though her body was telling her to *run.*

Nana looked up at her, pursed lips. "I don't move as fast as I used to, you know."

"I'm not trying to say that, I'm restless, that's all."

"Oh." Nana moved past her to the storage closet and unlocked the door. "There you go, need anything else?"

"No, thank you. I appreciate it."

"I'll leave it open so you can put it back when you return, ride safe!" she said with a short laugh and a yellow-toothed smile.

Soshana rode hard. She purposefully avoided the street that would take her past her mother's house and rode straight to the park that had biking trails and ponds. It was almost mid-October, and the wind had warning, the humidity dissipating, even when the sun was peeking around large puffy clouds. They were high in the sky and bright, no threat of rain today.

The trails were completely bare of humans or animals with the exception of some cheery birds and squirrels high in the canopy of the hemlock and sycamores. The leaves had mostly fallen, due to the thrashing of an intense storm while she was gone. Sunlight flitted through the branches as the earth warmed and felt cooler in places where it was completely shaded. She pushed herself up hills, harder than she probably should have. Out of breath, feeling the release of endorphins and the relief of anxiety leaving her aching body, she gladly and jauntily rode back to the apartment complex.

After cleaning off the mud from her bike and storing it back in the closet, she showered, got ready, made herself a real meal and had prepared baking materials, taking care to pay attention for any signs of a panic attack or episode. Mostly paying attention to Mr. Skittles and giving him the love he so deserved.

Dr. Linds called promptly at four. This time when an unknown number came up, her heart only quickened for a few seconds. Her heart did sink when it wasn't Kieran's voice answering on the other side, this she couldn't help.

They exchanged niceties, then he explained how sorry he

was for her, for what she had been through and what she continued to go through. He assured her that all her information was confidential and there was no one else who was working on her case, his specialty being neuropsychology and neuroscience. A doctor that had an advanced understanding of the human mind, unlike Ms. Erling who had retired a long time ago and wasn't always up to date with the latest developments.

He was professional, listened well and asked many questions, some were out of left field and didn't make sense to her, such as "Do you have a tingling sensation in your left foot?" They spoke for about an hour and a half, all the while taking cookies, scones and muffins in and out of the oven.

"Let's talk again next week. You have some more lab work coming in soon, right?"

"Yes, I had it done the other day."

"Great. Soshana, please be gentle with yourself. Treat yourself as if you were your best friend, remember that anytime you are feeling unhappy. Speak kindly when your mind wanders to having arguments that are not happening, when you have fear that is unfounded. Say things like 'Thank you for reminding me, or thank you for warning me, but I'm safe.' Hopefully that makes sense and helps in the meantime. Keep practicing your meditation, breathwork and exercise moderately. This isn't easy, in fact, it's the most difficult thing anyone can possibly do. And you're doing it."

She felt a surge of relief after they hung up. She truly felt heard.

Is Dr. Linds single? Taryn texted back.

Soshana had remembered to send her a message, it had

almost been a week. She couldn't imagine why Taryn was so interested in her life now. It had been ten long years since they had spent any real time together, and Soshana wasn't too thrilled about it.

Soshana replied, *I don't know? That was the farthest thing from my mind.*

LOL sorry! We need to get together and REALLY chat. The last meetup was BS. I need to hear what's going on with you. I was so freakin' worried when you said you were hospitalized. How about Oct 25th, ten o'clock? Want to walk in the park after we pick up some coffee?

That was two days away and she had the day off. Her work only wanted her to be there four days a week, six hours per day until the doctors cleared her to work more hours. The anxiety crept up to her throat, a dull ache grew in her stomach. She wasn't going to get away from it this time. They lived in the same city. Soshana had no plans to move away. She knew she needed to do this; it was one of those things on her list of 'things to do' according to Ms. Erling.

That sounds perfect. I'm glad we get to do this.

Soshana was telling a half truth. She was glad that she was fulfilling her oath to herself, to Ms. Erling, and the other half dreaded the inevitable. Telling the truth.

Soshana cleaned up, neatly packed her baked goods and prepared meals for the week ahead. She went to bed exhausted, but that didn't prevent the onslaught of nightmares and dreams to come.

She had dreams of interactions with her parents, some school scenarios, failing tests and also the unbearable feeling of being alone at college. They intertwined and flowed into a nightmare that made her feel completely out of control.

Kieran was outside, next to a tree that looked oddly familiar. She thought it could be one of the trees from the park that was closest to her family home. It was about to storm, and it looked like a terrible one. The clouds were coming in fast; they were the kind of dark that had you questioning if night had arrived too early. The wind was pushing the leaves, grass and flowers around ferociously, only there was no sound but her heartbeat and breath.

They were standing about twelve feet apart. His face, neck and body language were telling her that he was talking loudly at her, then yelling. His face showed remorse, sadness and pleading. He was moving his hands, palms up, in a way that showed innocence. Soshana felt confusion, fear. She wasn't able to move towards him, she wanted to reach him, grab his hands and tell him it was okay, even though she wasn't sure what he was concerned about. He disappeared. Then the howling, crashing noise of the wind exploded.

She awoke a few hours earlier than she wanted, again in a fit of sweat, breathless and paranoid. She looked at her phone. Nothing. She put it down then wiped the sweat and threw off the covers to feel the cold air. It had rained, she had left her window open a crack and the wind was whipping through. She could smell the dampness from her bed. She got up, grabbed a towel, wiped the sill and closed the window.

After a glass of water, she tried to fall back asleep but failed. Turning the event of the dream over and over in her mind, her heartbeat sped up, disappointment and heartache returning to her chest. He still hadn't called or text. It had been over a week. He had to have found the note. It was chilly enough for him to wear that coat. Her eyes burned, tears were threatening to form. She hadn't met someone like him, had never made a friend that fast, and hadn't felt like this with anyone before in her life. How could he just throw away that connection so easily?

Madness and rage were building inside her body. He was abandoning her, as if she was nothing. It was no use trying to sleep. Now she was fully awake and on the computer. She searched for him on the internet. She didn't have any social media, so she had to do what she could with the search engines and what they could offer. She looked up his name and discovered Kieran worked for a realtor, writing up contracts for the sale of residential and commercial properties in Detroit. But there were no photos to provide any evidence.

Scouring deeper, edging into the realm of stalking, she found an old site from another group of realtors. Her heart leapt, an old photo of him stood out, he was sitting with a group of people that were most likely co-workers. The photo was small and blurry but he looked healthy, younger.

Forty-five minutes later, her vision blurred, eyes aching. This had to stop. She needed to let him go. Over the years she'd heard "people come into our lives for a season, or a reason, sometimes it's for a while, sometimes it's not." Or whatever. Maybe he was one of those that was around for a short amount of time.

She sat more upright, cracked her neck, stretched her back and arms and folded her legs into a meditating position. She laid her arms gently on top of her legs, placed her palms upwards and meditated for a few minutes. After her heart rate slowed and she'd calmed, she pictured Kieran in front of her. She smiled and with all the love and care she could come up with, she said a sincere 'thank you and goodbye.' She released the image she had of him in her mind, turning into mist. She was able to fall asleep for a short while before her alarm went off.

They met up at L'Addition Merci for two Americanos to go. "Hop in my car, I'll drive us," Taryn insisted. Soshana 'hopped' into the passenger side. Her SUV was pristine, with the exception of scattered business cards, posters, personally labeled pink drenched SWAG items for clients, like lanyards, beer koozies and stickers.

They exchanged general small talk until Soshana opened her mouth to begin a most uncomfortable conversation when Taryn interrupted. "Why didn't you tell me you've been in town this whole time, that you had a job at the convenience store?"

She couldn't avoid it now. Tell the truth? Get shot down and chewed out by her old friend, then feel like shit about it? Lie and then feel like shit for the rest of her life? *Honesty, from now on, always.* She didn't have the energy to placate another person.

"I don't know, Taryn. I moved back here to take care of Marilyn. I needed money, I was tired of living off of her, even though she insisted but then bitched about it. I took the first job I could find, as close to the house as I could just in case I needed to run home quickly. Then she passed away sooner than we thought. I feel like... I think I've been stuck, lost. I don't think I know what I'm doing right now. You're supposed to know exactly who you are by this age, what you want out of life and at least know what you're doing."

It hit a raw nerve. Admitting to herself that she didn't know what she was doing and that she felt lost to someone other than Ms. Erling was jarring. Vulnerability was never an option. She waited for it, the irritation, annoyance, at worst, the disappointment.

Taryn nodded her head. Her face read complacency. No signs of any frustration. "I'm sorry I wasn't there for you during that time. Did you feel like you couldn't come to me? The last thing I want to be is unapproachable," Taryn said with a concerned tone, acting much different from their last meeting.

Soshana thought about what those words meant, what Taryn meant by them. *Was she trying to find a way to turn it around on me by being apologetic?* She calculated her response and spoke carefully and slowly, with care.

"I didn't want to bother you or for anyone to worry about me. You have a life, a family, a very successful business. You're busy. I didn't want to take you, or anyone else, away from their life. I don't like to be coddled, either. I can take care of myself."

Taryn didn't hesitate. "Why do you think you're so unimportant? You were like family to me, Soshana. You were the sister I wish I had. We had so many good memories together, and for you to disappear, physically and mentally, then to come back and act like you don't exist, like you don't matter... It hurts. I care about you; I care about you enough to make sure I carve out time and spend it with you. I'm not doing this out of spite or to make myself feel better. I can tell something is wrong, and I can't help you because you won't let your guard down."

Soshana's face was hot with anger. "You don't know me anymore Taryn. I've changed. I got help, I went to therapy and I got better. You don't know everything that happened over the past fifteen years. It's not like we can just go back to being best friends. We have different lives. You have it all figured out, I'm a college drop-out that has no life. I'm only able to survive, that's all I have to contribute to this world, my survival."

Taryn abruptly pulled up to the side of the road and slammed on the brakes, then put the SUV into park. She unbuckled her seat belt and turned to face Soshana, tears in her eyes.

Soshana was still hot with anger but was coming down from the boiling rage that filled her entire body. Taryn swiped away fast tears and took a deep breath.

"You're right. I definitely don't know you anymore, and you definitely don't know me. I'm not the spoiled, snobby, confident, bossy bitch you were used to throughout school. I also went through several years of therapy from what I endured during and after college, things *you* have no idea about. Your walls started to go up the last year of high school. You slowly stopped texting and calling me, but that's not all on you. I am guilty of that too. I felt us pulling away from each other. These things can happen. I'm sorry I stopped talking to you. I regret it every single day."

Taryn stared at Soshana for a few seconds, then continued when she didn't say anything.

"It sounds like you're assuming that I'm judging you because your life looks different from mine. Life is fucking hard, Soshana. It's more than enough if you can take care of yourself, take care of another living being, let alone hold a job, keep up with relationships, bills, taxes and maintain a home. I'm not judging you or comparing, however, you just compared yourself to me. I don't like that, it's not fair of you to do that. We had different lives, different childhoods and different paths. I was privileged as hell. I'm grateful for all that I do have, and I feel empathy for those who might not. Please don't put yourself down because you didn't get to where the level of success I am at. You're thirty-six for fuck's sake. Still so young! Your story isn't over, you have so much time to figure out what you want to do!"

She paused, eyes alarmingly serious, boring holes into Soshana's. "Sorry for swearing, I'm not used to it. Actually, I quite like swearing." She chuckled and wiped away more tears.

Soshana's heat cooled to a simmer. Guilt and shame arose in its place. "I'm sorry too," she said softly.

Taryn let out a small huff and shook her head. "I don't expect us to be best friends or pick up where we left off. I don't expect anything from you. But if you really don't want to spend time with me, why did you agree to it?"

Soshana came back quickly with a response. "I didn't intend for you to feel that way. I wouldn't have agreed to it if I didn't want to hang out with you. I'm working on being more authentic, on being myself. Which includes being truthful."

Taryn shook her head again. "Then what is it, Soshana? Why are you hiding away from the world? What happened? Only if you feel comfortable telling me. You don't have to if you're not ready either." Taryn said this with love and kindness. She had a sympathetic smile on her face that reminded Soshana of when they were kids.

Soshana fought back tears. With the anger in her body subsiding, crying was inevitable. They used to bare their souls, tell each other absolutely everything without hesitation. Open vulnerability and honesty. Soshana remembered the response she got when she shared her feelings with Mina, that it wasn't anything like what she experienced with Taryn. A crucial reminder to remember how people react when you expose your true self.

The tears fell fast. "I'm so sorry." Soshana let out a sob before she forced herself to stop. She wiped her tears on her gray Jimmy Eat World T-shirt.

Taryn patted her knee then squeezed it.

"I can tell you've been through a lot. There used to be a sparkle in your eye, a goofiness that would light up my day. That's all faded. I miss you, Sosh. Yeah, it's been a while, but that doesn't mean we can't try to catch up, right?"

Soshana nodded as she searched her purse for a tissue. She wiped her nose, took a deep breath and looked at Taryn.

"I think I've been through too much and now, maybe, it's starting to boil over. I feel like I'm losing my mind. I don't know what's happening to me. I was attacked and raped in college. My boyfriend accused me of cheating instead of believing me. I had a mental breakdown and had to drop out of NYU, and I also ran out of money. I moved in with my close friend at the time and we lived together for quite a while and that ended horribly." The tears threatened to never end. "She ripped my heart out when I chose to move back home to take care of Marilyn. We haven't talked since then."

Taryn was looking at her, touching her shoulder.

"I've been having these odd episodes over the past few weeks. They come on suddenly, I pass out and I lose time. The doctors have no idea what it is and I'm so frustrated. I don't like my life, I don't know what's happening."

They sat quietly for several minutes, each catching their breath.

"You've been passing out? That's really serious. You've been through so much, and I'm sure that's just the tip of the iceberg.

Everything you went through recently, plus how much you went through with your parents, it never goes away. It can and will resurface. If you ignore it, it festers and boils until it explodes. These episodes sound horrific and very scary, and you live alone!"

Soshana nodded in agreement and continued, quietly, slowly. "Not to change the subject but, *in other news-*" Soshana imitated a radio broadcaster from the 1960s to break the intense conversation. "I met someone while I was in the hospital, recovering. We instantly connected, I felt like we became friends, true friends. I've never felt that so quickly before. It was so strange, uncomfortable, yet completely comfortable, and wonderful at the same time. It felt cosmic. As if the timing was just right. I can't shake him, I can't get him out of my mind, but I know I need to let him go. I'm trying."

Soshana looked away from Taryn, down at her shoes.

"Listen, you have to trust your instincts. What are they telling you about these episodes and this guy?"

Soshana knew but was hardly able to admit it out loud to anyone, or even in the quiet of the night when she was alone. It had to be the numbing she had done to survive. Suppressing her emotions, that's why she hadn't cried in several years, why she didn't cry at her mother's funeral.

"It's me. I'm not working on what I'm going through, I haven't processed my feelings, what I went through with my mother, what I went through during college and after. I'm not accepting of myself and I'm ignoring the cues."

Taryn nodded her head, as if letting Soshana know that it was the correct answer. "You have to learn to trust yourself. It sounds like maybe you don't trust anyone else, either."

Soshana nodded, still not looking at Taryn and not responding verbally to this obviously correct assessment.

"I get it. I'll shut up! I don't want to use this time to talk about myself, though. I think I covered the basics at the cafe a few weeks ago, ha ha." Soshana looked up at her. Taryn had a twinkle in her eye, a cheeky grin on her face. "Now tell me *all* about this gentleman suitor, I need to hear every juicy detail." Taryn put her seat belt back on and started the car.

They walked for almost two hours in the park, Soshana regaling her time with Kieran, remembering as much as she could. They laughed about their school days, remembering their time in the choir together, the boys they had crushes on.

"Remember Jason?! He's *bald* now! The poor man!"

"Oh that's sad, he was obsessed with his fluffy hair, always playing with it," Soshana said with sympathy.

Soshana's felt freer, lighter. Having more energy than she did before the walk, she knew instinctively that reuniting with Taryn was a positive thing.

They walked back towards the SUV in comfortable silence.

"Listen, I really *really* enjoyed doing this-"

Soshana interrupted, attempting humor, "It sounds like you're about to break up with me."

"Oh get over yourself! I want you to know that this is important. Reconnecting. Rediscovering who we are, outside of our boring routine lives. I would love to be in your life, especially if you're going to hang around for a little while longer. Am I right in saying that or are you planning to move back to New York?"

"I don't know what I'm going to do. Derek wants me to get the house remodeled and sell it, but we don't have enough funds to do that. I already got it cleaned out and repainted. It's just sitting there. I don't know why we can't come to an agreement to get it sold."

Taryn gave a knowing nod. "I deal with this with other clients. Let me help you, please. I can stop by and take a look at it, get everything in order and get you an estimate, as is. We can talk to Derek together to come up with a solution that works for you both."

Soshana paused to think. It made her feel uneasy, questioning her gut reaction. "Yes, okay. That's really kind of you."

"You got it, just let me know when the best time is, no pressure, no hurry."

They got into the car and before Taryn dropped Soshana off at her apartment complex, she asked, "What's the name of that guy again? I can look him up in our database and see if I can find a match, there has to be some sort of listing if he's in the Detroit metropolis working in realty."

Soshana's stomach jolted. She didn't think about Taryn's connections. She had only just tried to meditate him out of her mind and now he was back. *Great.*

"Only if you want. Oh and please come to my Halloween party next week! I know it's short notice, but it will be so fun, I promise." Taryn had picked up on Soshana's discomfort.

"Only if you find it entertaining and no trouble, otherwise it's fine. I am learning to let go of him, it may be for the best. And sure, I'll come, let me know what I can do to help," Soshana replied, unsure of the response, knowing how much she hated social gatherings with people she hardly knew. Dinner parties were as dreadful as funerals.

Taryn leaned over for an awkward side hug.

"Thank you, Soshana. Thank you for letting me back in. I've

missed you."

"I missed you too," Soshana said with a genuine warm smile, and she meant it.

Soshana texted Derek, she wanted to talk about getting the house ready to sell, that Taryn was going to get it appraised and inspected. She mentioned that it might be a good thing for her, for both of them to move on from it. They could definitely use the money, and they would be running out of funds to care for the upkeep in less than a year.

Derek replied moments later. *No need to talk about it, let's do it. I bet Taryn could get way more for it than it's worth, she's a firecracker.*

Relief settled in her belly. She took a moment to meditate, to recognize how wonderful this feeling was, she was grateful. *Practice, practice, practice. It's okay to feel this, to feel good.*

The next few weeks were uneventful. Soshana stuck with her new routine, recognizing when she felt good, acknowledging it and appreciating it, slowly adding in more exercise: weight lifting, drinking more water, and stretching before bed and when she woke up. Begrudgingly, she acknowledged that Dr. Linds was right. She knocked on wood when she thought of the fact that she hadn't had an episode. And the vivid dreams of Kieran had stopped. She started to feel less anxious and more at ease.

Taryn reminded her about the Halloween party. 'Adults only!' Soshana had yet to visit Taryn's house and hadn't formally met her husband. They had only met briefly at Marilyn's funeral.

There isn't a theme, but feel free to have fun with it! Are you still coming?! Was it possible for Taryn to sound excited through text?

Soshana hadn't dressed up for Halloween in quite a few years. There had been a handful of small parties at the apartment Mina and her shared. She was not great at social settings; a few drinks were necessary before she could ease her way into the crowd. What the hell did people talk about at these fluffy gatherings? *Oh, I love your couch pillows. And look at the sconces! I love the color of your backsplash, subway tiles are so hot right now.* Fuck. She would rather rip off her toenails with pliers.

She hadn't done anything outside of work, home, doctor appointments and the grocery store since she got home from the hospital. She still felt fragile, even though she had noticed clear signs of improvement. *A few drinks won't hurt. After a few drinks, I'll leave.*

10

Introvert in the Wild

Soshana showed up as Wednesday Addams. She had long dark hair and almost everything she needed for the outfit was in her closet. She found some black lipstick and nail polish at work; it relieved her that it didn't cost much. She contributed to the party by making jack-o'-lantern sugar cookies. She hadn't had a drink in a long time, she never really felt like it but she decided to let loose a little.

Cookie tray in hand, the jack-o-lanterns' grinning faces jeered at her appearance. She sneered at them. From the outside she could tell the house was expansive, luxurious. It was modern with tall windows and a dark blue front door. Taryn had decorated it with spider webbing, witches' broomsticks, carved lighted pumpkins and gourds on top of a hay bale. She rang the doorbell and waited with spicy, damp armpits. She thanked herself for putting on an extra layer of deodorant.

A male of average height, with dusty blond hair and green eyes dressed as a surgeon opened the door. He had a quizzical look on his face and didn't smile. "Did Taryn invite you over?"

Soshana was taken aback by the abrupt questioning and attitude. "Yes, I'm Soshana and you are?"

The man gave a huff and said with a hint of apathy, "Oh, so *you're* Soshana. I'm Sean. Come in."

She walked into the house, studying his face and posture as she passed him. Indifference, impertinence.

The home was opulent. Tones of white, tan and beige with contrasting black ornaments and decorations. Accents of glamorous glittering Halloween décor: black candles, ravens with life-like feathers, black and white pumpkins, silver spider webbing, and gauze ghosts around the stairwell. It looked expensive. It felt stiff, sterile and unwelcoming. Once again, she was entirely out of place. She walked towards the kitchen where she heard voices, hoping to find Taryn as quickly as possible.

"Wednesday!" A tall, dark-haired muscular male dressed in 70s style clothing called out. He was leaning casually against a wet bar, a bourbon in his hand, the other in his baby blue polyester pants pocket.

"Hi there," Soshana said.

"Haven't seen *you* around this small town before. Taryn told me to look for the goth, sad girl in pigtails. I'm assuming that's you?" He laughed, a phony salesman type of laugh.

Soshana kept her face blank as she replied, "Yeah."

He put a hand out and said, "I'm Tim. It's nice to meet you."

Soshana looked at his hand, then up at him. He had handsome features, energetic eyes and a charming smile. His broad hand waited; one eyebrow raised while she kept his stare. She grasped his hand firmly and shook it while maintaining eye contact.

"I'm Soshana. Thanks for the warm welcome." She did her

best to refrain from rolling her eyes.

"There you are! I'm *so* happy you're here." Clapping with vigor and speed, Taryn gave her excitement away and the fact that she had pre-gamed the party with a cocktail or three. She was dressed up as an 80s fitness instructor, blonde hair teased, heavy pink eye makeup and ruby red lips. She looked ridiculous but adorable. She came in for a hug and turned to look at Tim. "You weren't bothering her too much, were you?"

Tim smiled directly and only at Soshana then turned towards a few other men in the room to start up a conversation.

"Don't worry about him, he's a relentless flirt. Anyway, what can I get you?"

Soshana debated having another drink. "Gin and tonic, please. Extra lime."

The night went on as usual, awkward introductions, hiding in the bathroom, breathing deeply to regain composure and checking eye shadow smudges. Soshana put some white opalescent eye shadow all over her face to make her look pale, luminous, not dead. She received several compliments from strangers at the party for her dedication to the character. She was sure they meant she was sullen and apathetic.

After a few hours of niceties, small talk and real-estate banter, as most of the people at the party were realtors, the party became dull. Being in your mid-thirties in the Midwest means you are probably a parent of young children, and/or you're obsessed with your work. Soshana was neither, so she couldn't relate to anyone. Panic crept up her spine, to the point where she felt a dizzy spell starting. The lights flickered, her vision narrowed and she felt her stomach lurch. She ran to the half bath near the kitchen and waited for the episode to take over. *No. Not now.*

She took a few slow and steady breaths in as she braced herself over the sink. Closing her eyes, repeating "no, not now" over and over, she seemed to overcome the worst of it.

Someone rapped quietly on the door.

"Hey are you all right in there?" Tim said with a hint of concern. "Just checking in on you, and I kind of have to use the toilet."

Soshana checked her makeup, the more-than-usual pale pallor was subsiding. She felt stable enough to move and distinctly proud. She prevented an episode. Her insides felt fine, not that she would know what that in truth felt like. She opened the door with steady confidence.

"Sorry, thought the G&T was going to come up, the bathroom's all yours," Soshana lied.

Tim gave her a wink and walked past her.

That was quite enough for one night. Though she had made it past an episode, which excited her, it drained her to be at the party. She found Taryn and said goodnight, then drove home, reveling in her new ability.

Soshana was straight on the phone with Ms. Erling when she woke the next day. She told her about the episode that didn't happen. Ms. Erling congratulated her and told her to call Dr. Linds immediately. Soshana complied but it went to voicemail so she left a message explaining briefly what had happened. She hoped to get a call back soon, wanting some good news and answers.

A few weeks passed without a call from either doctor. Soshana did her best not to worry about it so she kept herself busy with little things. Cleaning, organizing her apartment, playing with Mr. Skittles, coffee at L'Addition and working. Work days were filled with the buzz of the approaching holiday, people discussing their plans.

Joe and Carol invited Soshana over for Thanksgiving. She was unsure about going since they were buddies at work but not outside of it. Relationships change after being in someone's home. Maybe she wanted to keep her relationship the way it was with Joe, it was safe and predictable. However, recent events had made them closer, albeit Joe being more fatherly than friendly. Carol had more than proved she was an incredible cook and insisted that Soshana show up with just a dessert. Soshana felt warmth over her shoulders and back, like a heated, weighted blanket. A feeling she wasn't used to, something she felt incredibly anxious and yet ready to experience again.

Yes, I would love to. She finally responded to Joe's invite text. She later thought about Derek and how he might want to make the drive up this year, though she hadn't asked him yet. *Actually, is it okay if Derek comes too?* Joe and Carol agreed with enthusiasm. They had heard stories of Derek and mentioned how they couldn't wait to meet him.

Derek and Soshana would have normally spent the holidays together in New York at Mina's flat, or at Mina's parents' lavish mansion in upstate New York. Soshana had stopped coming home many years ago: the travel was insane, plus she made the excuse that she had to work around the holidays. She would rather her co-workers with stable healthy family relationships get to spend time with their loved ones. And she would receive the time-and-a-half pay.

Derek quickly replied *YES.* He was the sociable, charismatic outgoing type that loved meeting new people and could get

159

along with anyone, as long as they weren't homophobic. Even if they were, Derek could usually turn them around with his wit and humor. Not all, though. This consistently worried Soshana as Derek was quite the daredevil and tested boundaries.

Thanksgiving was more fun than Soshana had ever imagined it could be. Carol's younger sister and boyfriend, her daughter, Carol's niece, and a close friend around Derek's age were there as well. The conversation and wine flowed freely and easily, they played several rounds of card games and laughed harder and longer than she could remember.

A memory of her and Kieran playing cards in the hospital and laughing until they cried came up. Bittersweet but grateful feelings helped her move past the emotions of missing him. Soshana refocused on what was in front of her, the joy she was feeling from being present and in the moment.

Derek was set up in the living room, sleeping on the couch with lots of blankets and pillows. He enjoyed being comfortable but couldn't afford a hotel room. Mr. Skittles loved it when they had visitors so he spent the evening sleeping next to him.

Mindlessly, she washed her face and brushed her teeth. No anxious chatter in her head, thinking over and replaying what she may have said to the others at dinner. Tranquility in her heart.

Suddenly she felt guilty and ashamed.

Why the fuck did I have this feeling after I just felt peaceful?

Her mind forced her to recall how uncomfortable and upsetting life certainly was.

Don't you forget, you stupid bitch. They will hurt you.

Her mother was dead, her father completely absent and distant. Her best friend was still not talking to her, angry at her for leaving. Soshana tried to shake it off but she couldn't, so she finished getting ready for bed then journaled. She fell asleep hours later, let down that her mind would be so cruel.

The next day, Derek and Soshana went for a long walk, it was cold with a touch of humidity, the sun peeking out through low snow-filled clouds. They found their way to the cafe and Derek chatted with the barista. When they got back to the apartment, Soshana realized she had forgotten her phone, so she checked it. She had three missed calls. One from Dr. Linds, two from Ms. Erling, a voicemail from each, and a text from Taryn.

Soshana read the text from Taryn first. *I hope you had a nice Thanksgiving! Wanted to let you know that I couldn't find anything from the name you gave me last month, sorry it took me so long to get back to you about it! When you have time, I want to talk to you about a conference in February in Detroit. I have a plan.*

Soshana was curious about this, it piqued her interest enough to text back immediately. *Sounds good, thank you for getting back to me and let's chat in a few days. Hope you had a great Thanksgiving too!*

Derek started packing his things, he had planned to leave in the early afternoon to beat the traffic out of Detroit back to New York.

"Hey, can you excuse me for a few minutes? I want to check these voicemails; they're from the psychologist and my therapist," Soshana said while looking at Taryn's text again, curiosity growing.

Derek gave her a thumbs up. She went into her room and closed the door behind her. She listened to Ms. Erling's voicemail first.

"Soshana, it's Ms. Erling, please call Dr. Linds as soon as possible, he has some insight that you may find helpful. Please take care. Call me anytime." She was short and to the point, but this time she was speaking with frenetic energy. Soshana felt exalted when she played Dr. Lind's message.

"Soshana, hoping you had a nice Thanksgiving. I wanted to talk with you about an idea that my colleagues and I came up with about your recent episodes. Please call me back at your earliest convenience. I'm out of the office but will have my cell by my side. Thank you."

Dr. Linds sounded apprehensive and almost defeated when Soshana called immediately after listening to the voicemail. "Look, Soshana, I'm not sure how else to let you know, and I know you're most likely not going to like this answer, but all your labs, imaging and bloodwork came back normal." He paused for a moment, Soshana becoming increasingly infuriated with each hair-splitting second. The whiplash of uncontrolled emotions, flying around from a few messages, all contained in one human cage is unfathomable.

"However..." Soshana took a breath. "However, I have a theory. You're not having amnesia during your waking hours, only after you have passed out. In my professional opinion, these are extreme panic attacks caused by C-PTSD and PTSD flashbacks that may be causing you to go into a Fuchs-like state. I'm curious to see what your brain scans would look like while you are having these episodes, not after. Now, nausea could be a plethora of things, it's well known that anxiety and stress over long periods of time can cause long-term digestion issues. I would suggest that you see a nutritionist or possibly take a holistic approach. Ayurvedic practices have shown some incredible results but aren't for everyone. I would never suggest anything that could cause harm, but at this point, a regular doctor is going to dismiss you with these kinds of results."

Soshana stayed quiet. Ire burned in her core; she was close to exploding. One extreme sensation to another, she wasn't shown how to take unpleasant information with grace. Once again, this was not an answer and especially not one she wanted to hear. This was 'all in her head.' *It's all my own fault; I am mentally ill.* She had been doing so well over the past few months; she hadn't had a single episode.

"Soshana, are you still there?"

"Yes," she said curtly.

"I'm so sorry I don't have any solid answers for you, there's a lot in science and health that we don't understand, unfortunately. Though sometimes doctors like to claim they know a lot, we truly know so little. I'm not giving up on you. I would like to follow up with you in a month to see how you are doing, maybe after Christmas and New Year if that's okay with you?"

"Yes, that's fine," Soshana replied, this time more quietly, with defeat in her tone.

"Do you have any questions for me?"

"No."

He paused. "Okay. Don't hesitate to call, about anything."

"Okay, bye." Soshana hung up before he could say goodbye, a recurring habit when she was upset. She then crumpled into a ball on her bed and sobbed quietly into her pillow, so Derek couldn't hear. After a few minutes she collected herself. She went to the bathroom and ran a washcloth under cool water, holding it gently to her eyes. It helped a little, but not enough for Derek not to notice.

She walked into the living room, determined not to discuss anything with him. He looked at her with concern. "It's fine, I'm fine." He kept staring at her. "I mean it, I don't want to talk about it right now. You need to get going before the traffic is horrendous."

He got up off the floor, where he had been lazily playing with Mr. Skittles, and hugged her tight. "I trust you." He pulled back, holding her shoulders then continued. "I really enjoyed Joe and Carol, and that group. So much more fun than Mina's. Those stuffy stuck-up people and their gold-plated utensils. I'm not sure I've ever heard you laugh that hard, for that long, like, ever. You became a different person yesterday; you became *you* again."

Soshana was speechless. She wasn't aware that she wasn't ever herself.

"You had a sparkle in your eye, you were engaging with Carol's relatives, you joked around with Joe like you had been old pals for years. It was something magical. I'm so proud of you, Soshana."

Tears, again. She didn't recognize herself, she was feeling ashamed and guilty because she had let go, let loose and found a way to be joyful when she had been unaware of how miserable she had felt her entire life. She couldn't stop herself from crying at the thought of how grown-up Derek had suddenly become, so mature and loving.

"You're my favorite," she replied after she blew her nose and gave him another hug. "Now get outta here! You have a long day ahead of you. Please drive safely and text me when you get in, no matter the time."

He nodded and smiled as he closed the door behind him.

She called Ms. Erling back and discussed how she felt after Thanksgiving, even after having a wonderful time, then the realization hit her that she hadn't made as much progress over the past decade and a half as she had once thought. How her mind constantly reminds her that she had it bad, and she has it coming.

"You are really quite intuitive and intelligent, you know. More so than any other patient and I'm not just saying that. You're right, the brain likes patterns and old stories, even if they are hurtful."

"I'm nowhere near fully recovered, am I?" she asked solemnly.

"No, I'm afraid not."

"We worked so hard, for so many years. I don't understand. I thought I was done with therapy. Am I... Is this schizophrenia?"

Ms. Erling let out an audible sigh. "I don't have the sense that it is, the indications aren't present. Don't fret. Memories can smack you in the face at any time. It's a constant daily practice to learn how to deal with the events of life and accept them in a way we are not kicked down by them. You have done a lot of hard work, and that is not to be dismissed. There are some loose ends we need to tie up and you'll be right as rain. You're a strong, capable woman. I know we can get you through this. Keep doing what you're doing because it seems to be working. Don't be too surprised if memories come up over the next few days, please remember to write them down. I have to go, but I need you to know that you can do this. Take care." Ms. Erling hung up and Soshana was left alone in her apartment, her stomach in knots.

There is no end to healing, to therapy.

Right as rain?

This she doubted the most.

How can anyone come out on the other side, "right as rain?" Soshana had convinced herself that she was done with therapy years ago, done with learning how to "adult." Hell, most adults her age were still as immature and with an almost intentional lack of self-awareness as they were in high school, but now with college degrees, mortgages and kids. Soshana had the decency to at least have some emotional intelligence and self-reflection, but not the other things. This wasn't an easy thing to accept. You think you're done learning, then life reminds you how wrong you are. The numbness, the myopic view of the world, dismissing her emotions and feelings, tucking them away, pretending she didn't care about her mom, Mina and Kieran.

It was all too overwhelming. She now acknowledged how much work she had put off over the past ten years. Ignoring the signs to "learn from lessons." Drinking, socializing with apathetic so-called friends, keeping herself busy with inane chores, other's problems and societies uninformed collapse. The oceans need saving, the trees need to be repopulated, the people are starving- right in this country. The children are being raped and molested, here in these churches and schools. The people of color are being systematically oppressed and constantly on guard from relentless discrimination and racism weaved into every corner of existence. Trans and queer people being killed just because they exist. These problems were always, and have always been, more important than taking care of herself. One can so easily become ignorant of their own needs, because there is always, *always* someone else who has it worse.

"No more numbing myself." Saying it out loud felt reaffirming.

This is going to hurt, then.

She got up from the couch and brought out her journal. Focusing on how she truly felt, rather than the description of the events. She had been *describing* her childhood, not writing about her emotions that came from the experiences. Once she looked over the events she wrote, she took out a page and side by side wrote her feelings next to each. Once she started, the pain rose and plateaued to a mild burn in her chest. The tears flowed consistently, some surprisingly when she wrote about her dad, others waned when she wrote about situations with her mother. She wrote freely and without restraint for several hours. She emerged from her emotional bubble shaking, starving and drained. It was well into the evening and she realized she hadn't eaten since breakfast at the cafe.

She didn't bother to warm up the Thanksgiving leftovers that Carol had made for her. Soshana stood in the kitchen, eating it cold, and groaned in relief from the nutrients that her body craved. Mr. Skittles chirped for some treats at her feet. Soshana felt so grateful for Carol and her excellent cooking. She rinsed off her fingers under the faucet in the sink and dried them on a towel. She needed to tell Carol how grateful she was for yesterday. They had exchanged numbers last night and promised to go out for coffee on their days off.

Soshana felt a chill of happiness run over her body, goosebumps from her shoulders down to her wrists as she texted Carol her sincere thanks for the invite, food and company.

She allowed herself a moment to take in how much she needed to feel these emotions, not push them away and tell her brain to constantly "shut the fuck up" about the shame and guilt that came after them, and maybe be more gentle, such as, "*please* shut the fuck up."

It's a start.

She took a long, deep breath in through her nose and out through her mouth. It's hard to describe the feeling, it feels like nothing, and it feels how you would after you receive a full body hug from a loved one. Relief.

Holding the meaty leftovers and chewing another few bites of turkey, this time she politely grabbed a fork for the sweet potato souffle. She replied to Taryn's text. *Do you have time tomorrow to talk about the conference?*

11

A Kind Gesture

"Would you like to come with me to the annual realtor's conference in Detroit in February? I know it's a stretch, and I know we just recently reconnected, but I think it would be a good time, all expenses paid, and I'm allowed to bring a spouse or guest. You'd have your own room, we're staying at a fancy pants hotel downtown. It has a spa, a daily allowance for food and drinks and lots of restaurants, bars and entertainment at night! It's only three days."

Soshana stayed quiet on the phone for a few seconds, pondering this rare opportunity.

Taryn continued. "Also, I want you to meet a few people, they're looking to hire someone to do accounting, scheduling and organizing emails and client files. I know how amazingly organized you are, and it would be a work from home job. I don't want you to feel pressured. Maybe take a few days to-"

"I'm in," Soshana interrupted her.

"Oh my God, yes! Yay! Oh I was so stressed thinking about asking you. It's going to be great. You can relax while I am at the conference during the day, then join me for dinner and drinks afterwards. This is going to be so fun!" Taryn sounded elated. She continued, "And I was wondering if you were doing anything for Christmas? Maybe you and Derek can join us at the house, my parents will be in town and they would love to see you."

"Oh, I... um," she stuttered. She was quite uncomfortable at Halloween. Thanksgiving was a fluke that it worked out so well. Taryn went on for a little while longer and explained a few things. By the end of the conversation, she said yes, but wasn't sure what Derek was doing for Christmas and needed to check.

Taryn let Soshana know that her husband's cold shoulder during the Halloween party was because Taryn had told him Soshana disappeared years ago and how much it hurt her. Taryn neglected to update him, but rest assured he was aware now. Christmas may not be as unpleasant, then.

The following day, Soshana made an appointment with a local holistic nutritionist. The practitioner had an opening that week and she decided to take whatever she had available. At this point, she didn't want to mess around with her health. Things were happening to her body that she had ignored in the past but having extreme out of body dissociations were nothing to mess around with. The practitioner told Soshana to bring in all her recent lab work, anything she would be willing to share. It seemed odd that someone who wasn't a doctor would want to see it since it was all normal, as she had explained over the short phone conversation.

June, the practitioner was in her mid-to-late sixties. She had frizzy long gray and silver hair, healthy skin, wore a flowing beige skirt with a gray top, lots of colorful beaded bracelets stacked on her wrists and gold necklaces against her thin neck. Calling her a hippie would be an understatement. She embodied the naturopathic village healer, though she didn't project that when she spoke.

Soshana explained everything, even the episodes. June asked about her childhood, what she went through in college, any trauma and illnesses. She asked about her diet (not so great after all), drinking habits (trying not to, for obvious reasons), exercise (not enough), bowel movements (too frequent), her menstruation (heavy, painful) and sex life (nope).

It was getting a bit too personal. She asked questions that had never been asked by any physician before, some didn't make sense as to why Soshana was there, but in the end the questions sort of came together. She took a whole approach rather than just asking direct questions about symptoms and prescribed medication to treat them. She reviewed all the labs and imaging. She studied it, excused herself and returned after a few minutes. When she came back in, she scooted her chair closer to Soshana and put a gentle hand on Soshana's knee.

"You are suffering. You may have been for many years. I'm sure there is so much more to tell. I hear you and I'm sorry for what you have been through." She removed her hand.

Soshana was unsure what to say, given that the standard response was always 'you're fine, drink more water, reduce stress and stop being anxious.'

"Thank you," she said quietly, so close to tears. Being listened to and validated by a healthcare professional was a rare treat. Often necessary but not always delivered.

"Even though it says 'normal' on your charts, there are a few things that are below optimal. Your D and B12 vitamins are at the very low end of normal but not optimal, that would make you feel dizzy, lightheaded, nauseous, bloated, fatigued and depressed. Your complete iron is low as well, and would also contribute to those symptoms, among many other issues such as ringing in the ears, insomnia, anxiety, weakness, fainting and hair loss. That's only *some* of the symptoms. I can recommend vitamins and supplements that are better absorbed than the crap you find at the grocery store. Changing the way you eat and when you eat should help you feel better in a matter of months. I can send you home with a printout of basic instructions to start as soon as you can. How do you feel about that?"

This was unfamiliar. Care, compassion, straight answers, a sense of hope. *Why am I worried?*

"Soshana?" The doctor leaned forward for attention.

"Yes. Good."

"Excellent. Let's get you all fixed up. Please let me know if you have any questions, anytime. I'll give you my email, I will try to respond as quickly as I can."

'Let's get you all fixed up.' Why do I need fixing? Why does everyone need to be fixed?

Soshana left with some supplements, vitamins and a plan for a healthier diet, as well as tips on how, when and what to eat to help with her deficiencies and digestion issues. Deciding that her worry was linked to unfamiliarity when it came to being cared for properly, she left the office with a plan. Ms. Erlings words rang through her mind; *you need to change in order for your life to change.*

The weeks went by with a renewed sense of accomplishment. It was becoming easier to smile naturally, though some days were still difficult. She had bi-weekly sessions with Ms. Erling and once a month she would check in with Dr. Linds with updates.

"Irreputable damage. That's why you have a constant bombardment of thoughts, arguments, memories of trauma. You were the peacekeeper, the actual adult in the family dynamic. Always staying quiet, not expressing yourself or having a safe place to express your needs. It is no surprise you have digestion issues. To me, it sounds like you internalized it all and now your body and your mind are screaming for help. The small child in you still needs to be taken care of, and now that you're an adult, you are responsible for what your mother dismissed, abused and ignored." Dr. Linds was precise, firm. Deadly serious.

"I've never been told that, or rather, Ms. Erling never explained it like that. To me, it makes sense." Soshana had a sense they were onto something.

"This is the most difficult work you can possibly do. You are actually physically changing the way your mind works, how the neurons fire in the synapsis of your brain, many people are not up to the task. If you succeed, you may be able to have a fulfilling life."

"It does seem extremely difficult. There are still times I want to..." Soshana paused. She had let Ms. Erling know how often she thought about killing herself, like pulling a heavy lever in her mind, she released the forbidden information. "I... I often have thoughts of suicide." It was jarring to hear herself say it aloud again, confessing to another person.

"I'm sorry to hear that, Soshana. I hope you can understand

that you are worth fighting for, and the work you are putting in should ease the suicidal ideation. I do need to know how serious these thoughts are, if you've made plans to act on them and if you have any weapons in your home. I apologize for the bluntness but it's important you tell me the truth." His words are as soft as a newborn chicks' downy feathers, and as grasping as eagles' talons.

"None, I mean no plans, no weapons and I have never actually acted on them. It's just imaginings and fantasies I suppose. It's just that, some days I just don't want to be alive. A coma sounds nice. Other days, I see glimpses of what real beauty is in the world. A flower petal with a droplet of dew and sunshine reflecting off it will stop me in my tracks in awe. Birds singing early in the morning, the sound of the Grand River flowing through the city, how it makes me feel adventurous when I pretend Lake Michigan is an ocean. My mind will focus solely on those things, the hyperfocus tends to block out any barrage of thoughts and I want to stay there, I want to live in that peaceful, quiet world. If I could just stay there, in those moments, if I could have that feeling most of the time, I think I wouldn't want to die."

"That's the goal, Soshana! That is exactly what you are working towards, it is possible. I see how capable you are and how your mind is shifting, it takes a long time with constant practice. Years, sometimes. And even after you get to that point, you still need to keep up with the new skills you learn. It's worth it. The hard work is always worth it. It's difficult to see it while you are feeling the depths of depression and anxiety." They ended the call shortly after he gave her a few more 'tools' for managing the symptoms of panic attacks. Soshana had little hope, but at least it wasn't any hope.

The convenience store was running smoothly, Joe had helped Soshana train a few new recruits that were enthusiastic and friendly. This gave Soshana some relief, knowing that in a few months they would be fully trained for when Soshana took some well-deserved time off.

Christmas came and with it a strange awareness surrounded her thoughts, not particularly exciting or upsetting. The last few Christmases weren't pleasant. She didn't care much for celebrating and didn't have a reason to, this year was different, she was meaning to make an effort to reconnect with people and thought she was doing a fine job of it. She agreed to spend Christmas with Taryn and her family. It was best to get familiar with Taryn since they were going to spend three days together. Upon arriving at their neatly decorated home that reminded her of the east coast and smelled of cinnamon and sweets, she decided to put her best face on and smile like she meant it. Taryn's husband and sweet little Jeremiah greeted her at the door. This time Sean had approached his attitude towards Soshana was a cool demeanor and a wry smile. He apologized quietly with an air of dismissal while Jeremiah reached for Soshana saying, "Soshi!" It made Soshana smile so big she hardly recognized herself.

The unease settled after Sean's weak apology. Soshana enjoyed seeing Jeremiah open his presents, it felt bittersweet to reconnect with Taryn's mom and dad, she hadn't seen them in a long time. They were like a second set of parents to her as a child, now aging and developing brittle bones. Their warm, gentle embraces were welcomed. They asked how she was doing, no one had time for that. "Fine," with a flash of a smile was all they got. They asked about Derek, they knew about their parents. Taryn's father used to be friends with their father, but they hadn't talked in many years either. They skirted around the subject, knowing it wouldn't go far and the discomfort would cause tension.

Taryn explained that Derek was working hard on his midterms and needed to stay in New York until he graduated in the spring. Christmas was not Soshana or Derek's favorite holiday, they didn't enjoy celebrating it. Taryn's parents didn't need to hear that bit of useless information, and she didn't want to tell. Oversharing is not a virtue.

New Year's Eve was spent in silence. It came along dragging its feet after a yearlong marathon. NYE was the exception for socializing back then, in her earlier years. She'd had plenty of fun New Years in New York with her friends, but she was getting to the age were staying up past eleven was for the young folk. The store was closed on New Year's Day, so she used it as a day to cook and prepare meals.

Kieran had reappeared in her dreams over the past few days like a hammer that had come down on glass. She caught herself daydreaming about seeing him again, thinking about what he was doing during the holidays. She wouldn't allow herself any wasted time on him, but her subconscious was unable to release him from her thoughts. The dream was simple. He was talking with her as if they were old friends, he was younger in the dream, discussing his future. They were in an unrecognizable location. It was short, but long enough that when she woke up, it gave her the same melancholy feeling of loneliness. She wished she had someone she could share her life with, as simple and as dull as it was. Though it was proving to be a difficult task, she was physically feeling better. She hadn't had a nightmare or bad dream in almost two months. This dream of him that broke the ice felt like a setback, a failure given all the work she had been putting in over the past few months. An unwarranted but forced plunge into the cold, dark, wetness of Lake Michigan.

She did her best to get up but couldn't find the will. Tears fell down her cheeks, silent, damp and fast. She rolled over to get her phone. No calls, voicemails or texts. No new emails. No contact whatsoever.

Silence.

Emptiness.

Drowning.

Darkness.

She was tired of crying, tired of remembering, worn down by the constant fake arguments with her dead mother, her not-so-dead friend, with her disappearing-act dad. Numbing yourself for so many years has that consequence. She placed her phone back on the nightstand and pulled the covers over her head. Today was not a good day. She had hoped to start the new year off on a high note with high hopes.

Each passing day was a step towards healing but her emptiness was ever present, despite having Joe, Carol, Derek and Taryn to keep her company. She was able to exercise more, eat well and stick to the plans that Dr. Linds and the holistic doctor created for her. She had a sense of unease, misplaced guilt and shame that kept crawling into the back of her mind that she would ignore most days. Some days were harder than others, most days were 'fine.'

Practice. Practice. Practice.

Please shut the f– please be quiet.

Thank you for reminding me of that memory. It's not happening now.

Thank you for the reminder. I'm safe, nothing is happening.

Look at the cat. Look how sweet he is.

Thank you for the reminder, there is nothing happening to me.

That isn't happening to me right now, I am in a safe place.

Stop, thank you.

You don't have to constantly remind me of that thing my mom said to me over twenty years ago.

She isn't here. She isn't hurting me anymore. She can't hurt me anymore.

Why are you reminding me?

Thank you for reminding me. I am safe.

I can take care of myself.

I am a smart and capable woman.

I am a fucking mess.

Thank you for reminding me, but I'm in charge now.

Day in, day out. Some days it was relentless. A constant battle with her own mind to recognize the obsessive thoughts, accept and release them. It was agonizing, exhaustive work.

February came sooner than expected, and Soshana wasn't prepared at all for her trip with Taryn. She wasn't ready emotionally, mostly. Soshana had asked Taryn if she needed a few nice outfits for outings and dinners, she responded with 'most likely' which was not helpful. Taryn heard the hesitation in her question and offered clothes she could borrow and to come over that evening while she was packing.

Soshana arrived around seven after work and dinner, hoping

this would be a quick affair. Taryn was all too eager to get Soshana undressed in her own massive walk-in closet. Her husband had his own, which was of almost equal size. She had already laid out several dresses, even though Taryn was smaller in size, she had some dresses from when she was in her first trimester of being pregnant, which didn't make Soshana feel any better, until she tried them on.

"Wow, that one looks fan-fucking-tastic, Soshi. Look!" She closed the closet door; it had a mirror on the backside. The dress reached to mid-calf and was long-sleeved with a sweetheart neckline, peplum lace around the height of her hips, in dark plum with matching colored lace covering the bodice. It wasn't too dressed up, but enough to be casual. "Damn, woman, you have some hips on you. Why have you been hiding that figure, it should be illegal!" Taryn looked her up and down. She took Soshana's hand and lifted it, encouraging her to spin. "Let me get a good look 'atcha."

A spring of confidence flowed over her body. Then she looked at her tired, slightly puffy face. She stared at it for a few extra seconds and then looked down at her toes.

"Will you allow me to do your hair and makeup when we're there? Only if you want me to, I'm not saying you need it or should do it. Totally up to you, friend."

Soshana looked at Taryn with less confidence and nodded.

"I also have some cute shoes, I think we are still the same size, right? 7.5?"

Soshana nodded again. Taryn went around the back of the closet where she had a wall of shoes. Sequined silver opalescent pumps, sparkling black stilettos and some peep-toe white stilettos.

"I think any of these will knock the socks off any guy

179

checking you out."

"Why are you doing this for me?"

Taryn signed and gave her a look of disbelief. "I hope that someday you finally see how much people care about you. I want you to believe it. And I want to do this because it selfishly makes me happy to see you smile, to see you come to life."

"Thank you," was all that could come out, but it was as sincere as she could muster.

"You're so welcome. Oh, and I booked you a massage and facial the next morning!" Taryn giggled.

"What?! You're going to spoil me, I won't know what to do with myself after this trip!" Soshana laughed. "I mean it, thank you so much. I don't know how to repay you."

"You can repay me by having the absolute best time and enjoying yourself at every moment."

"Deal."

They left on a Wednesday afternoon, after Soshana completed an early shift at the store. She had packed as best she could, she did take Taryn up on her offer of borrowing the few dresses and shoes that she had her try on. Living in New York ran her account dry, so she only ever purchased thrift store clothing or got hand me downs from friends, which were outdated and old, but she didn't mind. Clothes were objects to cover your bits, no one important would notice her or care. She needed that money for Mr. Skittles, books and food, in that order.

Soshana texted Joe again to remind him of when to stop by and feed Mr. Skittles and give him some attention. *Go! Have fun! I know how to take care of your little guy.* Soshana knew how well Joe took care of him and felt guilty for asking again, even though he had offered before the words could come out.

She took a long look around her stuffy small apartment and hoped she would come back feeling different. Happier. More confident and content with life as it is. This was the first semi-vacation she had since she went to the Bahamas with Mina over six years ago, a trip that was Mina's choice.

The drive was a bit tense at first, Jeremiah having thrown another world-class fit before Taryn left. The energy cleared once they got into a rhythm in their conversations. They talked about high school, dealing with aging parents, missing being able to stay up late and wake up late, the simple little things about life that don't really matter but do at the same time.

They arrived at the Townsend Hotel around seven in the evening. Taryn used the VIP parking. Two young gentlemen dressed in fine redcoats with black trim came out to handle their luggage and bring them to the lobby. Soshana took in her surroundings, the biting cold tapping on her cheeks, the buzz of unknown adventures swirling between them. Taryn got them checked in. She couldn't believe she was able to get her own room. Taryn was a swindler, a charismatic genius at times. She never did anything that was illegal or took advantage of anyone, but if she said she was able to get something, she got it.

The waiting areas, the lobby and the dining room were a splendor of tasteful classical era decorations, wooden crown molding, the walls and decor were warm tones of burgundy, taupe, beige and off white. The furniture was wooden, with accents of metal, gold and burlap textures. The lights were dimmed, sensual and cozy. She felt like she was in a different country.

"We're ready!" Taryn turned from the concierge desk with

room cards in hand.

"Oh," Soshana said, mildly distracted, out of her element but pleasantly surprised. She gave a quick grin at Taryn as the two men that helped with their luggage gestured to guide them to the elevators. They were on the top floor. As they got to their rooms Taryn asked if Soshana wanted to go for dinner downstairs after they freshened up. "I'm starving," they both said simultaneously, giggling like their former teenage selves.

Soshana entered her room, knowing she only had about thirty minutes to freshen up.

It had a beautiful balcony, the window shades were open, they overlooked the twinkling lights of the city. The bed looked even more fluffy and comfortable than her own. She put her things down on the floor next to the bathroom and flipped the light on. It was a palace compared to her dingy dated bathroom. There was marble everywhere, the towels were inscribed, blinding white, neat as a pin. She touched the towels and turned to look at the glass shower and the large tub. "Oh I'm getting *deep* into you tonight." Soshana laughed out loud at herself and it caught her by surprise. She was funny when she didn't overthink it.

They met downstairs at the restaurant and were seated immediately. Taryn had only touched up her makeup, leaving her jeans, white blouse and running shoes on, though the restaurant setting called for floor length gowns. The tables and chairs were dark wood, there was a white starched tablecloth and on top of it a rose in a vase with a candle.

"This is bourgeois, Taryn, I feel out of place," Soshana said as she looked around at the waiters in white button-down shirts, black ties and black slacks or skirts, with shiny black dress shoes.

"It's Wednesday and it's slow, nobody will notice. Most of the people at the convention will be coming in tomorrow and staying at other locations. Oh, and we have money, so they won't care. Well, my company has money. Order whatever you want! Order stuff to take up to the room!"

The waiter came by with water, a menu and wine list. They ordered a bottle of wine, filet mignon, and loaded up on bread. They chatted and ate happily, feeling better after the first few bites. The wine may have helped too.

Taryn had printed out a schedule for Soshana to let her know what times she would be at the conference. She explained that a limo would be stopping by at ten tomorrow to pick her up and take her to the spa. Apparently, she would be spending most of the morning there, then there was a lunch break and she had the rest of the afternoon to do whatever she wanted.

"I'll be back around 4:30 pm so we can get ready before the dinner party," Taryn said to her while she sipped her last bit of red wine. "I hope that's okay?"

"Oh my gosh of course, it sounds like a dream. Thank you."

Taryn slapped her lap and said, "Well, I'm ready to pass out, how about you?"

Soshana was full in her belly and yet felt light. "Yes. There's a tub in my room with my name on it."

She woke the next morning, for a moment not remembering where she was or even what day it was. She slept unbelievably well for being in a new place. The sun was peeking through the blackout curtains; she had left them open a crack on purpose, for fear of not waking up in time for the momentous day that Taryn had set up for her. She sat up, stretched and took a moment to feel as much gratitude as possible for this moment. When Soshana was away from home, wherever it was, whatever time it was, gratitude always came to her heart so much easier.

She felt an obnoxious twinge of guilt when she ordered room service for breakfast, that feeling went away in a flash when she saw the bright face of the steward and the beautiful tray of steaming coffee, cream, eggs, bacon, toast and oatmeal. The oatmeal came with its own accoutrements of brown sugar, butter and star anise garnish. The five-dollar tip felt like a joke, but the steward smiled and told Soshana to call the service desk when she was finished.

She ate slowly, intentionally chewing, all the while feeling the waves of gratitude flow through her. "Mmm," she exclaimed while throwing her hands up and falling back into the bed like a playful child who just graduated from a kids bed to an adult sized bed.

She was ready for the limo driver a few minutes early. The frigid and breezy winter air scratched at any bare skin. The limo smelled like artificial rose oil and cheap cleaning solutions, at least it was roasting hot.

When she arrived at the spa, it felt like she had left one European country and stepped into another. She couldn't begin to imagine how expensive this was, and if Taryn was footing the bill or her company was. Another twinge of guilt, then a mindful reminder to "knock it off." This was okay, she was being treated and Taryn wholeheartedly insisted.

A ninety-minute massage, sauna, facial and salt treatment was more than a treat. She started off with the sauna, having been told the heat helps release muscle tension to prepare for the massage. The massage was off putting at first since she had a hard time with skin-on-skin touch, let alone a stranger, while being nearly naked. The woman was professional but made several off-key comments about how tight her back and neck were. She also told her to get more massages, the woman was probably right.

After three hours of relaxation, zen music, lavender, euca-lyptus and peppermint, she floated out. She didn't think it would help, but she permitted herself to relax and the whole point was to enjoy it. Even if it was difficult. She got back to the hotel, daydreaming about the plushness of the robe, the delicious scented oils and the touch of warm hands on her aching body. Divinity and tranquility delivered. She grabbed a pre-made sandwich from the lobby cafe and happily ate it in her room while looking out the window, watching the streets of Detroit flutter about while she sat still.

Back as promised around 4:30 pm, Taryn knocked on Soshana's door and when she opened it, she had a bottle of wine, two glasses, a bag filled with makeup and hair styling products and tools on the counter. "You first, babe."

Taryn happened to be nothing short of a miracle worker. Soshana's frizzy wavy hair was tamed with some simple products and a hot curling iron. The chair was turned away from the mirror, so as to reveal the work, or damage as Soshana thought. "Don't turn me into a clown, please. Not too much makeup, I'm not used to it."

Taryn laughed, taking sips of the GSM wine blend from California, a delicious blend they both agreed on. After half an hour, she was finished.

"Go put on your dress and then I'll let you see what a stunning hot babe you are! O.M.G. if I was single…" Taryn exaggerated, fanning herself.

Soshana laughed and walked out of the bathroom to the

closet where she had hung up the dark plum lace dress. She put it on and Taryn zipped up the back.

Taryn turned her around by the shoulders to face her and looked in her eyes. "You are so beautiful, Soshana, without makeup, without your hair done, without the need for fancy clothes. These are all just simple materialistic enhancements. You are gorgeous. Go look."

Soshana didn't initially recognize the pretty woman looking at her in the mirror. She leaned in and looked a little closer. The makeup was light but highlighted all her features in ways that were pleasing. She was curvy, with full breasts and moderately wide hips and the dress gave the illusion of a curved hourglass. She felt exposed and damn Taryn for noticing.

"I see you! Believe me, please try to trust me when I say you are a knockout. Don't compare yourself to another person for a second. I have to leave you now, I'm going to trust you to pick out your shoes and not touch anything, as long as you like what I've done."

"I look kind of amazing, you're a miracle worker."

"Not at all, the canvas was already beautiful." Taryn gave her a kiss on the cheek and said, "I'll be ready in about twenty minutes. I'll come and get you and we can go downstairs."

Soshana sat upright on her bed, staring at her reflection in the blank space of the flat-screen TV. A shadowed ghost, a person she may have seen in the past, someone who used to celebrate life, go out with friends, have nice dinners, laugh often... She felt like a fraud in this dress, the makeup was a mask, shielding herself from the world. She was frozen in place, time passing so quickly, her mind replaying old videos of hurt and betrayal while her heart was grasping for her to let go and move on. The gentle knock on the door startled her, she jumped up, grabbed the peep-toe white stilettos and her purse, and went downstairs with her friend.

As they descended the stairs, she could hear the chatter of people, glasses and utensils clinking, shuffling of feet and casual dining music. They went to the bar, Taryn whipping out her seller's smile at the middle-aged bartender. He splashed an extra bit of vodka in her drink with a half-smile. She turned towards Soshana and said, "Whatever you want, it's on the house." Soshana ordered a gin and tonic with lime. The bartender did not add any extra to Soshana's since she didn't give him a flashy grin, no hope for the wicked. Taryn took a first big sip, smacked her lips and said, "Let's do this. You ready?" Soshana took a sip of her drink and nodded, not actually ready but not much else she could do.

They walked around together, like people introducing themselves as a couple but not. Taryn rubbed Soshana's back every so often when she let her colleagues know about their long friendship and how happy she was to have her there. Soshana smiled painfully and nodded, and was asked at least a half dozen times 'well what do you do?' Soshana got tired of saying in a variety of tones and descriptions, "Nothing of importance, just general labor." The glances that followed were either dismissive, full of pity or apathy. Soshana excused herself to go back to the bar after asking Taryn if she wanted another drink. She was talking to another work colleague and shook her head.

Soshana approached the bartender, but this time with a toothy grin, and asked for another G&T. He reciprocated with a little extra gin this time. Soshana could tell there was someone nearby as she was always so sensitive to her surroundings.

"Fancy meeting you here," a man's voice said with sultry playfulness. She turned her head to see Tim, the friend at Taryn's Halloween party who was dressed in a horrific 70s outfit and had stunk of bourbon.

"Soshana, right? It's been a while, how's it going?" He leaned his elbow on the counter, shot a pointer finger at her. He stared at her face for a moment, then did his very best to not look her up and down but failed.

"You are looking fantastic, if I may, wow!" he continued after checking her out one more time. It took the will of the gods to not roll her eyes, it may have shown in her face this time.

"Nice to see you again, Tim," she said dryly.

Taryn giddily ran up to them through the cliques and groups, somehow escaping the dredge of realtors.

"Oh good, you two found each other!" She smiled at Soshana, a knowingly cheeky grin. One that suggested Soshana should flirt and socialize. "I'll have a vodka martini, please," she ordered. Taryn took her drink and left after a subtle wink towards Soshana, out of Tim's line of sight.

"So... what have you been up to? Looks like you've been taking care of yourself, not as pale as a few months ago." He chuckled to himself. Something about the way he stood, how he breathed was insidious: the fake laugh, the smell of his horrid cologne. It was painfully obvious this was a set-up by Taryn so she would placate her friend, after all she did for her. He wasn't bad to look at and he had glistening, polished teeth. That was all that was going for him at the moment.

Feeling a bit of disdain rising in her, perturbed at all the wealthy assholes she was surrounded by, she decided to be playful but also brutally honest. Soshana worked up her best enthusiastic, sarcastic but flirty tone.

"Oh, you know, working on myself. I was recently diagnosed with a mental illness! So crazy, right? I don't know what it is, but sometimes I see things. You already know I work at a convenience store, so that hasn't changed. So yeah, just slowly going insane, a bit deranged. Mentally fucked, but fine overall. How about you?" she said, wide-eyed and batting her eyelashes while sipping her drink.

She couldn't help but crack a smile and suppress laughter as he cleared his throat and tried to laugh. He started looking around, planning his escape.

Success.

Before he could run, another man's voice came from behind her. A quiet stillness took over the air surrounding her. Chills formed on her shoulders and spine.

"Is this guy bothering you?"

Soshana's blood froze.

That voice.

She took an imperceptible deep breath before she slowly turned to face Kieran.

12

Come Clean

The condensation from her drink caused it to slip from her hand as she looked up at him in wonder and bewilderment. Luckily, the sensation brought her back from the shock of seeing him and she caught it before it fell. She was taken out of time, location. Everything stopped in her universe for a few moments. All she could hear was the deafening ringing in her ears. Then he smiled at her.

God. It's him. He's right in front of me.

Tim spoke and broke her trance.

"What's up, man, it's been a while, right? How are you?" Tim shook Kieran's hand heartily and firmly. He clapped his other hand on Kieran's shoulder.

Kieran kept his eyes on Soshana until the last socially acceptable moment to look at Tim. "I'm good, man, I'm good. Getting better. It's nice to be out," Kieran replied.

"So you know Soshana then?" Tim said with a great sense of relief in his tone.

"Yes, we met a while back."

Soshana had begun to back away. Her body was moving for

her, instinctively. She stopped herself when she saw Kieran's face fall.

"Well I'll leave you to it then. It's great to see you out, alive and kicking." Tim gave Kieran another quick handshake and nodded phlegmatically in Soshana's direction.

Kieran turned to fully face Soshana. She was unable to form words or fathom a full sentence and knew she was blushing, but with the make-up and lighting it may be hard to tell. She looked down at her drink, then up at him. He was staring at her, unmoving, hardly breathing.

"Is it really you?" he asked gently, quietly, with a strained smile. His eyes were wide in surprise, sharp, glinting.

Soshana nodded slowly, swallowed hard and finally breathed. Disappointment and sadness began to well up in her belly, to her chest. Her breathing became more intense. She did all she could to prevent herself from breaking down.

They started talking at the same time. Kieran with "I'm-Soshana with "You-" Both watching each other, pausing, waiting for the other to speak. Pain formed in the creases of his eyes and eyebrows. He stayed quiet and gestured for her to continue.

"I was so worried about you. I left you a note in your jacket pocket. I tried calling the hospital so I could at least know if you were alive. But... Nothing. Radio silence." As she said this, her free hand sliced the air to motion being cut off.

He let out a deep sign and started to explain but is cut off by a thin but toned, dark-haired wild-eyed woman with shockingly blue eyes that glowed in the dim light.

"Dinner is about to start," she hissed. She darted her eyes to Soshana, looked her up and down with intensity, lips curled over her teeth before a glaring grin formed over her mouth, then glided away towards the tables.

Kieran's face was pale, his now cold eyes fixed on Soshana's. He waited until the woman was far enough away so that she nor anyone else could hear.

He leaned in quite close to Soshana. "I want to tell you everything. I promise. Are you in town tomorrow? Are you available to meet?" He backed away only far enough to scan every millimeter of her face, searching for any kind of flinch, movement or twitch.

"I don't have any plans for tomorrow," she replied.

"Meet me downstairs in the lobby at eleven?"

"Yes," she whispered.

She turned away from him, walked outside and steadied her breathing. Tears moved down her face, but she kept composed.

God damn it.

She dabbed them away with the cocktail napkin from her drink and took a few more moments to breathe. She folded her arms across her torso, pushed her back against the brick wall and tilted her chin towards the clouded sky.

Anger kept her warm. He could have called, and now all of a sudden she agreed to meet him. Alone. She knew she needed to go back in, Taryn would worry. She didn't have enough time to think this through, it was too much all of a sudden. She needed more time; the panic rose in her spine. She could drink it away, she thought.

Easy out. I have a valid reason to get fucked up.

Her eyes were closed as she turned to go inside and ended up slamming into a hard body. It pissed her off, making her hostile enough to want to punch the person. If she'd had her wits about her, she would have noticed and heard someone coming outside.

Kieran had followed her. The look on his face was frightening. Was he upset or scared? Without warning, he pulled her close to him and held her tightly, without giving her the chance to give permission to be touched. He whispered, "I'm so sorry." Then let go just as fast as he grasped her and went back into the hotel.

She was frozen in place, confused as fuck and quite frankly giddy with excitement. Then furious at being excited. She stood for a few moments to bring herself back to earth, back to her body. This whiplash was maddening.

As apoplectic as she was, it was nothing compared to what her sense of smell had triggered. His scent was a hundred times more intoxicating. He didn't have the faint smell of medication, hospital laundry detergent, musty smells from the room and acid on his breath. He smelled like a warm fall afternoon, earthy and spiced. Soshana allowed the feeling to overtake her senses. She was dizzy and not just from the alcohol. Taking deep breaths, concentrating on the moment and being in it, she remembered where she was and what she was doing. Picking up her drink and finishing it in one gulp, she headed indoors.

She found a bathroom to make sure her face hadn't melted off from the crying and cold. She did look attractive. She never took the time to notice. Not when she wore the face of her abuser since becoming an adult. The older she got, the worse it was.

She relieved herself, half hoping she could vomit and get out of this mess but plucked up the courage and entered society. The smell of food, and the sounds of people chatting and clinking utensils brought her back to the present moment.

She sat next to Taryn who sloppily exclaimed, "Who's this hot bitch sitting next to me?!" Then planted a wet kiss on Soshana's cheek. *She smells combustible*, Soshana thought. *Absolutely sloshed.* She loved the kiss anyway. As silly as the compliment was, it was genuine.

"Where've you been, babe? We missed you!" Taryn said with more of a slur. A couple of her friends, also hammered, smiled in Soshana's direction, raising a glass and whooping to honor her presence.

"I needed some air, I'm good!" Soshana said with a smile.

Soshana daren't look around the room to see Kieran. But she did and it didn't take longer than a moment's glance to see his face across the room, two tables over, staring directly at her. He quickly looked away. Soshana looked away too, heart quickening and forming an ache. The kind of ache that was forlorn, the husband was lost at sea, the dog that ran away feeling.

Tim was sitting diagonally across from Soshana, his face paralleled across the room from Kieran. Every time Tim decided to pipe up and say something stupid, and Soshana looked, Kieran's face was in view. *Great.*

"Another drink, ma'am?" the waiter asked. Soshana replied by shaking her head.

"Oh come on, Soshi, you're not driving!" Taryn patted her thigh.

"I'll have a martini," Soshana replied, begrudgingly. She gently tapped the waiter's arm and turned to mouth "and two waters, please." He nodded in response.

The dinner was impressive: freshly caught wild salmon with a white wine butter sauce, capers and steamed veggies, one of her favorite meals. They poured Sauvignon Blanc with dinner, it made Soshana's stomach churn. She took a few sips to appease the people around her. Tim seemed to be less afraid of Soshana and wanted to chat more, the alcohol was messing with his short-term memory.

"I'd like to get to know you better," he said, winking. She stared at him, only so she could get another chance to meet eyes with Kieran. There they were, warm. He smiled quickly; she returned a small smile. They played this little game all night, it soothed the ache in her chest somewhat. Unfortunately, Tim thought the sweet little smile was for him, Soshana reassured Tim that he would be making a huge mistake.

They finished dessert, Soshana had to hold her friend up and help her to her room. She was so full and had to pee in the worst way but wanted to make sure her friend was going to be okay. She helped her to the toilet to have her vomit before turning her around, lifting her skirt and gestured for Taryn to pull her panties down first before she exited the bathroom.

Taryn came out of the bathroom, swishing mouthwash, forgetting the sink was back in the bathroom, held up a finger, turned and went back in to spit into the shower.

Jesus. Soshana may have to wait a while.

"I'm fine, I'm fine, I promise. I've been drunkier. Drunker. Before." It was apparent that Taryn was working hard to speak clearly, she blinked hard and pried her eyes open. She sat on the bed next to Soshana and patted her back firmly. "So what do you think of Tim? He's a handsome fucker, isn't he?"

"He's handsome, but not enough to tempt me," she said, attempting a male English accent.

"Okay, Mr. Darcy." Taryn laughed.

Soshana chuckled and replied, "He's just not my type. I

appreciate you trying to set us up, but there's nothing there. I don't feel it."

Taryn kept tapping Soshana like a small child being playful, now on her shoulder and her back. "I totally understand. He's a good friend, but not for everyone. You do you, boo." With that said, Taryn fell backwards onto the bed and started snoring within a few seconds.

Soshana sighed. She sat there, contemplating flailing backwards and falling asleep as well. Responsibility and caregiving came first. Feeling buzzed and tipsy herself, she tapped her friend to tell her to get back up and at least take her shoes off. Soshana helped her into bed and covered her up.

"I love you, Soshi Roll," Taryn mumbled before she passed out again.

"I love you too, Tare Bear."

Soshana walked to her room with confidence in her steps. Mostly because she had taken the high heels off and felt great relief from it, but also because she was told she was loved, whether or not she felt or believed it.

Something else to work on.

She filled the tub with hot water, washed her face and brushed back her hair into a high ponytail. As she soaked in the bath, she paid attention to the pain in her body. The areas it took over, where the anxiety held itself. Her core, the base of her hips, her stomach and throat. She breathed, closed her eyes and concentrated on those areas. Her mind constantly slipped back to Kieran.

It was pointless to try to ignore it. She flicked her eyes open. Her mind was buzzing, restless and anxious. He looked healthy, alive. He was right in front of her. She kept going over how his body felt against hers, as brief as the moment was. It felt solid, strong, a little shaky but firm. His face and body had filled out, was no longer thin. His hair had grown out enough so no one could tell he had brain surgery just five months before. His clean-shaved face, his beautiful calm brown eyes, masculine but also soft face, and full shapely lips. His *smell*.

Jesus fucking Christ, that scent.

She felt a pleasurable aching in between her legs. She moved her hips to help ease the sensation away. The water sloshed gently around her chest. She giggled thinking about how big his nose looked when he was much thinner, and how it now looked smaller, more aligned with his features as he had gained a healthy weight.

She thought about how they agreed to meet downstairs in the lobby, her heartbeat picking up at the thought. She remembered going out to the courtyard at the hospital with him and how excited she felt. Her mind wandered to the note and how he never responded. *There had to be an explanation*, she pleaded with her mind. The mind that tries to keep her safe from harm. The mind that constantly has an argument against anything good, anything joyful. *Something could go wrong, it usually does*. Her thoughts went dark. Her heart sank. She couldn't ignore those thoughts either.

She waited in the tub until the water cooled and her fingertips became pruned and wrinkled. She got into her pajamas after flossing and brushing. She laid awake, turning over every detail in her mind until she became restless. She looked at the clock. 1:27 am.

The acid in her stomach was building, she needed to sit upright. She brought her knees to her chest and put her hand on her forehead. She knew she wasn't going to get much, if any sleep tonight.

13

The Privilege of Feeling Alive

Falling asleep sitting upright caused her legs to go numb. Her alarm went off at ten. She shook and smacked her legs to inspire blood flow.

She quickly got ready, despite nit-picking over what outfit to wear and if she should put any makeup on, before deciding it wasn't worth the effort. It didn't matter. Her heart was heavy this morning and her head was throbbing. She gulped down some water, ate some mixed nuts from the snack bar and flew downstairs a few minutes early. She checked her phone. Taryn had texted her to let her know how much she appreciated her help last night and hoped she wasn't a burden. Bless her heart, she was out and ready. A hell of a trooper.

"Hi," Kieran said quietly, startling her.

"Hi," she returned, trying to look like she wasn't fucked out of her mind from a hangover and anxiety. "So what's going on, what are we doing?"

She needed to keep her eyes off him for fear of staring but she couldn't and her mind wouldn't allow it. Unshaved, his hair tousled, he was a sight. He had on a dark gray coat, not the one from the hospital. A ready to be in a business meeting kind of outfit.

Soshana looked ready for a yoga retreat in California. She instantly regretted how she had decided to dress. He didn't seem to notice though, so she did her best to move past the degrading thoughts about herself that invaded her mind.

"I called a cab; there's a great art museum. Then I wondered if you would like to have lunch with me? My treat." He said it with a tone of hope, calling back to the days at the hospital together.

Soshana couldn't decide if she was upset that he made these plans without asking her, or if she was thrilled.

"If you want. If you don't feel comfortable, we can stay here, I don't mind," he said within seconds after the last sentence. He looked uncomfortable, he was pressing his left thumb into the palm of his right hand, then rubbing it.

Soshana looked at him and said, "It's fine, that sounds fine."

Kieran didn't look relieved, he glanced up and around then down at the floor, his breathing uneven. "Are you okay?" he asked with compassion, eyebrows raised, rubbing his hand harder, faster.

Soshana shook her head. "I don't know, Kieran. I guess I have a lot of questions. It's shocking to see you, to put it bluntly."

The cab pulled up, Kieran gestured towards it. They walked silently towards it. She hadn't felt this discomfort with him when they were together at the hospital. Something was off and she couldn't pinpoint what it was quickly enough to relieve her symptoms. In the car, Kieran told the driver to take them to the Detroit Institute of Arts. They sat in the back seat together, arms folded gently on their laps, staring forward. She hardly knew this man, but also felt so much emotion for him. What did he feel about her? She could tell he was anxious too. She evened her breathing and thought about how she could comfort him as that would help ease her discomfort. She needed courage more than she needed to give into her anxieties right now.

Say something.

"I'm so happy to see you're recovered, at least I hope you are?" Soshana started with an easy question.

He piped up, relief in his voice, "Yes, I'm in remission. Everything looks good."

She turned her head and body towards him, looked directly at him, wanting him to know that she meant every word she said and that she was intently listening. He turned to look at her.

"I was so scared, Kieran. I was supposed to see you, have lunch with you, then you were gone. Then I was told I needed to leave. I didn't know what to do." Soshana's cheeks flushed. He nodded, seemingly unable to respond verbally to the emotion in her voice. Looking at her hands, staving off an uneven emotional response, she continued, "Why didn't you tell me that day how serious your condition was?"

Kieran was quiet for a while. Then he talked slowly, taking pauses between thoughts while Soshana listened intently, "I was worried about the results from the latest surgery. I wasn't feeling better, the headaches were worsening, and the desire to leave earth had waxed and waned, though those thoughts quieted when you showed up." He paused to smile at her. Then his tone became softer, the pace slower, as if the words were dropping into a well.

"I didn't have the courage to tell you everything about my

life, I was worried you might not want to speak to me and I wasn't about to risk ruining what we had built in those precious few days. I convinced myself that day, after the gazebo, that you were the positive force in my life that kept me alive. I didn't want someone else to worry about me though. Going into this health crisis, I convinced myself that I wasn't going to make it. Desperation set in, the biological need to stay alive was stronger than the depression and pessimistic attitude."

The car stopped in front of the art museum. They were both frozen in place, staring at each other.

"Okay we're here." The driver interrupted their thoughts, his tone suggesting they should get out. Kieran paid and they exited the car. At the museum entrance, Kieran held the door open for her.

They clumsily stood next to each other as Kieran paid, Soshana feeling like a child. She had enough to cover some expenses. He insisted.

They headed towards the first exhibition: ancient Greece.

The lights highlighted the figures, pots, and framed artwork. It was warm so Soshana took off her oversized sweater, again regretting her clothing choice for what was now feeling like a date. She wore a low-cut green tank top underneath. She broke the silence as she wrapped the arms of her sweater around her waist. "Thank you for telling me all that in the cab. Thank you for being open and honest."

Kieran nodded, hands in his pockets. They walked around, each one taking a moment to comment on an image or statue they admired.

Kieran started to say something, then stopped, a huff of air coming out instead.

"What is it?" Soshana asked, genuinely curious.

He smiled, a little embarrassed. "I missed you."

She smiled generously. "I missed you too."

He stopped to look at her, a curious twinkle in his eyes. He told her, "I couldn't believe it was you last night. I saw a beautiful woman standing next to my old friend. I noticed your body language, then heard your voice and put two and two together."

"Beautiful woman?" Soshana said with one raised eyebrow and a chagrin smile.

"I mean this in the most sincere and genuine way, you looked amazing. You *look* amazing."

She pressed her lips together in an innocent smile and slowly nodded her head.

"I thought you looked beautiful at the hospital too, you know," he said. She shook her head now unconvinced of his compliments. "I mean it. You shocked me last night. I'm sorry for my awkwardness and shyness. I'm usually quite loquacious." He wiggled his eyebrows and smirked.

"Since we're complimenting each other, I think you look pretty great too." Her heart started pumping faster, heat rising to her face. She gave him a quick smile and turned towards another painting. They were in ancient Asia now. Remembering that he hadn't told her about the letter, the thoughts ran through her mind, warning her to make sure he was being truthful and honest.

He definitely doesn't see what I see in the mirror.

Still facing the painting of a warrior on a horse, she asked carefully, "So why didn't you call or text me? I left you my information in the letter."

He sighed and waited to respond. No doubt thinking what

he was going to say.

"I only just found the note last week. I dropped the coat off to have it dry cleaned. It reeked of that musty hospital stench."

"Why not then?" Soshana had an edge to her response.

"I thought about it many times over the past week. My insecurities told me that you had forgotten about me and moved on. I wanted to. I'm so sorry."

Soshana felt some relief. If he was telling the truth, which he seemed like he was, then he hadn't forgotten about her just as she suspected. She was unsure what to say next, she felt that pull, that familiar magnetic urge to be near him, touch him.

"You kissed me on the forehead before you left."

Soshana's eyes popped wide open. Thankfully, he was directly behind her and couldn't see her horror. She could tell he was smiling. His tone gave it away as he said it.

"I didn't know what else to do. I wanted you to know I was there and that I cared. Wait, how did you know? You were in an induced coma!" Soshana blurted out as she turned to face him. She was definitely blushing now. Her ears were steaming hot, her scalp sweating. No makeup to hide it today. She needed to steer the conversation away from what she could only describe as dangerous flirting. It was getting too close, too real.

He winked in response. She changed the subject. "So, you were invited to the realtor convention? Are you still working with the local group or firm? Whatever you guys call it?" Her feelings for him were shifting rapidly, evolving into territory she wasn't ready for. She convinced herself that he only had feelings for her as a platonic friend and he was being friendly. *Just a friend.*

He stood next to her and talked about being accepted back into the position a few months ago, and being invited to the convention by his boss, even though he isn't a realtor.

They walked around the rest of the exhibits, asking each other safe questions, commenting and joking on pieces of art. Soshana explained how she recently started spending time with her childhood friend since she got back from the hospital, how she invited her as her 'spouse' since her husband wasn't able to come. She talked about the holidays, how she had the best Thanksgiving she'd ever had with Derek, her friend Joe from work and his girlfriend, Carol. Kieran asked how Derek was doing and to tell him that he said hi. The conversation flowed easily and casually, returning to the old pattern and comfort they had had in the room at the hospital.

"I'm famished," Soshana said as they exited the last exhibit.

"Let's get something to eat! I'm starving too. What kind of food are you craving? Again, it's on me. I want to pay, please."

She gave him a look that told him it wasn't fair.

He gave her a look back, folded his arms and mimicked Josette. "Now darlin', you aren't going to win this argument."

Soshana laughed. "Don't make fun of Josette!"

He laughed with her. "She was great, wasn't she?"

"I miss her. She gave the best hugs."

"You know, I've been told I give pretty great hugs, but I don't give them out to just anyone," Kieran said as he leaned in with a grin.

Soshana gave him a half smile and said, "I could go for a Reuben and fries."

He clapped his hands in excitement. "I know just the place." He requested an Uber from the app and they headed down the stairs to wait.

Mudgie's Deli. It felt like going to your favorite mom and pop restaurant anywhere in any small town. The staff were welcoming and the food was fast and hot. They ate without hesitation and enjoyed each other's company. She thanked him for the meal. He stuck out his belly, patted it and grunted. He knew in doing this it would get a hearty laugh out of Soshana, which he seemed to enjoy a little too much. Soshana felt lighter, easier and much less queasy than earlier. They were almost back to themselves, the way they were before. The lightheartedness in their playful banter gave her hope that they were truly friends. It made her happy. It felt different now, better.

"So what now?" Soshana said while wiping her mouth.

"I definitely need a mint, that's for sure, then... I don't know... Do you want to walk around town for a little, work off the food?"

Soshana nodded, that sounded great to her. She fished through her purse and found a tin of winter mints. "Yes," Kieran said with his hand held out, then thanked her. She popped one in her mouth too, she felt the grease, onion and garlic seeping through her teeth, tongue and gums.

The sun had been out most of the day, warming the concrete, buildings and asphalt. They went into a couple stores, a pet store then a bookshop. They gasped and made obnoxious squeaky noises at the kittens, then pursued the isles at the bookstore. She glanced at him every so often, he did the same. She had the urge to hold his hand, to have his arms wrapped around her waist while she had her head on his shoulder, sifting through the first few pages of a fresh new book. She shook herself out of those feelings and distracted herself by pulling a random book off the shelf.

The evening hours were beginning to set in. She had completely forgotten that she was there with Taryn, and hadn't checked in with her since before she left. Kieran requested another Uber to get back to the hotel. She checked her phone as they were leaving the bookstore. Taryn had texted her a few times, with the last one saying *Where are you?! Please just text me that you're safe.* Taryn explained that she had made reservations for dinner then wanted to check out a local bar that was funky and modern. Soshana assumed there would be mixologists and the like. Handlebar mustaches. Suspenders. Bulging muscles. Tattoos.

"Shit," Soshana said out loud.

"What's the matter? Everything okay?" Kieran said, concerned.

"Yes, it's fine, I just left Taryn hanging. I have a terrible habit of either leaving my phone at home and/or not checking it. I think we're going to have dinner then go out to a bar later. Maybe you want to join us, if it isn't intended to be a girls' night of course."

"That sounds fantastic. Let me give you my number so you can text me after you talk to her."

She put his number into her phone and texted him a smile emoji with her name.

"Got it," he replied, grinning. "The ride's here."

They got into the car and headed back to the hotel, chatting about what a nice time they'd had, agreeing they were both glad they did it.

Soshana found herself smiling all the way up to Taryn's hotel door. She knocked twice, it was opened soon after.

"You made me worried sick!" Taryn briefly hugged Soshana without warning. Soshana gave her a wry smile. "Geez, I sound like my mom. Sorry, you're an adult. What kind of trouble did you get into today?" she said with a brighter attitude.

"Well, since you asked... Remember that guy I had you look up for me? The one that shared the hospital room—"

Taryn interrupted her with an exclamation of excitement. "Oh my God, you mean Kieran?! He's here?!"

Soshana couldn't help smiling. "Yes, we ran into each other last night and we actually spent the day together."

"You have to tell me everything over dinner. This is amazing."

"I was wondering if he could meet us at the bar later?" Soshana said with a sheepish smile.

"Oh absolutely! That would be great! I'm so excited to meet him. The bar's name is The Caregiver. I know it's weird, but it is in an old building, there's a speakeasy and they have the best-looking bartenders in town. So go get ready!" Taryn said as she turned Soshana's shoulders around and pushed her out the door. "You've got exactly thirty-two minutes!"

Soshana did want to feel a bit more dressed up after looking sluggish all day. She scrubbed the inside of her mouth and tongue to get the rancid garlic and onion breath to diminish. Energy renewed, she texted Kieran the name of the bar and pulled out the other outfits that Taryn brought for her. The black lacy long-sleeved top that went over a silky V-neck tank top with high-waisted jeans called out to her.

They went to an upscale French restaurant downtown and chatted about the day. Taryn was surprisingly quiet and wanted to hear every detail of Soshana's afternoon with the mysterious Kieran, which was quite unlike her. Taryn was always the spotlight of every conversation. Soshana was becoming increasingly anxious to see him again as she described the day with him.

She texted him when they were getting the check from the restaurant to give him the heads up.

It was bitterly cold; she regretted the lace shirt until they got up to the bar and the inordinately handsome bartender's bulging eyes bored into hers for just a second too long. She felt the heat rise in her body. Women consciously choose to dress a certain way when they want to grab attention. Soshana knew what she was doing when she selected the clothes she was wearing, she knew when she applied the light eye shadow and tinted lip balm. She knew instinctively that Kieran was her target, yet she doubted herself. She doubted his attraction. He still had not spoken of a significant other. She doubted what she saw in the hospital. Who was the alien-eyed woman at the dinner reception last night? She left out that little detail to Taryn, potentially subconsciously to ward off any other doubts niggling into her mind.

Will he show up? Yes, he said he would.

The atmosphere was electric. It was dark and moody with red lighting, dark green velvet drapes adorned a small stage. Art Deco-esque. Taryn got her drink, only after leaning in to show off some cleavage and flirt with 'tall, broad shoulders and perfect hair' behind the bar. She started swaying her hips to the synthetic dreamy pop music. With her free arm, she linked Soshana's and guided her to an open space.

She kept eyeballing the bartender and whispering how attractive he was to Soshana and showing off her blanched white teeth with a sultry grin. Soshana did her best to seem like she agreed but couldn't have eyes for anyone, until they landed on the ones she was hoping to see.

A warm hand hovered on the lower middle part of Soshana's back as a greeting. She turned and smiled at him. A forlorn look cast over his face then vanished when Taryn yelled out "Hi! You must be Kieran! Tim and you go way back, right?"

Kieran nodded and responded with a handshake. "And you must be Taryn. It's so wonderful to meet you."

They chatted about Tim for a few minutes then Taryn looked over at Soshana and smiled. Taryn whooped when a familiar song came on and danced more seductively towards the bar.

"Do you dance?" Kieran asked Soshana.

"Not unless forced, you?" she said shyly.

"Yeah, no. No thanks," he said, grinning and looking down at his feet. "How about swaying in one place?"

"Sure." she said, pleased.

They chatted, Soshana watching over her friend at the bar from time to time. It didn't surprise her that she was flirting, but she knew she wasn't going to break any marital promises to her husband. She just liked to rebel when given the opportunity, it gave her a boost.

"Well, I'll be..." A familiar voice came from behind Soshana and Kieran.

Josette was a sight to behold. She was stunning, straight out of a glamorous magazine shoot. She wore a red sequined floor-length gown, hair done up atop her head 60s beehive style, full face of makeup and an award-winning grin.

Both Kieran and Soshana exclaimed, "Josette!" Josette went in for Soshana first and gave her a big squeeze, then Kieran. She was almost as tall as him in the jet-black stilettos.

"My dears, I can't express to you how delighted I am to see you both. I thought I was dreaming when I saw you from backstage. I go on in a few minutes but I just had to come see you beautiful people. Look at you! My *word*." Josette had a hand on her cheek and shook her head, looking them up and down. "Both of you look good enough to *eat!* Mmm!" They all laughed together. She had that familiar jovial laugh, one that gave a start to people's hearts. She touched both of their shoulders and before she turned and winked, she said, "See you on the other side."

Taryn had eventually ripped her attention away from the bartender and rejoined them, asking who that was. Kieran explained how they met in the hospital and that she was their nurse from time to time. Their favorite, he said. The pop music faded and the lights dimmed, the velvet green curtains were drawn and the vintage lights that lined the base of the stage glowed a dull electric yellow.

A male voice came over the crowd. "Without further ado, you know her, you love her, your evening's entertainment begins with the incomparable, the incredibly talented Josie! Give it up!" The crowd screamed, whooped and clapped loudly. Kieran and Soshana looked at each other with wonder and excitement. Taryn linked arms with Soshana who stood in the middle of the three of them.

The spotlight illuminated on Josette, who began to sing a swanky, jazzy version of Nina Simone's "Sinnerman" accompanied by a live band. The effort they made to stop their jaws from dropping to the ground was punishing.

They all looked at each other in astonishment and mouthed "I'm not surprised!" "She's incredible!" The song immediately led to another and after a few rounds of dancing, applause, screams and exclamations, Josette announced she would be slowing it down a bit.

A muffled silence fell over the room in respect. The band's pianist began a slow melodic tinkering on the keys. Eventually, Roberta Flack's "The First Time Ever I Saw Your Face" formed. Josette sang with a profound accuracy and vibrancy one couldn't have imagined. Soshana was in awe, the chills she had all over her body, especially on her scalp were near agonizing. She was so moved by the singing and lyrics her eyes welled up. Strange sensations coursed through her, it was enduring. The simplest way she would be able to describe it would be that she was alive. *This is what it feels like to live.* Soshana felt like Josette was the only other person in the room and she was singing for her and Kieran. It was unbearably beautiful.

Soshana turned her head toward Taryn and discreetly wiped a tear away. She didn't want Kieran to see how emotional she was. She wasn't sure why; he had cried in front of her several times. Soshana knew she had a need to show people that she was the strong one in any situation, she could handle anything. She needed to tuck this revelation about herself away until she had time to dissect it. Right now, this was all about being present, here, with two people she was growing to adore in many different ways.

Josette finished and the crowd lost their minds. Josette threw her head back, laughing and clapping with them. She waved to Soshana and Kieran, then blew them a kiss. Several people in front of them turned and asked with wide eyes, "Do you know her?!" They both nodded, grinning with pride.

Josette continued with another soul-stirring song. Kieran gently palmed the back of Soshana's elbow and asked if she wanted to take a quick break outside. He said he would get uncomfortable in loud crowded rooms sometimes. She nodded and let Taryn know they would be right back, "Just need some air." Taryn gave her eyes that screamed 'go get 'em.' Soshana worried for a moment if she should leave her alone, then Taryn said, "Get out, I'm fine, I'll stay right here." She pushed her back and continued dancing.

They grabbed their coats from the check-in and went out a side door that had an enclosed patio, for summer no doubt. It had to be around twenty degrees Fahrenheit. Soshana started shivering immediately. Kieran pulled off his coat and put it around her.

"Stop it, you need this coat! It's freezing!" She looked up at him while she began to take off the coat but he stopped her.

Kieran's face was intense and solemn again. It reminded her of the day at the gazebo, but with more melancholy. First, he looked around, looked at the starless, clouded sky. Possibly looking around to see if there was anyone else there. The energy between them was palpable. You could grasp it, if it had substance.

"Everything okay?" Soshana asked with concern in her voice, calm behind the concern.

His face was flushed, chest moving steadily with each strained, shuddered movement. He lightheartedly laughed, what came out next was something Soshana never thought she would ever hear.

"When I'm near you, I feel like I'm on fire," he huffed out in ragged breath.

Soshana's eyes burned, along with her chest and base of her spine. Nearly choking on her response, she managed to ask, "What do you mean by that?"

He took several moments, while stepping a little bit closer towards her.

"You make me feel so alive and also like I want to die, but in the best way. I adore you, Soshana. Every moment of every day since I met you was spent daydreaming of you. Admiring you, your loveliness, your kindness. Your beauty is..." He laughed, embarrassed, rubbed the back of his neck vigorously.

"I know I'll never meet another woman like you in my lifetime. I would be a damn fool to let you slip away again without telling you how I feel. I understand if you don't feel the same way, I wouldn't know what to do with myself if I..."

This was her chance, the signal she was waiting for. Alarms blaring in every sense of the word, her body was not able to contain itself any longer. She was still unsure of what she was doing or going to do. She knew she needed to be as close to him as possible. She pulled him towards her and clasped her hands on his face. Their breath mixed in the cold air. Her eyes were heavy, his eyes half closed as he looked into her eyes. He looked down at her lips and met them with his, so painfully gently. Then suddenly intensely, with gasps and small moans of desperation he kissed her harder, moving his mouth to open hers. They kissed deeply and passionately, while using their hands to carefully explore parts of their bodies. Soshana was aching to feel his hair through her hands, touch his arms and feel their solid strength. He felt his way up her back, starting at the base of her spine, stopping above the narrow part of her waist. His hand went into her long hair, holding the back of her head firmly but still softly. Their bodies were shaking, vibrating from the excitement.

They paused to catch their breath, the air surrounding them was electrified and pulsing with anticipation. They both searched each other's faces for any sign of being uncomfortable or disappointed. They smiled at each other at the same time. He leaned in to kiss her, breathing heavily into her face while holding his lips to hers. She let out a satisfied soft moan and pulled away, laughing breathlessly.

Imagine being out in the long winter, walking alone, frost biting at your fingertips, thighs and toes, darkness surrounding your vision. Numbness sets in. Imagine years of this. And after a while, you become tired of the numbness. Nothing else matters. You finally make it home and it is cold in there too. A fire heats the skin but not the life force within you. One morning, you find yourself opening the blinds to a warm colorful sunrise, the rays of light thawing your shuddered thoughts, filling the depths of your agony with joy. An example of what life could feel like, if you just let the heat from the fire warm you. At least, for now, Soshana forgot about life before, and cared less for what life was to come, until today.

They stared at each other for a few moments, this time without the anxiety or mystery of not knowing how each other felt. Their bodies' reactions were sign enough that the feelings were mutual.

"We should go back in," Kieran said. He wiped smeared balm off his lips, then attempted to help Soshana with hers. She smiled at him and checked for a mirror in her purse.

The door swung open and a couple of women came out, cigarettes at the ready. One of the women looked Soshana up and down and huffed. The other couldn't care less. People will be critical, humans are complicated. It didn't bother Soshana. She felt the energy of being alive and safe enough. She needed to stay in this moment with him, nothing could ruin it, not even the stench of cigarette smoke. He kissed her once more before they went back into the bar.

The crowd was roaring again, the song ended before Josette

began her next tune, they reached Taryn. It felt like a lifetime since they stepped outside. The excitement of the past two days was beginning to weigh on her. Soshana felt heavy, body vibrating and mind buzzing, she knew she was running on adrenaline.

"Did you run for mayor while you were gone? That song was better than the last! I'm so glad we came here tonight!" Taryn was lit but not like last night.

Kieran was staring at Soshana in wonderment and admiration. "Can I get you anything at the bar?"

"Water for me and my friend, please." Soshana's face was now in a permanent smile. His, too. He nodded and walked away, she enjoyed watching his backside as he left.

"Dang he's cute, you know. I mean, a little interesting-looking and quirky for sure. Did you two just make out or something?" Taryn said sarcastically, grasping the straw from her drink, looking at her with all-knowing eyes.

Soshana's face couldn't possibly turn any hotter or redder.

Taryn sighed and said with a slight slur, "Oh honey, your hair is tousled and your lips are red. Also, he has a sheen on his lips from your lip balm. It's so obvious, I love this. I LOVE THIS for you!" She annunciated and screeched out 'love this' just a bit too loud, several people turned around to check out the offender. Soshana may need another fresh breath of air.

Kieran returned with the water, the closeness of him made her ears hot, the adrenaline pump harder, vertigo set in. She took a sharp breath in and chose to listen to her body and speak up.

"I think I need to head back to the hotel, if that's okay. I'm feeling dizzy." She looked up at Kieran who nodded immediately.

"Aww come on, Soshana! We just got here an hour ago!" Taryn nudged Soshana with her elbow. Soshana shook her head, the swimming and vertigo now taking over since she claimed her voice and told her truth. It's funny how the body relaxes and lets go when you admit to yourself that you need rest.

"Ah fine." Taryn sucked down the rest of her lemon drop.

"Sorry," Soshana replied. She did feel remorse. She knew Taryn didn't get to let loose like this since her little one was born.

"It's okay. I'm keeping up appearances, I'm fucking ex-hausted." Taryn let out a haughty laugh. She patted Kieran's arm and said, "It was so nice meeting you. Hope to see you sooner than the next convention!"

Soshana and Kieran waved to Josette on stage, she was in between songs and blew them a kiss. Soshana regretted not being able to spend more time with her, hoping that this wouldn't be the last time she saw her.

"Great to meet you too, I agree. I can call for a ride?"

"*That...* would be great," Taryn replied, slurring.

It arrived quickly and they set off to the hotel, Soshana wondering the whole time if they would get to have another moment before they left tomorrow morning. The thought of leaving gave her a sinking feeling deep in her body. Her heart started pumping, beating hard against her chest. What did that kiss mean? What did he want from her? She wasn't ready for sex, which was the opposite of what her body was saying. Her mind was scrambling with energy and chaos. Fear crept in as they approached the hotel. Steam was pouring from her face and ears. She was grateful that he took the front seat and left the ladies to sit together.

They got out of the taxi, Taryn insisted on paying. She went ahead of Soshana and Kieran and said, "I'll see you tomorrow morning, Sosh, right?"

Soshana nodded, feeling queasy. Taryn pinched her lips in a thin and innocent smile and with a dramatic fling of her arm said, "I'm off to bed!"

That left them alone in the quiet lobby. They stood awkwardly for a few moments, then they both began to speak, Kieran signaling for Soshana to begin first.

"Look I-I'm..." she stuttered. She shook her head. He waited patiently. "I don't know what this is." She gesticulated between them.

"I don't know either. Maybe we can figure it out as we go? I do know that I don't want to see you leave tomorrow."

"I don't want to leave either. I haven't felt this... like this... ever. I have to process it. I hope you can understand that."

Kieran nodded, a beautiful smile spreading over his face.

Her body wanted to press against his but her mind prevented it. She swallowed and took a deep breath. "I really, really like you. Please don't misunderstand when I say I need to... be alone... Tonight."

His eyes opened wide and he shook his head briskly.

"Oh, no, no, that is not my intent. I don't... I will respect whatever you need to do."

Soshana felt such relief, while also aching to touch him. It was too much to handle right now.

"May I at least see you safely to your room? With the promise of not entering and leaving right away." He smiled, she smiled back and nodded.

He held up his hand, palm up, indicating he wanted to hold her hand, she accepted. They walked in silence.

She looked at her door, knowing the other side would mean he wouldn't be there. Her heart started back up as she turned to face him. His eyes were pleading.

He leaned in, kissed her on the cheek and whispered in her ear, "Goodnight, then."

"Goodnight," she replied. He backed away from her, they stood staring at each other, a soldering brimming heat forming between the space of their bodies. She moved a little closer to him, eager to feel his lips again, telling him to move closer to her. He did the same, then they came together softly, briefly, hanging on to each millisecond before they parted. His face lingered near hers, she could feel the heat of his breath on her cheek as he kissed it while wrapping his arms around her and embracing her tightly for several moments, taking in his scent. She held him tightly, then moved her body away from him.

"You promise to call or text me, right?" she said quietly to him with a cheeky smile.

He smiled. "Yes of course!"

She needed to peel herself away from him before she made a decision she could regret. She nodded and turned away to open the door. Through the crack of the door, she dared to look at him again. She needed to find the willpower to close it.

Do it. Close the door.

The adrenaline had finally worn off, she felt her body loosen, bones and muscles begging for rest. She smiled and closed the door. She stood in front of it for a few moments, then peeked through the hole, he was still standing there, looking down at the floor, then he shuffled off.

Exhilarated and lost, manic and scared. Blissful yet sorrowful. Sitting at the edge of the bed, she went over the entire day, minute by minute, remembering as much as she could. Wanting to sit in each moment, convincingly telling herself that it had all happened, and it happened to her. The buzz and energy were wearing out quickly. She didn't have enough time to wash her face and change before she felt she was going to pass out. She set her alarm, took her top and pants off and crashed into the fluffy bed.

She slept deeply until the alarm rang too soon, getting in about six hours of sleep. She awoke with a painful headache, a dry, sour mouth and fuzzy teeth.

Did yesterday happen or was it a fabrication of her post booze-addled mind? She audibly groaned as she pulled herself upright out of bed, turning the blaring alarm off. She noticed several texts, one from Joe with a photo and update on Mr. Skittles. He was sleeping, curled up in a tight, what she called, 'cinnamon roll' on the couch next to the window. A wink face emoji from Taryn. The last text was from Kieran, saying *I hope you slept well, beautiful. I hope it's okay that I say that.* Her heart leapt. Her mind reminded her that no man had ever called her beautiful, outside of her father when she was a child. Her boyfriend said she was pretty once or twice, but only after she asked him if she looked okay before they went out for dinner or to a social event, as if obligated to say so.

Her mind reminded her that this could be a trap, a manipulation. The thought traveled to her heart and crushed it. She shook off the feeling, put the phone down without responding and headed to the bathroom to get ready.

Taryn and Soshana met outside of their doors at seven. The sinking feeling had turned into a drowning feeling. She felt heavier and heavier as they descended the stairs to the lobby and out to the VIP parking area outside. Each step searching for him, each step taking her away from him. She started to feel angry at herself, inwardly she called herself obsessive, impulsive, foolish and careless.

"What's up, buttercup?" Taryn said from behind large sunglasses. She hadn't showered, smelled of day-old booze, and her hair was wrapped up in a careless bun.

"Nothing, just ruminating about the last few days. It's been… incredible. So much fun." It was and she meant it. She didn't mean to hide behind dark gray clouds of negativity so often, it happened naturally.

"So… anything you want to tell me about last night?" Taryn said.

"No!" Soshana barked out with a laugh. "No, we're trying to figure things out, I guess. I mean, we've really only known each other for a total of what, two weeks? It feels so much longer than that since it was long enough ago that we met. I don't know." Soshana's doubts returned.

"Look, I'm really glad to hear that. It's just… Well, I don't know how to put this other than bluntly. I care about you and I don't want to see you hurt."

Soshana was put off by the tone in Taryn's voice.

What did she mean?

Does she know something about him that I don't?

Did Tim tell her something?

Taryn's car pulled up and the attendant put their luggage in the back. Taryn slipped him ten dollars and in no time, they were headed west. Soshana felt a raw lump form in her throat as she watched the hotel disappear in the rear view mirror.

They were silent for a few minutes after getting settled in the car and taking off.

"Are you going to leave me hanging, or is that all you needed to say?" Soshana piped up.

"I've been trying to figure out how to tell you since last night. I was up early this morning going over it in my head." She sighed, a half-hearted, half-disappointed exhalation. "Kieran is apparently married. Tim and I texted last night. When I saw you two come back from being outside, I realized it was more than a friendship. I told Tim that I met Kieran at the bar and asked if he was cool, you know. If he was a good man for you. I just thought you should know, in case you didn't. I don't mean to assume in asking Tim, but you don't seem the type to be with a cheater. I'm so sorry, love."

Her fear was realized.

Her over-medicated induced eyes weren't playing tricks on her at the hospital, she did see a ring on him that day. He had said nothing to her, he was leading her on. Something was always a little bit off, he so often looked like he was about to tell her something she didn't want to hear. Her mind reeled, out of control, rage building, her head started to shake then the rest her body followed

"Hey, are you okay?" Taryn said, she glanced over at Soshana, then back at the road.

Soshana couldn't speak just yet. She wasn't sure what to say anyway, feeling emotionally raw and bewildered by what her friend had just revealed. Soshana's phone vibrated in her hand. Kieran's name popped up.

I need to talk to you.

14

This Will Be the Last Time

You're married?! Why didn't you say? she texted him, punching the keys with accelerated fervor. She didn't think the oncoming conversation through and cared even less. Soshana was always the one to hold back her feelings to spare others, so they wouldn't get upset at her. Never again. Enough of the gaslighting, lying, being used, treating her like she was an object. The only way through this pattern of behavior was by her changing. Settling into her mind, she felt a shift in her body.

I need to change in order for my life to change.

Kieran called immediately after the text was sent. She rejected the call. She stared at the phone for several minutes, heart pounding, thinking of what else she would say, seeing if he would text or call again. Instead, a voicemail notification popped up.

Soshana broke the silence, nearly forgetting she was riding in a car with her friend.

"I'm processing what you said. I'm obviously pissed and confused. He didn't tell me. I knew something was off; he has been secretive about his past and only gave me a few details about his work." Soshana shook her head slowly, irritation obvious in her tone. "What the fuck, here I go again, just blindly trusting people and giving them the benefit of the doubt. I'm so tired of this happening. I'm fucking done with letting people get to me."

The lump in her throat was unbearable. She coughed out a sob then cried as quietly as she could.

"I'm s-s-sorry," she stuttered. "I had such a wonderful time the past few days with you and with-"She stopped before saying his name.

"I'm sorry too, love. It's hard, I mean, Tim said he's a great guy, known him for years. He seems like a genuine person. It's a kind of feeling you get when you first meet people, you know? I had a good feeling." Taryn sighed with remorse and pity.

Soshana kept a steady pace of streaming tears and shuddered sobs, sucking in air when her body reminded her to breathe. It amused her in a way, she wasn't necessarily crying just over Kieran, it was the betrayal, the same anger she had felt when Mina betrayed her. The many, many times her mother lied, the way her father left and cut himself out of her life. She was more than hurt, this cut her in a way she hadn't experienced before.

"I don't think I've ever liked someone so much, in that way. He saw me, understood me, the real me. And I chose to show him." She found a ratty old tissue in her purse to wipe away the liquids pouring from her face.

"Maybe he will have a valid explanation, if you feel like hearing him out. I wouldn't blame you if you didn't want to, though. There really isn't any excuse that would make up for that kind of behavior. If Sean did that, I would cut his dick off."

Soshana managed to laugh at that. "I think it was that dark-haired, wild-eyed woman. She was very thin, and her tone was sharp, unpleasant. Disturbingly attractive though. I saw the look on his face when she approached us at the dinner reception. He could have passed out from fright. She gave me a look that may have melted my face off," Soshana divulged with malice in her tone.

"Huh? Maybe I know her? She sounds awfully familiar. I know a shrill bitch when I see one." Taryn seemed a little too excited with all this gossip and drama. Soshana never had an interest in name calling or making accusations against someone she hadn't met or had the chance to get to know first, it wasn't fair. She felt extreme resentment when someone made assumptions about her without getting to know her. Still, she couldn't help but feel regret for kissing him and feel bad for his wife. Whoever she was, it didn't matter.

A hot coal was burning the lining of her stomach, vertigo pulling her head in circles. The corners of her lips started tingling, her mouth pooling with sticky saliva.

"PULL OVER!" Soshana yelled through clenched teeth, then covered her mouth as the vomit started to work its way upwards. Taryn did her best to weave through cars and pull onto the laneway. Some of the vomit did hit the door but not much before she spilled the contents of her stomach onto the gravel. She coughed up as much as she could while bent over, hands on knees, dry heaving and gasping for air between takes.

"You okay, honey? Do you need me to come out there?" All Taryn could see was her backside hunched over.

Soshana gave her a thumbs up before turning to the SUV. Taryn was at the ready with baby wipes, a bottle of water and some mints. The kind, doting mom. She wiped her mouth, swished water around, shuffling it through her teeth, then spilled out the rest on the gravel. She took several labored breaths as she sat back in the seat and buckled in. She laid her head back, closed her eyes and said, "My life is a goddamn shitshow, isn't it?"

Taryn smiled but didn't laugh. "Your life is your own, you just have to make do." She handed her the mints.

Soshana replied, "I'm grateful that you showed back up in my life," then popped a few winter mint flavored sweets in her mouth. Taryn reached for her hand and gave it a squeeze.

They stayed quiet for the rest of the trip, listening to a few different radio stations. Soshana fell asleep and woke up when her stomach ached, making her worry that she would vomit again. The surroundings became familiar after a few rounds of napping. Taryn pulled up to Soshana's apartment complex.

Soshana wasn't in the mood for a long recap of the past few days with a heartfelt goodbye. She just wanted to brush her teeth and crawl into bed with her cat and forget what happened over the past few days. It had drained her more than she wanted to admit.

"Thank you so much, for everything. I can't begin to tell you how much it meant." Soshana leaned over and gave Taryn a side hug.

"You are so welcome. I'm here, please let me know what happens. Go and rest though." Taryn rubbed her back and gave her a pitiful smile.

Soshana grabbed her items out of the trunk and headed towards the entrance. She turned to look at her friend, seeing her in a different light, differently than she had when they were kids. She was a beautiful woman, slightly neurotic, but funny, mature and loving. Soshana admired the woman she had become, wishing she could be better for her. They waved at each other, Taryn waited until Soshana was safely inside before she took off.

Soshana trudged up the stairs, letting herself into her small safe home. No one here hurt her. This was entirely her own, she decided who came in and what energy she brought into it. This was not a new feeling she was bringing in today, though. The feeling of being let down, lied to and used.

The apartment was more frigid than she remembered, she hoped that Mr. Skittles wasn't too cold, she found him curled up next to the radiator, he came running when he heard his name. Purring, chirping and meowing until she picked him up and nuzzled in his face. "Hi, buddy," she said.

She unpacked a few things and grabbed some Pepto-Bismol out of the refrigerator, shook it and took a swig.

She sat on the couch, feeling extreme exhaustion, sadness and anger boiling through her body. Her first instinct was to make a double vodka seltzer. That would help with the mental anguish, if just for a few hours. Then her stomach lurched. She swallowed the excess saliva and kept it down, for now. She thought about how her mother would drink after a hard day, it would always be worse on days where she was frustrated from work, or if one of them pissed her off or didn't do what they were told. Drinking wasn't the solution to revolving issues. She knew Ms. Erling would be disappointed if she gave in to a binge session.

She sat quietly with her feelings, paying attention to her breath, trying to meditate. Her eyes started burning, her breath shallowing, then crying, then loudly sobbing. She found her way to the floor and sobbed there in a fetal position until she started to feel something other than devastation.

Work was inevitable the very next day. Heartache, stomachache, headache or not. She still hadn't listened to Kieran's message and had ignored his text message after the voicemail. Part of her felt satisfied.

See how you like it, asshole.

Thinking of how he ghosted her, even though she knew it wasn't his fault.

Was he lying about that too?

Part of her wanted him to feel pain, the other part wanted to soothe and comfort him because she could feel the tension in the text. Getting through the workday was proving to be more difficult than she planned. She had hoped it would be a good distraction, but everyone wanted to know about her girls' trip, and Joe could always tell when something was off.

"I don't want to talk about it right now, but I promise I will later." Joe wasn't satisfied. "Thank you again for volunteering to watch Mr. Skittles, as always the place was in excellent shape." She forced a smile. He nodded in response.

She went home after picking up some groceries and grabbed a sandwich for dinner. She had a missed call and voicemail from Ms. Erling. She listened to it, she just wanted to check in and to call back when she could. It reminded her that she hadn't had an episode in quite a long time and even though yesterday was horrendous, even with the fatigue and the vomiting, no sort of funny vision or episode happened. Maybe she was getting better? Although it certainly didn't feel like it right now.

She got back into the routine of working and coming home, slowly feeling better each day, crying less. She told herself that she needed to practice trusting herself more, trusting her instincts and that not everyone is going to be her version of perfect. It helped her to say kind things to herself, about herself, instead of beating herself up over a guy. She couldn't take her mind off him for more than a few minutes. And with the next day being her day off with nothing to do, that was going to be a challenge. Even though she was feeling slightly better, she was beginning to get anxious about not responding. You can't get through life ignoring people and your emotions. It's not fair to those who care about you and want to be in your life. She wasn't convinced that Kieran kissed her just to get laid. Their connection had to mean something and ignoring it wasn't working. She was determined to have a lovely day off, so today she needed to do some work.

The voicemail waited with heaviness; it was time to let it loose. He sounded serious while pleading in a way that didn't sound desperate.

"Soshana, please understand, it was so difficult to figure out how to tell you. It was my intention to tell you as soon as possible, it never seemed like a good time. I was so afraid of you running away that I panicked. Yes, I'm sorry, I am technically married. I can't tell you the specifics at this time, please know that I really, really wanted to tell you. It's a complicated situation. We're currently separated, working out the logistics of the divorce. It's been hell, especially over the past few years. I want to tell you everything, but I have to wait until the divorce is final and I promise I will tell you everything you want to know. I have nothing to hide from you. Soshana, please. I…" His voice cracked; he cleared his throat. "I'm doing my best here. I'm asking for patience, if it's possible. Please call me."

It irked her that she enjoyed hearing his voice, and also hearing that he was going through a divorce. Her first thought was, *is it cheating if they are going through a divorce?* trying to justify their actions. It sounded like they might be headed towards the end of it. She bounced back and forth between being relieved but still upset that he hadn't been honest up front. The desire to call him came over her like the sun rising over snow capped mountains. She fought hard but gave up. Without thinking about it any further, she called him.

He didn't pick up; she didn't leave a message. She texted him and all she said was *Call when you have time.* Her heart was pounding, she needed to move her body, so she flitted around and cleaned her apartment to near godliness. The phone rang as she was washing the dishes. Heart pounding resumed, she dried her hands and swiped to take the call from Kieran.

"Hi," she said. It came out colder than she had intended.

"Hey, thank you for texting me back," he said, not matching her coldness.

"Is there anything else you want to tell me?" she said, standing her ground, reminding herself that she deserved more of an explanation.

He sighed into the phone. It sounded like he was outside, the wind was picking up through the microphone, crackling and hissing. She assumed he had gone outside to talk to her, away from someone potentially. She heard a car door open and close, the wind ceasing.

He sighed again. "Are you upset with me?"

Soshana didn't want to say anything.

"I'm assuming your silence means yes. You have every right. I'm an idiot. I can't begin to describe how mad I am at myself. I fucked this up. This amazing, intelligent, beautiful woman finally comes into my life and because I was scared. I get it. I wouldn't trust me either." The sound of a hand smacking a leg rang through the line.

Soshana kept her silence, tears burning, throat threatening a painful sob. She could tell by his tone that he wasn't finished.

Exasperated and with a quiet intensity, he continued. "I filed for a divorce within days of returning from the hospital. I couldn't take it anymore. She went insane. She is the worst person I have *ever* met in my life. She has to be a narcissist. She controlled my life. Everything has always been about her. Can you believe she was mad at me that I got cancer?! The attention was on me, which pissed her off. She was the slithering snake that came up to us at the reception. She knows about you. She found the note in my jacket pocket right before I took it to get dry cleaned. I told her that we were just roommates at the hospital and friends. She tried to use it against me and said I cheated. She threatened to take me to court to get something out of it. I peeled her off the ceiling and she backed down, for now. Somehow, she put two and two together and figured out that it was you at the realtors' reception. We have a deal in the divorce proceedings to pretend we're still married until it's final, and especially during work events. She's obsessed with image and appearances. She disgusts me. We sleep in separate bedrooms, I promise." The last sentence was thrown in with intent.

He was silent for a moment. "Soshana?"

She replied, "Continue. I'm listening."

He took a long deep breath in, signaling some relief.

"Soshana, I don't know how else to say this except I'm begging you to believe me. I know I crossed a line at the bar. My feelings for you are out of control. When you didn't respond I thought I'd lost you again. I don't know what else to say, and I can't say too much more about the details of the divorce without jeopardizing it. It fucking *kills* me that I can't tell you right now and I know how bad that sounds. All I can say is that I promise it's nothing bad. There are only a few weeks left and it's over."

Soshana took a few beats and a breath before she responded.

"I'd like to have some time to think." There was still a tinge of coldness in her tone. She didn't like this version of herself. She was always the one to comfort and coddle people. It didn't feel right, but she knew this was who she needed to become to protect herself and show herself respect.

"I understand. Thank you for listening to me," Kieran said flatly with some defeat.

"Okay. I'll talk to you later, then." Soshana hung up without waiting to hear him say goodbye. She felt strong and proud of herself. Her past self would have groveled, said "oh it's okay, I believe you." And then probably invited him over and had sex.

He respected her boundary, the invisible and unspoken one where she was in charge, she determined where this relationship would go. She wanted to be with him, he ran laps around her mind over the next few days. It didn't get better, but it got easier to deal with.

Eating, sleeping, exercising, daily routine items fell to the backburner again. The numbness fell over her mind and body again, routine became survival. She went to work, slapped on a fake smile only when she absolutely needed to, then it drained from her face at the first given opportunity. Soshana knew her moods better than most, she knew she would eventually move on from this, though her chest still ached every day. She didn't call Ms. Erling back, she didn't see the point, there wasn't much to tell. Dr. Linds had also fallen out of touch as well. She was surprised she hadn't had an episode given the whirlwind of emotions over the past few weeks. Some days the ache from the fall would sting in her back, feel sore in her neck and unusual headaches caused panic. She hadn't had an episode in a while, maybe they were gone. Maybe they weren't real in the first place.

Taryn had been MIA until Soshana received a text. *WE NEED TO GET TOGETHER ASAP! COFFEE?! WHEN?!?!* Even with the unnecessary drama, this had to be good news and worth showering for.

She met up with Taryn at the usual cafe that afternoon. They discussed the phone conversation first. Taryn had that excited look on her face when she had a bit of juicy information she couldn't wait to unleash. She interrupted a few times, bouncing out of her chair, unable to hold back the information she learned. Barry the barista was making it clear that he was listening to the soon-to-be-spilled gossip by hanging around their table and "cleaning."

When it was finally her turn to speak, she could have powered a city block with the amount of enthusiasm.

"Okay, *so!* I dug deep into this whole scenario, the marriage, his wife, his background, *everything.* You have to keep this quiet, because it could get him into trouble, but…" She leaned in, palms on the table and whispered, "…it's most likely a green card marriage. They have been 'technically' married for about six years. I know exactly who she is, I've met her a few times. She is one cold son-of-a-bitch. Ruthless. She is one of the top realtors in Detroit. I could almost admire her. They met at work, he was about to be shipped back to Canada and she had eyes for him for a while, I guess. She proposed to *him!* He agreed but said it was a platonic marriage, only for convenience until he could get citizenship. Well, *that* never happened. I don't know much more, but obviously it isn't working. Tim found out yesterday that they are going through a divorce!" She opened her arms wide and smiled with her entire face. "This is GOOD NEWS! Why aren't you happy? You look... actually, I can't get a reading off you." She laughed. "You're like a marble statue sometimes. What are you feeling right now?"

Thrown around, like a baseball between kids in mid-summer with nothing else to do. No one stopped to notice if the ball was splitting at the seams, torn and frayed. What did it matter at this point how she felt? No wonder he couldn't say anything. This was an agreement with severe consequences, he could get kicked out of the country, fined and jailed, they both could.

"I had no idea. How the hell did you figure that out? He wouldn't tell me, he said it was serious and that there was no way he could tell me or anyone." Soshana felt relief as weight lifted from her burdened body. How miserable he must feel. Maybe his admiration for her was authentic, and maybe he was telling the truth.

"Tim said he just made a wild guess and then we both dug into the wild west of the internet. He knew Kieran was from Canada and that his work visa was expiring. Then all of a sudden he married this woman, after only 'dating for a few months.' He said, 'no one in their right mind would marry that woman, and especially only knowing her for a few months. She's a banshee' and then laughed."

"So, there's no definitive proof," Soshana said with not an inch of hope left in her heart.

"No, technically not, but it's a hunch, and I gotta tell you, Tim is a talented sleuth. I believe him," Taryn said definitively. She had known Tim since they were in grade school, she trusted him with her life. How can people trust like that? So convinced in their belief in others, there had to be a flaw in these people. Thinking this way was a trap, one she had fallen into repeatedly.

Soshana nodded her head, her mind was elsewhere. It had been several weeks since their last conversation. That meant their divorce must have gone through. Chest burning, heartbeat quickening, she wanted to squash the joy rising in her body that she just couldn't control. She hadn't texted or called him since she told him she needed to think about it. She was proud of the way she was finding ways to respect what her body was trying to tell her, upset that her anxiety still ruled in many ways.

It was early afternoon when she returned home from meeting with Taryn. The sun was shining in the bitter cold of late February, it typically gave locals a jolt of energy. She was in desperate need of maintenance: her fingernails had grown and splintered, the ends of her hair were crispy and raggedy, legs could pass for a wooly mammoth. The tightness in her joints screamed when she bent over to pick up the shampoo bottle from the base of the shower, then a crashing wave of vertigo caused extreme nausea as she stood up.

"Well fuck," she said out loud. She braced herself in the shower and did whatever she could to rinse off then stumble to the toilet. The sensation waned.

Disappointed, she wrapped herself in an old gray robe and fell into bed. She waited for the dark human-like creature to show itself. It was high time it returned. Twenty minutes passed, the only shadows she saw were Mr. Skittles bathing himself by the window and a passing cloud in the sky that reflected off her sheer curtains.

Weariness settled over her shoulders, tightening them. The vertigo was slowly returning to steadiness, her stomach grumbled in warning of hunger. She hadn't gone to the store for fresh food in a while. She had eaten horribly over the past few weeks and this was her punishment. She kept fighting with her internal monologue on what she should do. She didn't want to seem desperate; she wanted to be seen as strong when she knew damn well she was at a weak point.

"Me, first. I need to take care of myself first. This is what all the doctors are telling me, and I left myself behind. Again." she said aloud, pretending to talk to someone, anyone who would listen.

She got up, dressed in comfortable clothes and went into the kitchen to make a cup of peppermint and ginger tea. Sipping it tenderly, she started writing to-do lists, which calmed her frantic mind, practiced somatic breathing and gently stretched her aching joints. She had been laying and sitting for too long. This was a good start. As she wrote and contemplated, she became aware of the slightest barometric shift from behind her in the living room.

The hairs on the back of her neck and spine tingled, awakened with warming. She knew she wasn't alone in her apartment.

15

Dimensional

Violently shaking, she screamed, "WHO'S THERE?!" while still facing away from the living area. No response, no feet shuffling, no breathing, nothing. She allowed herself to take a few quick breaths in. Once the oxygen went to her brain, she remembered she had knives. She dove for the closest and largest kitchen knife and spun around; arm extended in the direction of her front door.

There, in the corner of her living room, next to the couch was the shadow. Taking it in, sizing it up as quickly and calculating as possible, she let out a scream and dropped the knife. The shadow was standing, shoulders rounded, head bowed. Taking another moment to assess, preparing for the inevitable pull towards the darkened figure, Soshana noticed it looked like it could be breathing, or rather... pulsing. The shadow was not black or misty gray, it was a thousand shimmering colors that surrounded the figure, pulling in towards the center torso, pulling out and circulating a kind of darkness that couldn't be described. It was hypnotizing and devastatingly beautiful.

Nothing happened. It didn't move. Soshana didn't move. Remembering that each time she moved away the shadow pulled her in like gravity, there was no escape. Courage built slowly as they seemingly stared at each other. Soshana kept her eyes on the figure as she bent down at the knees to pick up the knife that had just missed her bare feet. This time, she took a small step forward. Her eyes widened with each step. The figure stayed in place, but the scintillating colors sped up, it being swallowed into the blackness of its body even faster. Soshana stopped, assessed, then proceeded again, knife at the ready. One step further and the figure vanished instantly.

The light flickered back into the living room, the chill in the air dissipated. Soshana stayed locked and frozen in place until Mr. Skittles let out a loud low growl. It startled Soshana out of her daze. Mr. Skittles never growled or hissed.

"So you saw it too!" she said, feeling silly for even thinking to exclaim out loud to a feline. She had convinced herself that she must be insane. Tears of relief ran down her face as she began to unwind from the event.

She sat, eyes still wide, still on high alert, and took a sip of her tea. She wrinkled her nose on discovering it had gone ice cold. She shook her head in spite of herself, wielding a knife to a ghost. She called Ms. Erling as she had promised every time she had an episode.

She picked up after a few rings. "I'm so glad to hear from you, it's been a while. What's happening." *Right into it*, Soshana thought, *as usual.*

She explained that she had been doing well, discussing a few highlights about what had happened during the realtor convention with Taryn and how she ran into Kieran.

"I felt something more than numbness. It was like waking

239

up from a decade of sleeping. I thought to myself, 'this is what it feels like to be alive.' Then it all changed so quickly. I thought the dark shadows had left until just now."

She explained how instead of resisting it, she stood her ground and moved towards it. There was no pull or epileptic type episode.

"Fascinating. Fascinating! It sounds like a singular event. Have you tried to move towards it before?" Ms. Erling sounded more enthusiastic than ever before.

"Well, no. I was scared. This time I thought, what do I have to lose? Plus, I had a knife so, you know. I would have stabbed the air, but it gave me some confidence at least." Soshana managed to drum up a smile, thinking of how stupid she would have looked.

"I'm so proud of you, Soshana. You stood up for yourself with Kieran, and now standing up to the misty figure and abandoning your fear." Ms. Erling paused.

She was *proud* of her and Soshana believed her when she said it.

"I need you to do something for me, I think this is a breakthrough, truly. I need you to continue to take care of yourself as you have been, and next time try talking gently to the figure, and keep stepping forward towards it, but slowly, and *without* a weapon. Be careful. Listen to the signals your body is giving you. If you feel it's unsafe, try finding a safe and comfortable position, close your eyes and breathe through it. How does that sound?" Ms. Erling said in a motherly kind tone, very much unlike her own mother.

"I think that's a great idea. I'll try it. Ms. Erling, you must think I am insane. Right?" Soshana agreed. What *did* she have to lose at this point?

"Insane? Not a chance. Mentally disturbed? Perhaps." Ms. Erling let out a quick laugh to provide ease. "I'll reach out to Dr. Linds and give him an update, if that is fine with you. I think it would be wise if you rested for the remainder of the day. Is there anything else you remember or want to talk about?" Ms. Erling replied.

Soshana thought about telling her more about the situation with Kieran. How she felt like her heart had broken and that things had come to light. She pursued it further with Ms. Erling.

"Reach out to him, Soshana. Be kind to yourself, find compassion for him. Yes, what he did was wrong but there's always another side to the story. Good luck. Rest now."

Soshana didn't like needing reassurance or permission to do anything. She was a goddamn adult, she had been taking care of herself since she was in high school, possibly before then. No one was going to tell her what to do anymore. Unless she needed to pay rent, taxes and bills of course.

Phone in hand, she began to type out a greeting to Kieran, like she had over a hundred times over the past few weeks then deleted. Perhaps he was already staring at his phone and saw the (. . .) 'typing' message that pops up. She started with, *How are you doing?* then erased it. *Can we talk?* Then erased that. She slapped her forehead with the palm of her hand several times to try and awaken her thoughts.

She added *I'm sorry it has taken me a while to respond* then pressed send.

Waiting, eyes unmoving from his name, did she think he would respond instantly? She put her phone down and turned on the TV to distract her buzzing mind. Every two to three minutes she checked her phone for a response. Nothing yet. Frustrated with the obsessive thoughts, she turned her phone on silent and tossed it into the pile of clothes on the floor. She couldn't pay attention to the TV show. Spunky and empowered, she ate a small snack and proceeded to resume her self-care: lighting a candle, turning on mellow spa-type music and letting go of all expectations. She pushed away the thought of him hating her for ignoring him for over two weeks. She replaced it with realistic thoughts of *he's busy, he's at work. It's okay.* She got through most of her to-do list and started the laundry while cleaning her kitchen. She grabbed the phone off the pile of clothes and saw two missed calls and a text from Kieran. Her cheeks flushed as she looked at the text.

Can we get together, please? I have to tell you something in person. I can drive to you.

Soshana wasn't expecting such a fast response and him wanting to get together so soon. Though it was recommended she should rest, she felt it was safe to see him. She had started to let him go, but this was now going to be difficult if he was near and in her space. She looked around her room and swallowed, anxious. They could meet somewhere public, maybe even halfway.

Okay. I'm off today. Do you want to meet in Lansing? That way it's halfway.

Yes. When can you leave? I can start to drive in about an hour. We can meet at the Blue Owl Cafe off 496.

Okay, I'll see you around five? Does that sound right? Soshana calculated the driving time versus the meeting time.

Yes, that works. Thank you so much, Soshana, Kieran texted back.

She changed out of her pajamas, touched up her hair and

applied a little bit of makeup, deciding it was appropriate that she wanted to look nice for him, and for herself. She had felt like shit since they left Detroit. Her heart started racing as she began to leave. How is it possible she hasn't passed away from all the anxiety and heart palpitations? People die of heart attacks in their thirties, it wasn't unheard of.

I don't want to die right now.

I don't want to die?

Pausing at the thought, she realized this was the first time in years she had wanted to be alive. Just in this particular moment. This was a type of joy, she thought. She was going to see him again. This person she now felt was as much of a ghost as her dark shadow. The comparison between the two was startlingly different. One gave her a reason to live, the other had her begging for death.

The sunset was arresting, as striking as they can be at that time of the year. Hot pink and deep rich purple stripes set against a dark blue sky, stars blinking into view. The colors were brighter, more eye-catching than she had remembered they could be. When was the last time she watched a sunset? A calmness from her past sat with her. Such an odd sensation that moments from a traumatic past could have a calming effect in your present. Trying to figure out when or how those moments happened is a losing game. She accepted the feeling and enjoyed whatever it was. Most people would make the excuse of being too busy, distracted by the routine of life. It's easy enough to find a place to pull over and park on the side of the road and spend no more than ten minutes. There's no excuse worth missing being present.

She pulled into the parking lot of the cafe and saw him through the illuminated window, elbows on the table, checking his phone. She sat there for a couple of minutes; she was early anyway. This helped her relax her relentless heart and allowed her to look at him without having to think or speak. Even at a distance, watching him unencumbered by distractions was insightful. Who is he when no one is watching? She noticed his body language with the waiter. Respectful, attentive. This gave her no reason to believe he was deceiving her. She watched as he looked at the parking lot, then looked at his phone. It was time to go in.

He watched her with anxious eyes as she settled in the chair across from him. She could see that his leg was shaking. She ached to comfort him, to relieve his worry. *Me, first.* She reminded herself.

"Hi, Kieran." Soshana spoke first, it was apparent he wanted her to be in control of this meeting. He huffed out a relieved sigh and returned the greeting.

He looked down at his phone and while putting it in his coat pocket, he said, "Thank you for meeting me here." The shaking began to slow.

"How- how have you been?" Soshana hesitated, uncertain how to start this sure to be uncomfortable conversation. She looked away from him, rubbing her hands together in order to provide some comfort to herself.

His eyes were tinged with bloodshot redness. He looked disheveled, worn out. The scruff on his face told her he hadn't shaved in a few days. Drained, but still handsome.

He let out a miserable low cough disguised as a laugh. "Awful." He looked away from her. The headlights of cars outside shined into the restaurant windows, showcasing the splayed sunburst of wrinkles around his eyes. He caught his breath. "I'm so sorry. I'm so, *so* sorry."

Soshana reached out her hand and held his, then squeezed. "It's going to be all right." She didn't want to mislead him; she believed that whatever happened would be okay. There's not much anyone can do in times of crisis, other than remember to breathe.

He pinched the top of his nose then wiped his eyes. He nodded and proceeded in a deadly serious, low voice. "It's done. It's over. We're divorced. It was hell but I wouldn't change the nightmare I went through if it meant I got to see you one last time."

Soshana was taken aback, her face dropped. "What do you mean, one last time?"

He said quietly and sharply, "I can still get into trouble but I owe it to you. It was a marriage of convenience. A green card marriage. I'm from Sudbury, Canada. Six years ago, my work visa was about to expire so we came to an agreement. We pretended to date, then after a few months we got married in a small ceremony at the courthouse. We convinced our family and friends it was real, we played 'house.' Moved in together, kissed and held hands at public gatherings. I was scared to death the entire time. She told me she had fallen in love; she convinced me that I was in love too. Over the last year I felt nothing but contempt. It wasn't worth the pain I was going through. She blackmailed me, called me a cheater, convinced her friends I was a liar and a piece of shit. All because I would rather get deported than stay married to her. Then the cancer, then you. It was all too much. I didn't think I was going to make it. Until you. *You goddamn beautiful thing*. You created such a mess for me and I can't help but feel grateful. You gave me my life back. And now I have to go. I have to go back to Canada. I have until tomorrow night before I run the risk of getting arrested, it's unlikely but I prefer to be cautious. My work visa expired and the only thing that was keeping me legally bound in the country was our marriage."

Soshana pulled her hand away from his and leaned back in her chair. She promised herself she would stay focused, composed. She held her hand to her forehead and closed her eyes.

His foot reverberated waves in the flooring that reached her senses. She took a deep breath and looked at him. "What are you going to do?" she asked gently.

He shook his head and huffed out an incredulous laugh. "I don't know what to do."

Soshana then asked, "Where will you go?"

"I'll stay at my brothers' for a while. I'll need to find a job there."

His breathing quickened. "I don't want to leave. What I mean is, I don't want to leave *you.*" He pressed his left thumb deep into his right palm, twisting and digging into the tendons.

There's nothing Soshana could do to help him with this scenario. All they had was tonight, and she didn't want him to leave either. "Do you want to go out to dinner with me?" She asked with a kind smile.

He laughed out a sigh with a wonderful smile. "I would love nothing more than to spend every single second with you until I can't," he said, studying her face.

They hugged for a few minutes outside and shared a brief kiss, only after he asked if it was okay. She just smiled at him, which was answer enough.

Her chest started to tighten at the thought.

Until I can't, she repeated on their way to a restaurant close by, in his car.

It was a local mom and pop, nothing extraordinary or romantic. They each ordered a beer. He reached out from across the table in a silent request to hold her hand, an act of familiarity. The paper napkin, the utensils, the plastic cup of water, his hand. A comfortable unease. An instinctive feeling of being safe, the mind battling against the body. She took the hand easily and smiled at him.

"Is there a possible universe or other dimension where you can find the will to forgive me? I know I don't deserve it. I betrayed you and I brushed over the truth. I can't say how sorry—"

Soshana cut him off by holding up a hand and nodding her head slowly, showing her understanding. "I don't want to be mad at you. I was, though. Disappointed, hurt. I will not allow myself to be treated like that, not anymore. I have to treat myself with compassion and I don't deserve to be lied to. This is all new for me, standing up for myself. It's entirely possible that I might cause hurt and disappointment with my actions too," Soshana said firmly, though her voice wavered towards the end.

He nodded, teeth clenched, jaw flexing. She watched him, getting a sense he was becoming mad, though she had to remember it was not at her or because of her.

"However..." She trailed off purposefully to watch his face change as she continued. "...I do forgive you. I'm sorry you went through all that. I had every instinct in my body telling me to trust you and then it was betrayed. Please know that I never gave up on you and I want to try to figure this out. Whatever this is."

He smiled, his hand tightening on hers, he placed his other hand on top and pulled it close to kiss the back of her hand in a sweet gesture.

They ordered and ate; they talked about where he came from. Kieran showing eagerness to discuss his past, his family, including older brother, Abrams, and his ex-sister-in-law. How he hadn't seen them since before he gave them the news of the cancer diagnosis. "They have a daughter, his six-year-old niece who's a firecracker at her worst. At her best she is adorable, endearing, and wiser than me some days."

As they got closer to finishing their meal, nerves began to build, she could see it in his demeanor. They ate slower, easily flowing through conversations, laughing and getting back to the comfort they once had in the hospital.

She needed to make a decision, to not think, but act.

"Do you want to stay at my place… tonight?" The thought of not seeing him again surpassed the nervousness.

He rubbed the back of his neck and said with hesitation, "Sure, I mean, if you're comfortable with that."

She nodded and said with a sweet smile, "No expectations, I just want to spend as much time with you, too. Before tomorrow, you know?" Saying there were no expectations caused great relief between the two of them, it showed in relaxed shoulders.

He nodded with more confidence. "Okay. I can follow you back home." The color returned to his face. His handsome face, genial smile, and kind eyes. No wonder his wife, now ex-wife, fell in love with him. How could you not? He paid the bill and they left.

The drive back to her apartment was excruciatingly slow, and simultaneously too fast. Speeding up as they approached her apartment. Uncomprehending every action made without thinking, she knew she wasn't ready to take things to a new level with Kieran. Yet she had an insatiable urge to be near him, link her arm with his, look into his doe-like eyes. They had such an effect, so much that it made her hesitate and question if she even knew herself properly. The sensations that encompassed her body from the thought she would be near him caused her to shake uncontrollably. Though, when he finally was near enough, when she was with him, her body released tension. A soothing, healing balm that coated her insides. It was insane. She didn't like it. And she needed it.

They arrived; he parked in the guest spot near her car port. Soshana surveyed the windows to see who was home, she knew some of her neighbors were busybodies, rubbernecking to get the gossip on anyone in the neighborhood. "Did you hear about Justine's boy? He was caught with that dope stuff, you know, I think they call it Milly."

"No, no, no, it's called Molly!"

Soshana would overhear the two older women on the bottom floor cackling over someone's misfortunes, or someone else's business. The subject of someone else's hot tea. She could hear the rumors swirling and in a nasally mid-western tone she imagined, "Soshana came in late with a strange man!"

They walked up the stairs as silently as possible, which was deemed impossible when the old wooden stairs creaked and whined beneath their feet.

Soshana opened the door, flicked on the lights and pushed through, not looking back at Kieran, wondering if she made a smart choice.

Kieran immediately put his things down and called out for Mr. Skittles.

"He's a bit shy with new people," Soshana explained.

Soshana, feeling vulnerable, looked around at the areas of

her apartment she had neglected, and the dark corner where the shadow had appeared earlier. No ghost or specter in sight.

"Do you want something to drink, coffee, tea…"

"Whiskey?" he asked.

"Sorry, no whiskey. I have a bottle of Petite Syrah?"

"Perfect."

She did a once over of her face in the bathroom, wiped the excess makeup from underneath her eyes and took a beat to ground herself. Constantly analyzing and trying to understand what another person is thinking and feeling, then responding in a way so there is no misunderstanding would wear anyone down. If she could only just fucking stop it. Stop caring, stop worrying, over thinking.

She came out of the bathroom and went straight to the kitchen and opened the wine. Kieran had found Mr. Skittles who had warmed up to him.

"Here you go." Soshana handed him his wine.

He sipped his drink and let out an approving "mmm" sound.

They smiled gingerly at each other then looked away. The only sounds were tenants scuffling in their areas and the wind pushing through the trees.

The silence between them was heavy, laced with unease. Soshana turned some generic radio station on and leaned back into the couch, sitting one seat away from him.

"What do you want to talk about?" Kieran said.

Soshana frowned and looked straight ahead instead of at him, even though she wanted to. "I don't know how to move forward." She paused. "Or backwards, or side to side, up or down, left or right. I don't know what to do with my life."

He took another sip and nodded his head. "I feel the same. What the hell am I doing?"

They finally looked at each other and smiled, they hadn't since the restaurant. She was locked in. She searched her body and mind for any indication of discomfort, unease or fear. Nothing. She prided herself on being able to sense danger in people. Instead of feeling safe, she was disappointed that she couldn't feel any warning signs.

Tuck it away, save it for later. Don't be rude.

Soshana changed her position on the couch, uncrossed her legs and leaned forward to help shift the anger rising in her body. She had no reason to be mad at him anymore.

"Tell me how you see your future. Where do you want to be, what do you want to do?" she asked sweetly.

A stoic look fell over his features. Digging deeper into his private life was part of the deal if he was going to be in her private space. She could tell he had a hard time revealing any kind of weakness, though he admittingly declared to her several times that she had the ability to bring it out of him.

"I just want to be content. I don't reach for happiness anymore. It's too far away and seems impossible to find. I don't know what that should be like. Society seems to think that when you're in your thirties and forties you're supposed to have it all together. What a joke. Everything is falling apart and I feel mentally broken."

I know exactly how you feel.

It's too close. The dam would break. She would break. Not in front of him.

He continued, "I'm really grateful for my brother. He's a good guy. I'll admit I'm looking forward to playing princess and dragons with my niece." He grinned genuinely.

Soshana smiled with him. What she would give to see him with his niece. She wished she could have something so dear to her, something that could bring her that kind of effortless joy. She wouldn't allow it, though, anyway. Who was she without her anxiety, pain and discomfort? These thoughts were unwelcome and blurring her vision. She took a large sip of her wine and returned to the scene in front of her.

"He sounds like a great guy and your niece sounds like a lot of fun," she said robotically.

"Will you visit me? It's a long drive from here... I know that's asking a lot. I mean, I would come and visit you but I won't be allowed back into the country until the paperwork's documented and everything's in place. I mean, of course if you want to..." He trailed off, looking less hopeful as the sentence concluded.

"I don't know, maybe." Soshana wanted to say more, she wanted to say how much she enjoyed being with him, how she adored him.

I would ruin his life with my issues, my pessimism. He doesn't deserve that.

He nodded then finished the wine.

They sat for another uncomfortable moment until Kieran stood up and headed for the kitchen to pour another glass of wine. He stood there for a moment then turned to face Soshana.

"Why did you invite me back here? It seems to me like you think you made a mistake."

"No! No not at all. I- She got up and walked over to him, stubbing her toe on the coffee table in the process. "Shit!" she said, leaning over to grasp her toe. Kieran immediately responded by grabbing a towel and some ice. He corralled her back to the couch and sat next to her, quite close. He held the towel out towards her foot, she went to grab it and he pulled away.

"Can you let someone help you for once?" he said with a smirk.

She stared at him, anger boiling back up, spilling over this time.

She grabbed the towel and ice out of his hand and put it on her foot. The anger came out hot and fast. "I don't need anyone's help. I don't know why I asked you here. I think I did it out of fear. I don't want to lose you. I also want you to go. I'm too fucked up to try to figure out if I want to have some sort of a relationship with you. I don't understand why I'm this way and I'm *scared.* I'm scared out of my mind and I am drowning in it." Soshana's eyes poured out hot tears. A sob let itself loose then another until she caught her breath. She felt like throwing up. How could she let herself be seen like this? Waves of shame flooded over her.

"I'm so sorry. I'm sorry. I'm not mad at you, I promise. I'm mad at myself."

Kieran carefully put one hand on her shoulder, she twitched so he pulled it away then slowly placed it back. "Thank you for telling me that. Though I'm not entirely convinced you aren't upset with me. I wish we could start over, go back to the day we met, and I would do things differently."

She looked at him, face covered in wetness and dread. "We can't go back there. We're here now, this is all we have, right now."

His gaze softened as his shoulders lowered. "Will you let me be with you, then? Can you be present with me? There are so many times I see you leave me, even when you're right in front of me, looking at me." He swallowed hard. He is treading on dangerous ground, telling her who she is and how she acts.

No one gets to tell her who she is.

He continued carefully, "You won't let me see you sometimes. I saw glimpses at the hospital, though you kept yourself far away. I want to know you, I want you to understand me and if anything, *trust* that I'm not going to ever knowingly hurt you. There are times when it seems like you just don't want to try. I get it, everything I went through with my wi- ex-wife."

"No, I don't think you get it." She said, looking at her clasped hands. His face turned from understanding empathy to confusion. She continued, "the pain and trauma that comes from a parent is completely different than when it comes from a partner or spouse. I'm not undermining what you went through with her, please understand. It's just different. It's deep-seeded, ingrained. It's in the very fiber of my everyday life, threaded through every thought, every decision. Every waking hour. It's hard to overcome, if it's even possible. This is what I am talking about. I don't have the ability to discern between your kindness and my inability to decipher if you're trying to take advantage of me. Or guilt trip me."

"Is that how I make you feel? Like I am trying to coerce you into doing something you don't want to do? Like I'm some sort of asshole who only cares about… about what? Getting laid? Using you then leaving you?" His upset now turned into anger, his frustration with his ex-wife showing its bruised and beaten face and reflecting on his own.

Soshana scooted a half seat away from him, his anger felt too close, she felt it on her skin and deep in her chest. This was comforting, strangely enough. If someone was mad at her, at least they were feeling something, and it was true. Anger was always, always truthful. Love was cunning, used for manipulation. Anger was the only acceptable emotion in her childhood so it felt real.

This interaction was turning cold, bitter and unbearable as the seconds passed. His disdain wasn't what she had expected although he had shown his moodier side at the hospital. Heat rose and fell in waves in her body. She didn't want this to be a fight, she wasn't sure how she would handle it, if she would fly into a rage like her mother used to. Her breathing became erratic and uneven. She turned her body slightly and moved far enough away from him so she couldn't feel his heat. She was shutting down and tuning out, the disassociation now crawling through her blood. Not unlike what happened when Marilyn screamed at her when she was a child. Soshana was eleven again. Scared, hurt, misunderstood.

"Damn it, I fucked up again. I'm sorry," he said in a hushed tone. Eyes closed, hands covering his face, elbows on his knees. He took a few labored breaths and let the last one out like a gust of wind.

She knew she needed to say something to defuse the tension.

Softly she said, "It's not your fault. I have a lot to work on. This is what I'm trying to tell you, I will most likely hurt you because I am hurt. I'm damaged, no one wants this." She gestured over her body, sweeping her open hands from her head down to her feet. She stifled another sob. Feeling her own words and admitting them out loud were two very different actions. Proclaiming the known is damning, foundational. It makes it real.

Soshana got up and went to the bathroom to blow the snot out of her nose. She dared to look at her hideous, monstrous face. The face of the bitch that was now dead and currently ruining her life. Her lip snarled, then pouted.

There you are, you dumb little girl.

She spat at the mirror, looking directly into her eyes. "Fuck you," she whispered. Breathing heavy and slowly, chest aching, her eyes burning and leaking, she closed them and sniffed. She couldn't leave him out there for too long, the fear of him leaving right now was too much for her to bear.

She kept her eyes down and her face solemn as she walked back to the couch and sat closer to him. She took another breath, hopefully signaling to him that she was 'okay,' whatever the fuck that looked like right now.

"Please look at me," Kieran begged, his voice cracking.

The pain in his face caused her to suck in a breath, gooseflesh rippling through her back, arm and legs.

"You are worth loving, Soshana. You are loved, I know you are. What could you have possibly done in this life to deserve to feel like you are less than?" He confidently laid his hand on her knee.

She had nowhere to run, no excuses or insults to hurl at herself at this moment. She hated herself for constantly doubting him, his feelings. How dare she do that when she hated when others did it to her. She immediately clasped her arms around him, hugging him tightly and breathing into his neck. He adjusted his position so he could hold her closer, breathing into her hair and rubbing her back.

"Please try. I want you to believe how much people care about you. I know you think it's difficult, but it's everywhere and in front of you. Please try for me if you can't do it for yourself right now." His voice was mellifluous, honeyed with care.

They hugged until they both stopped shaking. They each took necessary healing deep breaths, then letting out a soft sigh when they broke apart.

"Thank you. I will try harder. For you," she said, smiling at him, sniffing, dabbing her nose on her sleeve and wiping the mascara from under her eyes.

"But most importantly, eventually, for yourself. At the end of the day, *we* are all we have. It's just an extra bonus if there are others in our lives that have our back." He smirked. "Let's not worry about the future right now. Can we watch something pleasant?" He nodded his head towards the TV.

"Yes, please," she said with a grateful smile. They sat back and watched *Somebody Feed Phil*. Partway through a few episodes, another glass of wine, some cheese and crackers later, they fell asleep holding hands and leaning into each other.

Soshana woke several hours later, neck tight and back aching. Kieran was sleeping soundly until she moved. She drank some water, mouth parched and sour from the wine and crawled into bed where Mr. Skittles had waited for her all night. "Sorry, little man. I'm here now."

She fell asleep within seconds.

Falling fast, gravity pulling her hard for what felt like hours, she could hear her breathing echoing through a tunnel that smelled of rotting earth. The tang of the filthy walls snuck into her nostrils. Every so often her elbow or knee would scrape against the stone wall. No sound came from her mouth when she tried to scream. The walls of the tunnel opened at some point and in the vast blackness, her body plunged into a temperate liquid. Unable to sense the depth, the viscosity of the liquid or the temperature and it being so dark, she couldn't tell which way was up, which direction was air.

She gulped the liquid, flailed her arms and legs until buoyancy pulled her to the surface. Coughing and spluttering, gasping for air, she was finally able to scream for help. For the entirety of falling, she couldn't tell the difference between her eyes being shut or open. She found the will to peel them open to see if there was any sign of light, land or surfaces. There was light, but it was coming from the liquid. It swirled in streams of an indescribable amount of small fuzzy dots, opalescent and *alive?* She thought of natural bioluminescence. This wasn't an ocean though, it had a musty smell, ancient and primordial. Through the ripples and rolls, a reflection of colors started to form in the outer edges of the darkness. Catching her breath, she waded in the lukewarm waters. Instinctively, her senses forced her to turn her head upwards.

When her eyes connected with what she assumed was the night-time sky, a sense of connectedness and belonging infiltrated her dazed mind. Immediately following this recognition, infinitesimal bolts of light poured out from her eyes, mouth, nostrils and pores in an unfathomable amount of brilliant swirling colors in the shape of clouds, smoke and sand in all directions. At the very center of the unfolding of her vision was an old sycamore tree. It was familiar and had reminded her of deep longing and love. The ripples of undulating colors quickened back down towards the liquid she was wading in, that's when the tree began bending from hurricane-like winds. Its' limbs were being tossed in several directions, fresh leaves peeled themselves from the branches. The tree rooted firm and she thought of the strength it took to survive a storm. Overawed by the events unraveling before her, she had forgotten there was no sound until a high-pitched whistle formed, growing louder. Each moment that passed released a cacophony of whistles and whines, tree branches snapping and cracking, tires screeching, glass breaking, people screaming. The intensity of the sounds caused unequivocal fear and exhilaration, her body vibrating and shaking from the built-up endorphins, she couldn't contain herself any longer. Her eyes wide, mouth agape, the brilliant colors, shimmering and bright both enveloped her and excreted from every fissure.

She felt a light tapping on her shoulder and saw a faint blue light through her closed eyelids.

"Soshana, are you all right?" Kieran said in a whisper.

Soshana was halfway between the dream and her own world, unsure which was real. The whiplash of terror of falling through darkness, then the pure ecstasy of the water and colors were enough to question reality.

She pulled herself up, taking notice of every movement, every sensation. Her emotions felt categorized, not frantic. At least for one moment, until she realized this was it, this was when she had to say goodbye to Kieran. It was five in the morning.

He was ready, too. She hadn't prepared herself for it. She felt it in her gut, deep in her chest, a lachrymose aching that was there when she left him to return home from the hospital.

"I have to leave soon," he said, not looking at her.

"Okay, give me a few minutes," she said quickly. He left the room and she got up, still reeling from the dream, absolutely unsure what to think about it. There was a haunting familiarity to it.

She brushed her teeth, combed her hair and pulled it up into a ponytail, all while avoiding looking at herself directly in the mirror.

He was sitting on the couch, right leg bouncing quickly, hands clasped, elbows on his legs. He looked beat up. When he saw her come out of the bedroom he leapt up and walked directly to her and held her tightly. She indulged in his warmness, breathing him in, taking in his scent as if it were life giving.

He kissed her on the cheek and whispered into her ear, "Please don't forget me. You will never leave my thoughts, no matter where life takes us."

You would be able to hear his heart pounding if you were across the room. The only thing that she could think was *I don't think I could forget you even if I had a lobotomy*. She kissed him gently on the lips, knowing it wasn't a good idea, but it was the first and last thing she wanted from him.

He looked at her through the darkness and shadows of the room. His chest moved wearily with each breath, her body was too controlled and steady. He looked like he wanted to say something more as he searched her face for a clue, a weakness, a crack in the stone. She couldn't move, couldn't speak. If she did, she would break.

He nodded, gave her a weak smile and left.

16

Unraveling

Going through the motions, getting through the day and getting through life was what Soshana knew best. She was great at it. She could 'feign it 'til you reign it.' That was her motto, she lived by that turn of phrase. She could have invented it. Fakery can only get you so far, though. It is a butter-cream frosted shit cake. It's the filters on apps, the lies we tell others and ourselves every day. Fakery is a weight that adds up slowly over time, so imperceptible, until one day it is a sword too heavy to wield and you give up your power.

You then have several options in order to 'clean it up.'

- Option one, change your name, move out of the country.
- Option two, tell the truth. Deal with the consequences.
- Option three, kill yourself.

The heaviness of faking it showed in obvious places. Lack of an appetite, in opposition a voracious appetite for wine and bourbon. She began to throw up again. Severe stomach pain that came in waves. She ceased exercising. Lying in bed, scrolling mindlessly through her apps when not at work. All her books, read and unread, were collecting dust and untouched. She couldn't bring herself to respond to texts unless they were about work. Calling in 'sick' at work, unable to find the will to shower so she could show up. Noticing that she wasn't paying attention to Mr. Skittles, sometimes forgetting to feed him.

Three weeks had gone by since Kieran left. He had texted her once, telling her he had arrived safely. She responded with *I'm glad* and left it at that. A goddamn expert at numbing. She was safe in that world. She was so numb that she stopped dreaming. The nightmares stopped too.

Pathetic, she was her mother's daughter, it was impossible to escape the fact. She convinced herself it was inevitable. Drinking was the only way she could feel something. Wanting to feel something for Kieran. Wanting to feel loved by her friends. Being obliterated helped her breakthrough the barrier she had put up. She felt raw emotion, recalling that she had promised Kieran she would try, and she would beat herself up, physically pounding her thighs, screaming into pillows, then purge the alcohol from her body, throwing up hard into the toilet or sink, whichever was most convenient. She would grunt and groan into the pillows again, then pass out. Work the next day, then repeat the cycle.

Her co-workers, Joe included, had asked her too many times if she was all right or needed help. One day it was too much and instead of answering 'I'm fine,' she walked directly to their manager, Wendy, and quit. Joe came to her apartment the next day; she could tell he knew something was off. Reassuring him that she had a plan and that everything would be all right, he gave her a disapproving nod and said, "if you need anything, you know you can always count on Carol or myself." His eyes pleaded, begged for her to allow him to help her.

There was nothing to be done at this point. She stared at him with lifeless eyes and said, "Go."

He shook his head and left.

Her 'ghostie friend' (what she drunkenly called the dark shadow from the episodes) had been missing since the day she had met up with Kieran. She couldn't feel it looming in the background. She welcomed it, even called out to it several times to come get her.

Concluding that the alcohol was keeping it at bay, she stopped drinking for several days just to try and toy with it. She cleared a space in her living room, lit a few candles, positioned herself in the middle of the living room, then turned the lights off. She faced the corner where she last saw it. Sitting crossed-legged and taking a few breaths, she waited. Her head and heart pounded from dehydration and alcohol withdrawals on the third day of waiting for it to show up. It didn't help that she wasn't eating and drinking too much coffee.

She had convinced herself to get up and grab a beer when her little seance in the living room worked. The shadow appeared. Out of character, she grinned, whooped and hollered at it, clapping. In a high-pitched reel of excitement, she yelled, "There you are, fucker! Where have you been?" It retreated, hiding behind the curtain. "What are you afraid of? Little old me? I won't hurt you."

But you will.

She wanted it. She wanted to physically hurt, she begged for it. Soshana became furious that the shadow was hiding. She stared at where it haunted, willing it to bring her down with her, into the darkness, away from herself. She thought of the place she went in her dream the night Kieran left. She thought maybe that's what death felt like. Falling, falling, falling. Ethereal effervescent colors, undulating through time and in perpetuity. Deeper into non-existence. Her thoughts shifted unconsciously to her mother dying.

The shadow pulled back the curtain and collapsed to the ground, its arms and legs popped up, it crawled toward her at a speed that was inhuman. Soshana's eyes widened, she let out a scream of terror as the dark shadow came within inches from her face revealing a blinding whiteness in place of the eyes and mouth. It bellowed a hollow, scraping bell tone at the same time as Soshana was screaming, then gravity pulled them together, crushing Soshana's chest.

When Soshana caught her breath and looked around, she was again in the kitchen of her childhood home. Clean, organized, neat and tidy. Everything in place, perfection. Not a crumb. For a second, she thought she could have mindlessly walked over there herself. The mixer was in the back corner, the very toaster that heated too many brown sugar pastries was there too.

It was dark, damp, musty and felt more real than it ever had, which aided her confusion. Everything felt too real, too close, even if she wasn't touching anything. She got up, looked over her body, touching her chest and ribs to be sure they weren't broken. She looked around to find the shadow but could tell that it wasn't downstairs. She knew, somehow she felt, that it had to be upstairs in her old bedroom. She didn't want to go there but knew she had to in order to get herself out of this memory, this vision. As she ascended the stairs, she heard a faint conversation. It grew louder as she climbed each step, then became deafening as she placed her foot on the landing.

"You fucking bitch! You broke this on purpose because it's my favorite, didn't you? You hate me so you want to hurt me, is that it? You have no idea how much I fucking hate you too. You selfish, ignorant, arrogant, dumb little girl. TURN OVER! MOVE YOUR HAND, MOVE IT!!" Thud, smack, smack SMACK SMACK SMACK SMACK SMACK. A deafening screeching and wailing came from a little girl in her old room. A whip like whoosh and a crack of metal on skin repeating over and over. Hysterical cries and sobbing, deep blood-curdling screams. The child was utterly terrified and alone. "STOP CRYING! You know you deserve this."

Soshana was a stone, petrified, bile rising from her aching throat, her heart pounded so loudly it had to have been heard. She held her breath for fear of her mother hearing her. She didn't dare move. Unless. *Unless this wasn't happening.*

But she knew it had happened; she remembered it. She felt the pain in her bones, the heartbreak, the resentment. This gave her an idea. She could make it stop; this was *her* memory. She was an adult and she now knew that beating your child is a criminal act. Without thinking further, she burst open the door and found her mother standing over the shadow, beating it on the back of its legs with a plastic clothes hanger, a broken vase on the ground. Soshana was shocked to see it, she thought she would see a younger version of herself. She looked at the shadow, its eyes and mouth still wide-open in horror, directed at Soshana. The mouth was turned in a way that told her it was pleading with Soshana. Its face morphed into a disturbing calm. It mouthed, silently, "Tell her."

Soshana didn't know what to do except grab Marilyn's shoulder and turn her around. The face she saw was her own. Soshana shuddered and fell into the hallway. Marilyn rounded on her, charging towards the landing. Soshana crawled backwards away from her.

"You are a fucking whore. You stupid bitch." Marilyn's voice was manic. Soshana had fallen weak against the spewing of hatred. She reminded herself it wasn't real, but she had just touched her mother, which was not possible.

"STOP." Holding her hand confidently in front of Marilyn, this caused her to halt, her face contorted, ugly with rage.

Taking several minutes to administer deep rib-fracturing breaths, she imagined she was invincible, impermeable, strong. When her mind was settled, she realized she was in control. She said, dangerously and carefully as she stood to face Marilyn, "You were supposed to love me unconditionally. You were supposed to protect me, care for me, not belittle, judge, name call, beat and gaslight me. But how could you know that, if it was yourself you were supposed to protect me from?"

Each sentence grew louder, she grew stronger. She charged towards Marilyn, who stumbled backwards into the bedroom.

"HOW DARE YOU TREAT ME LIKE THIS! HOW *DARE* YOU!" She pointed at the shadow that was now crouched in the corner, arms pulling its knees into its chest.

Moving within a few inches of Marilyn's face, Soshana screamed as loudly as she could for as long as she could, spittle exploding from her lips. She crushed her eyes shut, fearing they would explode out of the sockets. When she had exhausted herself, she noticed that the shadow had moved to her side and was cowering.

Soshana, now recognizing it was her, said to the shadow, "You're okay. You're safe, I'm here." She glared at her mother who stood in front of her with a face of stone. It was what she would always do whenever emotions ran too hot, she would turn to stone and give her the cold shoulder. It hit her hard. Kieran had told her she had a stoney emotionless face and that she was like a sphinx. She did it as a defense mechanism, to keep her mother from reacting and punishing her. Soshana hadn't been allowed to show emotion or feelings because her mother didn't know how to handle it. Her mother only knew how to be angry; it was the only acceptable emotion to display.

They stared at each other, sizing each other up, a pair of wolves ready to attack. Soshana had fought with her mother more as she got into her late teens. She'd had enough of the binge drinking and parentification. The fights were pointless and ended in screaming matches, not unlike what just happened. There was no use in screaming at her mother, though. It did no good, it changed nothing.

A small voice coming from the depths of her subconscious told her it wasn't entirely her mother's fault. It was her grandparents' fault for not teaching her how to be a decent fucking human. And it was her great-grandparents' fault for not knowing how to teach their children how to handle their emotions… and so on.

They continued to stare at each other. Marilyn was frozen in place, her face was stern, eyes unblinking. Soshana took a step away from her. Nothing happened. She waved a hand, still nothing. Confused, she turned to face her shadow. It had grown to Soshana's height, the eyes and mouth now closed. The shimmering, swimming light that surrounded it had moved inwards at a slowed pace. It reminded her of the liquid in her dream. The beautiful bioluminescence, the opalescent colors moving more calmly now. Soshana looked around, everything seemed frozen in place as well. The drapes across the open window had stilled mid-ruffle from the wind. The tick from the clock had ceased.

"What the hell is going on?" she said aloud. The shadow headed downstairs and as it descended, it disappeared. Soshana was left alone, with her mother turned to stone.

Soshana walked around the house after standing in the hallway for some time. She looked in every room. Checked every cabinet, corner, drapes and drawers. She wasn't sure what she was looking for, except her shadow. It seemed to be the only thing that got her in and out of these episodes and now it had disappeared. She tried calling out to it, she sat on the floor and meditated, just as she had in her apartment. Nothing.

Hours and hours went by. She tried yelling, jumping up and down, banging on walls. She couldn't open any windows or doors; everything was lock tight.

Starving, exhausted, nauseous, she climbed upstairs and went back into her bedroom, her mother was still in the same place.

"What do you want from me? Do you want me to forgive you? I already have! So many times over! But you know what? You don't deserve it. Forgiveness is for people who show true remorse, who actively change their behavior and prove it. You on the other hand…"

Soshana laughed incredulously. "You can't get through saying '*Sorry*' without sarcasm. Remember, Mom? Remember saying 'I *guess* I'm sorry, I don't even know what I did but *I guess* I'm sorry, *okay*? Do you feel better now honey?' Then laughing at me, as if you knew better than to forgive a child? You enjoyed abusing us. It gave you power. How's *this* for power? I have wanted to die every day since I became aware that this isn't how a child should be treated. How does *THAT* make you feel? Do you feel better about yourself *NOW*?!"

That did nothing either. Though it felt selfishly, sinfully delightful to get out. She sat cross-legged on the floor. She put her hand on her face and leaned her elbow into her knee. "I'm sorry." Soshana laughed at herself. She would apologize for the wind moving! Everything was an apology. Her existence was an apology. She was tired of living just so she could apologize for taking up space.

More time passed, uncountable. A feeling of deep sadness rose from the base of her spine to her heart and stopped there. "I'm sorry," she whispered again, but this time it was for herself. She continued, timidly and in a quite soft voice. "I'm sorry I treated you so terribly. I'm sorry I hated you my whole life. You don't deserve this. You didn't deserve to be treated like this."

She looked at Marilyn, still frozen, but with a duller, fuzzier appearance. Soshana looked at her own legs, her hands and feet. She stared at them in amazement, crying softly at her own compassion towards herself. She gently pressed both palms on her stomach and told her body, "You carried me through this, all of this, the whole time. And I have never been grateful for you." Her sobs became loud, a fiery mania, a fierce and powerful energy burst through her eyes and mouth, she glared at her mother with disdain, rage and resentment. She spoke forcefully, punctuating every word, her face drenched in sweat, snot and tears, "I never had to forgive you to move on with my life, I needed to forgive myself!"

She woke up in her apartment to the smell of acrid festering pools of vomit. It was light outside; she assumed she was out cold overnight. An empty bottle of bourbon was toppled over beside her. Mr. Skittles was hiding in a corner, his eyes were squeezed shut. He moved slowly and weakly, adjusting his legs to tuck them closer underneath his body for warmth.

Soshana panicked. She weakly got up, tumbled over herself, tripping from vertigo, and checked her phone. It was dead. She plugged it in to charge. She turned the TV on, scrambling to find a news station. Monday. Monday… fuck. Fuck! She was out cold for almost twenty-four hours. She looked at her sweet cat, he hadn't been fed in two days and the water bowl was dry. It could have been longer; she couldn't remember the last time she fed him. Pain started enveloping her body, beginning at her core then radiating out to every last inch of her existence.

She cried and wailed, she fell on the floor next to him and gently patted his frail body. "I'm so sorry, my love, I'm so sorry." She brought him some clean water and tried to feed him, but he wouldn't take it. After about fifteen minutes of running around trying to find something he would eat, she checked her phone to see if it had enough charge and called his veterinarian. The vet told her to take him to the closest emergency office. She gingerly picked him up. He was limp in her hands. He squeaked and let out a tiny moan.

"No, no, no, my sweet. It's okay you're going to be okay."

She drove as fast and carefully as she could. She hadn't changed her clothes; she smelled the vomit on her shirt and on her breath. Sharp stabbing pains in her abdomen and stomach rippled through her body. She arrived and did her best to explain that she was sick, and her cat was left alone for several days, lying through her teeth.

Lying like the piece of shit that I am.

The vet took him in without further questions, waiting in the office for longer than she hoped. Fears of his death, imagining the vet walking through the door with an empty cage caused her body to shake violently.

I can't do this anymore, it's too much.

She leaned her head back against a chair in the waiting room, she came in and out of consciousness over a few minutes.

The tech finally came out and told Soshana that Mr. Skittles had an IV in for fluids and anti-nausea medication that should help him feel better, but they needed to keep him overnight for observation. They would call tomorrow with an update, but he should be fine. Soshana asked if she could come back and see him, they hesitated but allowed it briefly.

She patted him a few times and said she was so sorry and that he was in good hands. Better than hers. She didn't deserve him. She patted him again, pain increasing in her chest. What if she left him there? He would be better off. She wasn't capable of taking care of herself, how could she take care of another living being?

Soshana went home, she felt defeated in a universal no-going-back kind of way. This last episode had been too much. The numbness was gone and in its place was an all-encompassing brutal pain.

That afternoon, Soshana decided she'd had enough. The pain from existing was too much. Nothing and no one could convince her otherwise.

She stood in her apartment, eyes unfocused, unsure of what to do, how to do it, where. If she should leave a note. The only thing that came to mind was to walk. Walk as far away as possible, for as long as possible.

The stillness outside changed with a wind that whipped through the trees, freshly bloomed flowers and bushes. Dark clouds formed and a few raindrops tapped on the window to announce its arrival. Thunder rolled lazily in the distance. She stared out onto the earth with a dull, myopic perception. The energy from a massive storm was building. A clairvoyant wasn't needed for this kind of violent storm, it was known to the most skeptical of skeptics.

Open the door and get out.

She left the apartment door open and began her descent. The only thought focused on was what direction to walk in order to head into the wilderness, northeast. Several vehicles passed her, some slowed down, the drivers craning their heads to stare at the thin woman with a distended abdomen and disheveled hair in a grease and armpit sweat-stained white T-shirt, pale pink pajama bottoms and bare feet. She kept her focus on the darkening clouds as she walked towards a patch of trees, the hovering storm approaching.

The lightning created surges of frazzled energy to keep her feet moving forward. Thunder crackled through the wind. The rain hit her body from different angles. A warm wind hit her hard, pushing her weak body around, followed by a sharp cold gust that came with extra rain and small pellets of hail that scraped across her face. Her ankle rolled at the edge of the sidewalk; she fell face first, mouth open, into the road. Teeth and gum scrapped the asphalt. Head splitting, ankle throbbing, she welcomed the sensation of fresh pain. A bolt of adrenaline shot through her body and allowed her to pick herself up and continue walking. Soshana stopped at the edge of the park, the very park her and Taryn had reconnected at not so long ago. Soshana looked further into the distance and noticed the clouds turning, circling around a mass of menacing dark green and gray clouds.

She hesitated, her body trying to convince her to turn around, seek shelter, her mind telling her to move forward, follow through with the plan. Instinct kicked in, her heart pounding faster, her pupils dilated as she held hesitation and studied the sky. This wasn't just a late spring rainstorm; this had the makings of a massive tornado, uncommon for that area.

Move.

Searing pain ripped through her stomach, she lurched forward, wrapping her arm around her middle, dry heaving with a dribble of sticky wetness coming from her mouth. Tasting metal and sourness, she knew it was blood before she saw the deep red stain on her fingers from wiping it away. This was encouraging. This was death, a slow death but one step closer. It was excruciating and final.

She pushed forward as the sirens blared in the distance, warning the city's residents to take shelter. Within seconds, the base of the funnel formed in the near distance, beyond the park. The energy in the air could split atoms. The internal fight of survival versus suicide was peaking, this was the ultimate test, she thought. She would force herself into death if it meant running straight into the oncoming storm.

The wind was building to a hollow screech, power lines began to pop in its wake, incredible sparks of lightning radiated from the peak of the sky like jagged talons towards the earth. The sky had darkened to twilight above the growing tornado while the edges of the massive storm showed deep blue and gray cumulonimbus clouds. The event was near, anyone near enough would feel it. Ultimate unyielding chaos.

Shivering, teeth chattering and soaking wet, she found an open road beyond the park with cars beeping and driving at top speeds away from the oncoming storm. She saw a few people scream at her from their open windows mouthing what she guessed was "take cover!" or "what are you doing?! Are you insane?"

She mindlessly, drunkenly swatted them away with one hand while clutching her stomach with the other, stumbling over herself. More blood splattered out of her mouth as she coughed. She was experiencing vertigo in sections of consciousness; at some point she couldn't tell if she was awake and walking aimlessly towards the peaking rage of the storm. The wind was screaming so loudly she couldn't hear the cars honking wildly, zooming by. The sky had become wickedly alive.

There it was. Salvation. Rampaging straight towards her.

Blood trailed from the corners of her mouth and stained her teeth as she screamed with guttural hoarseness. Over and over and over until she could feel her throat torn from the repetition and hear no sound coming from her throat.

She fell over; the wind whipped her clothes so hard they could have flown off if she hadn't had her arms wrapped around her torso. Somehow her weakened body found a last reserve of energy, a burst of adrenaline, the biological need to survive. Her eyes searched for safety: a tree, ditch... an overpass. She remembered there was one a few hundred yards from where she exited the forest. She ran like hell towards it.

As she reached the pass, the tornado had taken a turn and was heading towards town.

Allowing herself to settle under the overpass, flashing brilliant-colored lights swam in and out of her vision. Suddenly her sight blackened. Her lungs heaved shallowly and her heartbeat slowed. The sensation of pain had ceased, her body finally succumbing.

17

Kieran

Kieran hadn't spent more than a few days looking for a job before he landed accounting work at the University of Western Ontario. He was staying at his brother's home in Grand Bend, a small beach side town off of Lake Huron. His brother, Abrams or Abe, and niece, Sadie, lived in a small but comfortable cottage on the edge of town, overlooking the lake. Kieran had hoped to have a few weeks of adjusting and organizing his emotions so that he would be able to focus on what he needed and wanted from life but wasn't the kind of person to pass up an opportunity. The last thing he wanted was to be a burden until he got his 'shit' together.

The ever looming, pervasive and altogether haunting aware-ness of Soshana was always around. He went for walks in the afternoon and would catch a soft breeze that reminded him of her, her scent and the feeling of closeness. His heart had a weight of unease and despair. He knew, for certain, the day in the courtyard was his convincing factor that she was more than just someone special. She had been hurt, possibly traumatized, it was painfully obvious to him. It wasn't his place to pressure her into telling her story. He would wait. He wanted to wait until she was ready to come to him. He knew what pursuing a woman who wasn't ready or wasn't for him meant. Rachel had almost completely ruined any kind of trust in relationships for years, until Soshana. He had convinced himself that all women, and maybe even all people, had a motive, that they wanted something from him. Humans existed to be used and discarded. We are a selfish, self-serving species, but most of our existence is. Animals, trees, plants and flowers are opportunists. When you meet a human who wants nothing from you but your kindness, your capacity for compassion, your touch, how is it possible to believe in it? We brainwash ourselves into thinking those people don't exist, so we keep searching for the opposite to give ourselves confirmation bias. It feels better knowing we are right. Kieran often fought these thoughts; he knew it made sense to stay in the discomfort.

Three weeks had passed, and still no contact from her. He spent entirely too much time looking at old social media photos of her. She hadn't posted anything in several years. She looked noticeably happier, healthier and lighthearted then. Photos of her smiling with what he had assumed were her friends from New York at bars and restaurants. He checked his phone immediately upon waking, obsessively throughout the day and sometimes stared at it for minutes at a time, blankly, unmoving, hoping for something. His dedication to her never wavered. He never gave up. Abe had told him he needed to heal from all relationships and focus on his mental and physical health. Of course, the asshole would know, being a physical trainer and whole health 'life coach.' Irritating jackass that he was, sometimes he was right. He was quite successful, running his business online, working on a book and being overly handsome and attractive.

One afternoon, for reasons unknown to him, he turned on the news. It wasn't allowed on in the house, news was to be read from the most unbiased source possible. "News is entertainment, there is no information that those stations can provide." Or "Shut that shit off," Abe would say when Sadie wasn't around.

He had worked out for several hours with Abe at the gym, went home, showered and felt the need to rest. He hadn't exercised that hard in almost two years. It felt fantastic, he was exhausted while simultaneously feeling the energy running through his body. Imitating a gym obsessed body builder, "I'm going to be *sore* tomorrow, bro," he said to Abe before he left the kitchen, escaping to watch the news. Kieran flicked through the stations, landing on the local weather.

"...a rare and devastating category F4 tornado has touched down in East Grand Rapids, Michigan, over the last hour leaving four dead and thousands without power. Currently, there are seven people missing. Efforts are being made to find the lost residents..." The last sentence was drowned out by reckless thoughts in his head. His ears went hot, heart raced wildly, his vision narrowed. "No," he whispered, shaking his head. Louder, with fear and terror in his voice, he repeated, "No!"

"What? What is it? Another pointless war in another country?" Abe skidded into the den and looked up at the television. "Oh yeah, that's terrible, huh?"

Kieran didn't respond, he stood up and went outside to call Soshana. Her phone was off, he heard her voice saying her name as the voicemail message, his heart dropped. Panicked, he called Tim because he lived in that area. He needed to know if he knew anyone that had died, hopefully not him as well. He answered after a few rings, out of breath, saying how he was helping a neighbor move several fallen trees and debris from their front door. He said he was unaware that anyone had died or was missing. Panic rose in his voice, he said he needed to go to make sure everyone he knew was all right.

Kieran was unaware that Abe and Sadie were watching him the entire time. Abe came out and put a hand on his shoulder, Kieran jerked in surprise and sucked in a much-needed breath. "Uncle Kiki?" Sadie said in less than a whisper, feeding off her uncle's energy.

"What's going on? Are you okay?" Abe was capable of listening and understanding, just not great at problem solving when it came to raw, unexpected emotions.

"It's the town she lives in, on the east side, too. I tried calling her but the phone is off. I just spoke to Tim, you remember Tim, right? He lives outside of town and it hit hard over there too. I just... I just... I..." Kieran trailed off, panic in his voice. He started to shake and tremble. "I don't know what to do. I can't go back into the States yet. I want to leave..."

"Kieran, calm down. There's nothing you can do. She's probably okay."

"You can't know that!" Kieran was close to yelling. He had a dangerous look in his eyes.

Abe backed away, he held his palms out to him, signaling peace. "Okay, you're right. Let's try to figure this out. Is there anyone else you can call? Is there any other way to reach out to her?"

Kieran didn't have her friend's number, so he could reach

out to Tim again later, or at least text him. Kieran let out an air of defeat. "No, not really."

Abe looked at his 'little' brother, his friend. He would do anything for him, and vice versa. Kieran had been there for him through his uncomfortable divorce. Kieran was so proud of him for standing up for his daughter and himself. He had built a wonderful life, even though it was difficult.

"You really care for her, she's something special, huh?" Abe finally replied.

"I've never met anyone like her. She's… she has a wild heart. Uncommonly kind, so generous and sweet. She's probably a bit broken, not unlike me or anyone else. I don't know if she can see how wonderful she is and she won't allow anyone to reach her. I think she thinks if anyone gets too close, they'll be hurt. It's just the opposite, the closer I got, the more I wanted to be near her. It shocks me, but I feel safe with her." Kieran hadn't ever been this vulnerable with his brother. It was altogether uncomfortable and a relief. Like releasing a rusted valve, the water flowed easily.

Abe patted his shoulder a few times and smirked at his brother. His equally brown and soft eyes gave him reassurance that he was listening and comprehending.

"Let's go inside and get some calming kava kava lavender tea and ashwagandha in you. We can keep the news on so you can keep up with the reports." Abe's tea and supplement concoctions were typically disgusting or rarely worked as he said they would. But Kieran felt cared for, and that was enough.

18

The Living Tree

Platanus occidentalis. The sycamore tree had to be a hundred years old, providing shade and shelter over the last century to those who were in its presence. Soshana knew the tree well, it had brought her a sense of safety when she ran to it as a child during her parents' arguments and screaming matches. Some days the yelling was so loud and terrifying she would freeze in place, sometimes she would yell at them to stop, and other times she would run to the safety of that tree. It wasn't named; it was just the one that was located in the park closest to the house.

On days that were quieter, she would still want to be out of the house, the one riddled with broken eggshells, landmines and dark shadows. She would carry a book, blanket and snacks to read under its enveloping branches. As she grew older, she would listen to music under the canopy and daydream about finding someone to share her life with. She had so much love to give, unknowing of where to put it, she left it in the tree in the form of hugs, reading sweet poems, singing, smiling and trusting it with all her darkest thoughts and grandest wishes. She wasn't going to give those beautiful little things to her undeserving parents, she spared enough for her brother. Unbeknownst to her, the love she freely gave grew and grew under the tree.

She easily loved what the tree and the life surrounding it gave to her. She loved the ants making their way down to the earth with their offerings. She loved the contrast of the blue sky against the bright yellow leaves, veins glowing against the fall colors. She loved the stars at night, scattered through the bare branches in the winter. She loved the array of birds that hopped through its limbs, happily singing while searching for food. She loved the feeling of safety, calmness, peace, and often told the tree softly, "I'm so grateful for you. Thank you."

Soshana heard the faint sounds of beeping. For a long while, it could have been minutes or hours, she was unsure if she was alive or dead, where she was, what day it was or even what year. She took a few shuddered breaths in and activated the part of her brain that was meant to move body parts. First her fingers and toes, they wiggled and moved. She lifted her arms and weary legs only a few centimeters. Those were working. She gently turned her head left and right. Not entirely broken. Opening her eyes wider, she glanced around the room. It was unfamiliar, no one thing in her immediate area gave her an indication of where she was. It didn't matter much to her after a few more minutes. She tried to fall back asleep, or whatever this was. A few more hours or days could have passed without fully knowing.

On another plane of existence, maybe another dimension, she thought, she became bored with possibly being dead. She felt around her body and to her great terror, she felt a tube coming out of her abdomen. Suddenly, her mind connected to her nervous system and she felt a memory of extreme and intense pain. Pain that lasted weeks or longer? Unclear. She looked at her arms, they had several different IVs hooked up. A small yellow tube was connected to her upper abdomen, the pressure from the tube protruded into her body. She brought her hand to her throat, it ached, it felt raw, as if she had been screaming for days. A breathing tube was secured to her mouth, a contraption wrapped around her head, holding her hostage. Claustrophobia wasn't something she normally worried about, now it was emerging.

This is not the time to panic.

Her mind wandered.

Maybe I'm not dead.

This was disappointing at first. But then a tiny trickle of relief crawled through her body. Through the oscillating sensations of nausea, dizziness and pain, she searched her memory.

She tried to suck in a deep breath but couldn't. She felt the uncontrollable ache of insanity crawling up her spine. She wanted to run away again, but that was not an option. She had tried that.

No more running.

Soshana had almost been successful. She had come close, so close to bliss, darkness and her bitter end. It was an odd, new sensation, but she finally understood what it felt like to be proud of herself. Proud of coming close to accomplishing one fucking thing in her life. Alternatively, though she didn't recognize it at first, she also felt increasingly proud for surviving it.

Each passing moment during the next few days there were more examples of ways to celebrate and increase her new sense of pride. The incredible pain from removing the tubes and healing from them, she survived. The pain of passing a bowel movement without aid for the first time was an award-winning moment. Looking at herself in the mirror and not moaning at the sight of her diminished body, thinned hair and the dark circles under her eyes. Sitting upright by herself. Wheeling herself to physical therapy. Lifting more than ten pounds.

The next few weeks were in and of themselves a triumph. All the while she couldn't stop thinking of Mr. Skittles. Cradling his soft warm body, feeling the vibrations from his purring, gleefully watching him play with his orange mouse toy. The happiness he brought her for several years was priceless. She hoped he was still at the veterinarians. He was worth living for.

Then her mind would float to Kieran, then Joe, Derek, Josette then back to Kieran, then Taryn, even the simple conversation she had with the coffee shop barista. She thought of all the people in her life who had recently given her the freedom to be herself. They showed her that they cared about her, that they wanted her in their life. She would have taken that away from them if she had succeeded in her wish. Her thoughts changed to an alternate world, one where she did die. Yes, she understood it would make those people terribly sad, but maybe they had the tools and ability to cope with it, to cope with life. Something she lacked.

Kieran.

She had successfully screwed up that one. Shame, resentment for the argument they had at her apartment, guilt for ignoring him. Her mind pushed her to reject the emotions bubbling up. She had to trust how she truly felt, and how Kieran made her feel. It wasn't wrong, it wasn't uncomfortable. It was joyful, easy. She felt sunshine illuminating from her chest when she was around him, even when it was overcast outside. Her smile came easily, without force, when they spoke. His eyes glittered with amusement and interest when they had conversations. This wasn't flirting for the sake of flirting; it wasn't just someone she knew and would eventually forget. He was so much more than that.

Most days were too ugly for her, maybe because her mind was wired to only focus on the ugly. The anger that she felt, the projected arguments she had in her mind with people that didn't matter anymore. She was tired of arguing with her mind over her dead mother, her absent father, her ex-boyfriend, her friend Mina. These people did not care for her in the way she needed or wanted. And it was fine that she wanted to be cared for differently, it was okay that she asked to be treated kindly, with compassion and the truest form of love. It didn't matter that it couldn't come from her family, the people we are supposed to love unconditionally. As long as the conditions were worthy. Especially when those people demanded unconditional love on their terms and their rules. If you fuck up, if you can't own to your mistakes and make those behavioral changes to be better and do better, it's best to let go. She had finally found the people in her life that showed her love without conditions. She got to be herself.

Is it still worth it?

Her mind guided her towards a different path. She had envisioned the family home being engulfed by flames, a bomb dropping on it, a tree slicing it in half, many times throughout the past year.

What if the tornado took it?

There would certainly be an insurance claim, and she could sell the property. It is in a prime location, close to a park and school. A great place for a new family to build a home. A place where love could grow, not boiling hatred, anger and resentment.

Taryn said she would help. What if she did help? What if she truly did care and meant it when she said she loved her? It felt too big for her mind to handle. It encompassed her physical body and soothed her while she allowed herself to cry openly without restraint. Someone actually loved her, someone was looking out for her, protecting her and helping her. She no longer only had herself to rely on. She allowed herself to trust Taryn. She told herself it was safe, Taryn was safe, that help could be accepted and be rewarding.

A pulsing, warm and energetic feeling crossed over her chest, arms and back. This feeling reminded her of a time when she felt hopeful, a time when her mother sought help for her emotional outbursts and alcoholism. When she got accepted into college, when she looked forward to being with her friends on a Friday night in New York. She felt a spark of life. A thought emerged that helped her warm-up to the idea of continuing to live. It came from a place deep in the recesses of her mind. As if it were a memory, not her own, though. "Pain tells us life is real. Joy is a reminder that it is worth living it."

She held the thought and repeated it several times, knowing it was of vital importance. She begged herself, *please stay.*

It was only a lifeline for now, she knew she needed an

incredible amount of strength to face the aftermath of her recent decisions. She thought, *does anyone truly care? Truly?* Her mind wanted to numb how she felt but she knew better than to allow it. No more of that. By ignoring and pushing away uncomfortable thoughts and feelings, you do yourself and others a great disservice. It ends up coming back to you in damning ways, some you may not realize. She knew her stomach problems were most likely from internalizing all her childhood abuse, the rape, her ignorance. From not allowing herself to take the time to just *feel*.

Sit with it. Be here, now.

She breathed until her breath steadied, with her head gently held by the hospital pillows. It had been a bit windy and cloudy earlier and now, with the wind dying down, the sun was cracking through thin clouds. Sunlight hit the left side of her face, urging her to open her eyes. A tickle gently teased her right arm, a wisp of her hair was caught in her sleeve. She held it up against the sunlight to examine it. Before she tossed it onto the floor, out of the corner of her eye she noticed it glistening, sparkling as the sun came out past the clouds. Lifting her head towards it, leaning in, she studied it more closely. That single strand of what was supposed to be dark brown hair, a solitary color, had produced *many* colors. The colors reminded her of that wild dream. The bursting illuminated colors from the sky and the tree that she had forgotten, the unimaginable display of grandeur it held.

The colors are inside of me, I made these colors. They came from me.

A quiet thought, though not altogether unimaginable. She had held the spectacle of that dream world, that universe inside of her. She was capable of great beauty, even in the smallest of ways, in the softest of moments.

She decided to visit the sycamore tree from her childhood once she had recovered. Tell the tree how grateful she was for it during those traumatic years. In the meantime, she would daydream about it. Connecting her memories with its grandness and locking her mindsight on it until she reached its roots, she walked gracefully towards it. Studying it from ground to canopy, she admired the trunk, pressed her thumb in between the bark that weaved patterns from its skin. She watched the sun catch on the back side of the leaves while the wind tossed them about. She felt the warm wind gently kiss her face and tousle her hair. No words needed to be spoken; she felt the gratitude from her past returning to the present moment. She needed to be present, just be. That's what she instinctively knew as a child when she ran to this tree. That child knew what her adult-self had left behind, had forgotten. *Just be.* Mindfully, gently placing her palm against the flank of the trunk, she felt safe once again.

19

Derek

Even though Derek knew he shouldn't have, he ripped open the letter from Kieran to Soshana with impatient curiosity. It had a bulge in the center, and it was just too much to resist. He paused at reading the contents, the guilt washing over his actions.

The past few weeks of watching Soshana not making any additional progress in her recovery was wearing on him. The initial panic when the hospital called, his frantic drive from New York, the uncontrollable dread that came from the unknown, minute to minute, now day by day. Unknowing what to say to her while she was deep in a coma. He had tried everything. He watched her face countless times, scanning it over and over, looking for movement, an eyelid flicker, twitch of her mouth or a breathing pattern that changed. He would pick at lint on her hospital clothes, plucking one of her shiny hairs off her right shoulder. Anything to watch her come alive, be present. She was too far away, no one knew or understood why. Though the doctors told Derek that her brain activity was fine, her organs were close to shutting down when she was admitted. But now she showed signs of the ability to recover. "It's all up to her at this point. Let's wait and see." They told him multiple times.

He thought of how he begged Joe to visit her, speak to her. Maybe having people present would revive her in some way. Joe resisted initially but eventually came. Being at her side must have reminded him of his last days in the hospital with his own daughter. Finally having to make the decision to pull the life support after many months without any brain activity. Derek saw in the lines of his tired face that he was grief-stricken, heartbroken.

"You can do this, Soshana. We're here. We want you here. Please try." The last of the words hardly sounded audible through the shaking in his voice. His movements were robotic, his words punctuated. Joe did not return after that day or stay in contact.

Taryn had also stopped by and explained how their family home had been destroyed by the tornado, how the insurance would pay out soon and that the listing for the property would be up as soon as the debris was cleared. She said Soshana had a room in her home, ready for her when she was well enough. The strain from holding back sobs was evident, though she was there to discuss business with Derek she also wanted to tell Soshana, in the hope that she had heard as well, "Hang in there, love, we are here waiting."

In those last few weeks, he had visited her apartment with the intention of taking care of Mr. Skittles. When he had arrived that first day, he noticed the door was ajar. He figured he must have escaped. Derek walked around the building, knocking on doors asking if they had seen him with no luck.

Ruth had handed him a letter stating that she hadn't paid rent in several months and needed to vacate. She showed remorse after Derek explained Soshana's situation and didn't ask for the back rent, but did indeed ask for her things to be packed up and moved out.

Derek worked tirelessly over the course of several days to get her things packed, the vomit cleaned from the floors, the empty bottles recycled and had to constantly remind himself that he wasn't cleaning up after another dead relative. His disappointment from her binge drinking faded when he gradually figured out why. In her stack of books, he found many labeled 'self-help.' Several of them were about narcissistic parents, emotionally immature parents, PTSD, depression and anxiety. Pausing from his work, he sat on the floor cross-legged and flipped open a book, choosing a random page that read:

"Emotional abuse cuts to the very core of a person, creating scars that may be longer-lasting than physical ones. With emotional abuse, the insults, insinuations, criticism, and accusations slowly eat away at the victim's self-esteem until she is incapable of judging the situation realistically. She has become so beaten down emotionally that she blames herself for the abuse. Emotional abuse victims can become so convinced that they are worthless that they believe that no one else could want them."[1]

Neurons firing, bells alarming, he continued reading on, desperate for more insight. He hadn't touched a single self-help book and only went to therapy for a few sessions, believing that his mental health was his problem to fix on his own, his sole responsibility. And partially because of being gay in a world made for straight people and not having been on this earth long enough to have the maturity to understand the complexity human nature. He knew that Soshana had issues, this had proven that it was beyond anything he believed. He now knew that Soshana didn't have a drinking problem, she had an issue with being alive.

Curiosity got the better of him. He pulled out the contents of the envelope that lay waiting to be opened. The front of the card had a watercolor print of a beach, tall grass and deep blue water resembling Lake Michigan in the summer. Taped on the inside was a small plastic pink heart-shaped bead with holes on either end. It looked like it came from a child's necklace.

The handwriting was neat, small and slanted, some in cursive. He scanned over the brief letter and decided Soshana needed to hear this read to her, whether it registered in her or not. He left for the hospital without a second thought.

Soshana,

I hope you don't mind me writing you. I wrote down your address after I sat in my car the last morning when we were together. I heard of the storm in your area and I am worried something happened since I haven't heard from you. I'm making one last attempt to reach you.

I'm not sure what to say, except that you are in my heart, my thoughts every day. The short time we spent together was some of the happiest days of my life so far. It was a privilege to have been in your life and to share moments with you that most will never get. I don't want this to end, whatever we had. Every instinct in my body is telling me not to let go, so I won't. I will wait. You are worth it.

My niece gave me this little bead heart to carry with me when I was going through chemo and surgery. She suggested I give it to you in case you need it. She is quite charming when she wants to be. We both hope this helps you.

If you need to move on and/or you are not interested in keeping contact with me, I understand and will honor your wishes, respectfully.

Yours,

-Kieran

Derek stood up quickly to remove himself after reading the letter aloud to Soshana, his uncontrolled sobbing bursting out when he entered her hospital bathroom. He pressed his palm across his throbbing forehead and wiped away the tears from his cheeks. It had been extremely difficult to control his emotions and reactions lately. The letter sent him over the edge. It had been a few weeks since anyone else had visited Soshana, even their father hadn't visited. The undeniable disappointment that Derek felt could have shaken the earth. He had cursed his father and his mother for being so cold and unfeeling. They had left their children behind to suffer alone, to figure out everything on their own. They knew nothing and hated everything and everyone because of it. The one person Derek loved was Soshana. She was lifeless in front of him, while someone was loving her from a distance. She couldn't see it and Derek knew instinctively that she rejected Kieran in spite of herself.

He returned to her bedside and stood over the letter that he had left on the chair. He picked it up and stared at it blankly, unseeing but engulfed in a kaleidoscope of feelings.

"Don't you see, Soshana? This right here, it's proof! I know it's hard to understand, to comprehend that someone could *love* you." Derek gripped the handwritten letter tightly and shook it in front of her face. Tears formed; his throat tightened.

"Our love wasn't enough for you. I don't think you're capable of understanding, I know that now. I'm not angry at you for that. The hardest thing you can possibly overcome is accepting yourself, loving yourself. It doesn't make sense. We were only taught to love others if we did what we were told. We are nothing without their approval. But that is just not true! You are enough by just existing; there's nothing to prove to anyone. But you have to accept yourself. As you are. You have to learn to love yourself. As you have loved me for exactly who I am."

Derek fell into the chair and grasped her left hand, sobbing into it, begging for a response. He whispered into her hand, "I don't want to be left without love right now, please don't go. Stay with me. Stay with me, stay with me. Don't leave."

On the other side of the bed, unseen and unaware, Soshana's right hand flexed and relaxed.

Cited Work

1 *Stop Walking On Eggshells* Third Edition by Paul T. Mason, MS Randi Kreger

Acknowledgments

To my darling husband, thank you for your endless love, acceptance, kindness, laughter, compassion and friendship. Your unwavering support and belief in my wild adventures are only possible because of you. There's no one better than you. I love you so much.

To my dear family and friends, your love and support mean the world to me. Thank you for being a part of my life and making it joyful, I love you.

To my editor Abbie Rutherford, this novel would not have come to life without you. Your expertise, thoughtful insight, support and knowledge have been instrumental in the making of this book. I have a feeling we are going to be working together for a long time.

To my cover artist Pixie Thorpe, your friendship and artistic creativity is as much a part of this book as the writing itself. I am so grateful for your talents and the discussions that brought this stunning cover to life.

The music from the incredible artist *Gordi* played in the background as I wrote this book. Your music continues to stir up deeply felt and important emotions with every song. I admire you and always look forward to your next release. Thank you.

To everyone that makes it to the end of this book, please know that my heart is exponentially expanded by your trust in my words and support in my writing. I wrote this book initially for myself, to get my feelings out in the form of a novel, but at the end of it all, publishing it was for you. I dream of being able to hug all of you (with permission) to show my gratitude. Thank you, thank you, thank you.

About the Author

Maggie currently lives in Michigan with her husband and rescue pets. When she isn't writing you can find her tending to her garden, reading antique novels, hugging trees, smiling at flowers, singing, painting, traveling, working on puzzles, spending time with her favorite people. She studied Psychology, Sociology and English language in college. Living the gentlest life possible, she continuously works on her mental and physical health.

You can connect with me on:
- https://www.maggieyore.com
- https://www.instagram.com/maggieyoreauthor